THE
HERETIC
WIND

A story of Mary Tudor, Queen of England.

JUDITH ARNOPP

St James' Palace – October 1558

I hate autumn; I always have. It heralds the onset of megrims, endless days of gloom, nights of frozen misery. *It is so dark.* Why haven't they come to light the torches or stoke the fires? Where on God's earth are they?

I move my arm, dislodging a pile of books, and a tankard of ale crashes to the floor. A dark stain spreads like blood. The noise alerts my women, who should be attending me. The door opens and a face peers tentatively around the edge. Expecting it to be Susan, I frown vaguely at the child who creeps forward.

"Who are you? Where are my women?"

"You sent everyone away, Your Majesty, on pain of death."

I grunt acknowledgement; I had forgotten. My damned women are always fussing and fiddling, whispering and watching. Waiting for me to die. I get tired of it. I squint at

3

the blur of her white face that seems to float in the darkness. I wave my arm again.

"Get someone to light the torches and then do something about that fire."

She bobs a curtsey. I hear the door open and close, and know I am alone again. A scattering of raindrops peppers the windows, a draught eddies around my ankles. It is only October. The thought of the long winter months ahead fill me with gloom. Perhaps I will not live to see the spring. I let my chin drop to my chest and close my eyes. Sleep will help me forget; it is a refuge, my only friend.

The present blurs, music plays in the recesses of my mind – music and laughter … I am slipping into oblivion when the pain bites deep in my gut. I cry out and clutch my belly.

"Your Majesty, should I call the physician?" Susan Clarencius, who is braver than the rest, bursts into the chamber and bends over me. I feel the anxious hush of her breath against my cheek. I push her away.

"I told you I wanted to be alone."

She stands over me just as my lady governess used to do. Folding her hands across her stomach, she sniffs dismissively. "But if you are sick, Your Majesty…"

"I said I wanted to be alone. Get that girl to stoke the fire. I will tolerate nobody else near me tonight, do you understand?"

The effort of anger makes me cough and she takes a step forward, but I point toward the door. "Out. Now."

She hesitates for just a moment before curtseying low and leaving me in peace. I close my eyes.

When I open them again, I become aware of stealthy movements. My neck is stiff from sleeping in my chair and there is drool on my chin. I turn toward the hearth where someone is kneeling, trying to silently rouse the flames.

"Is that you, girl? Are you still here?"

She rises.

"Yes, Your Majesty." By her voice, she can be no more than twelve. My eyesight is so dim I have to imagine how she looks; a child in grubby skirts, the beginnings of a hole on her left shoe. What must it be like to be such a person, so lowly? I doubt it can be as hard as it is to be queen.

Maybe she would make a better job of ruling than I have. When I came to the throne I had such good intentions. I meant to put everything right but ... I can't even pinpoint when the trouble began...

"Do you think it is easy being queen?"

I speak suddenly. The girl gasps and drops her poker, rolls to her feet in a flurry of petticoats.

"I – I beg pardon, Your Majesty?"

"Being queen..." I poke my head forward, trying to bring her features into focus. "I suppose you think it's as simple a task as lighting fires or fetching buckets. Well, you're wrong. It is hard. Hard, do you see? I – I thought the people would love me ... they loved my father, didn't they, despite everything he did? They always loved him."

I glare at her. She thinks I am crazed, and she is not alone. It is a question I have sensed frequently in the voices of my women and the quizzical brows of my physicians of late. It is their pity I hate the most. I narrow my eyes.

"What is your name?"

She clears her throat before replying. "A–Anne, Your Majesty." She has the grace to sound apologetic.

Surprising even myself, I let out a bark of laughter and find it difficult to stop. She waits while I rock back and forth, showing my gums, tears dampening my cheek.

"My least favourite name," I explain as soon as I have adequate breath to speak. I mop my watering eyes on my sleeve. "Was your mother an admirer of the Boleyn woman? You were named in her honour, I suppose?"

She steps forward determinedly. "No, no, Your Majesty; not at all. My mother was a good Catholic soul. I was named in memory of my granddam."

Hmmm. Choosing to believe her, I indicate that she should pass me a cup of ale. It is the only thing that soothes my raging thirst.

"Should I not fetch your women – Lady Susan or...?"

I shake my head. "No. There should be a cup on the tray. Pass it to me."

She hesitates, wiping her hand on her apron before doing as I ask. I sip the liquid and

6

let it flow wet and warm down my parched throat.

"She started it all, you know. The Boleyn woman. The misfortunes I have suffered are all due to her. I was happy, we all were. My parents were contented before she danced like the devil and stole my father's eye. We were all content. She bewitched him, changed him, and forced him to follow where she led. Were it not for her, there'd have been no division of the church, and my mother would have died in the royal bed where she belonged. My childhood would have been blessed. I'd never have been sent from court and forced to remain unmarried until I was past the age of child-bearing. It is ALL her fault. Everything!"

"Yes, I see, Your Majesty." She inches away until I raise my hand sharply and order her to stop. I struggle to focus. My eyes are sore, weary of opening and closing – I might as well let them remain shut. I beckon her closer and at last her face grows a little clearer. She is very young; her eyes are youthful and vigorous. I sense hope in their depths, and a sort of triumph.

"You think you'll never get old, don't you? You despise me because I am wrinkled and raddled with disease."

"No, Your Majesty. I don't. Indeed, I love you. You are my queen."

I laugh again, without mirth.

"I'm not as old as you think, you know, and I haven't always been like this. I was young once. As young and fresh as a newly opened daisy…"

<u>Summer 1523</u>

There has been a recent shower; the roses are spotted with shining raindrops, the grass is wet and my toes grow damp inside my slippers as I tiptoe through daisies. Above my head, the voices of my mother's women buzz like lazy bees, their conversation irrelevant as long as my hand is held fast in hers.

As we walk, her skirts brush against mine, the scarlet velvet of her gown clashing with my yellow. This is my favourite gown and, according to the women who helped me dress this morning, it is the exact shade of gorse blossom. I enjoy the way it swings like a bell when I walk, just as Mother's does, and one day I know I shall be as beautiful as she is.

I glance up at her face and notice that her smile is tarnished with sadness today. My heart dips in pity. I know from my gossiping servants that Mother longs for a son, an heir to my father's throne, but … she has me. *Why won't I suffice?*

I squeeze her hand to make her notice me and instantly her melancholic expression is replaced with love; love that lights up her eyes and stretches her mouth upward into a bow. I smile back, and gently swing our clasped hands as we progress through the garden.

We turn a corner, pass beneath an arch of yew and come face to face with a party of laughing gentlemen. Mother halts, her women gathering around us, the murmur of conversation ceasing. The gentlemen break apart and bow elegantly low to my mother, and then to me. One man, taller than the rest, steps forward in a flurry of velvet and fur. He grasps me beneath my arms and swings me high into the air. I am really too old for such games, but I scream with laughter and grab for his collar to save myself. I know he would never really let me fall, for I am his Mary, his sweetheart, his little pearl.

Belatedly, he lowers me to the ground. I reach out, fingers splayed, as my world continues to spin while he turns to greet my mother. Instead of swinging her in the air he offers her his arm and, as we progress along the pathway, he relates his morning prowess at the hunt. Slowly, my world stops spinning and becomes stable again. I walk between them, one hand in Father's, the other in Mother's; I am a link in a royal chain.

The courtiers fall behind. "It is a fine day for a walk in the gardens, Madam," my father says, and Mother murmurs in agreement.

"Oh!" She halts suddenly to admire the roses that cascade like warm honey over the ruby brick walls. Father plucks one and tucks it into her cap and she smiles up at him … but the sadness in her eyes does not lift.

A butterfly drifts across my path and I hurry in pursuit, the laughter of the courtiers floating across the garden as they watch me.

"So sweet," I hear them murmur. "Such a perfect princess."

It is always so. I am Princess Mary, and one day, when I am wed to my cousin, I will be Queen of Spain. I will have the finest gowns, the most lavish jewels, as is my due. Since I am my father's only heir, if no brother comes along to take my place I will inherit the throne of England. As the granddaughter of English kings and the granddaughter of kings and queens of Spain, I shall embrace that day when it comes.

I know these things, although I have not been taught all of it. The conversation of my elders is informative, and I know that my mother's sadness is because I have no brother. It seems she has failed in some way, but I do not understand why I am not enough. I am certain no boy could ever be better than me.

The butterfly flutters over the high wall and I give up the chase. I stare after it in dismay, irritated at being thwarted in the hunt. When Mother catches up with me, she exclaims at the green stain on my skirt, but I know she is not really angry. She takes my hand again and I hop and skip at my parents' side until we reach the sundial where a man is waiting.

The red robes of Cardinal Wolsey put the roses to shame. My heart sinks, for I know from the sheaf of papers beneath his arm that he means to claim the king's attention and lure him away. After a short consultation, Father kisses my nose and bids the queen farewell before taking his leave of us. I stand with Mother and watch his departing back, and feel as if the sun has ducked suddenly behind a cloud.

"Come," the queen announces. "It grows chilly out here; let us return to the palace."

She takes my hand again. Although it is not in the least cold and there are many hours of daylight left, no one dares complain and the company follows obediently behind us. Once inside, I am passed into the care of my lady governess, Lady Margaret Pole, who takes my hand. Mother retires to her state apartment while I am taken to my own rooms, which are situated alongside hers.

My clothes must be changed. My hair must be brushed, and I must take a nap before supper. Lady Margaret removes some of my pillows, bids me lie flat and close my eyes. I do as I am told but my mind still leaps and dances with a will of its own. I stare at the bed canopy while my fingers trace the outline of the embroidered leopards and lilies on my counterpane.

The shutters are closed, extinguishing the sunshine, and two of my women settle at the hearth to watch over me as I sleep. After a while, their lulling voices soothe me and I relax. My eyes grow heavy and my breathing slows. I cannot prevent my lids from closing.

"Her Majesty seems distraught today…"

Immediately, I am alert at the mention of my mother, their whispered words scrawled large across my mind. Wide awake now, I squint my eyes and cock my ear the clearer to hear. I had sensed Mother's sadness in the garden today; perhaps my women know more about the cause of it.

Hetty shifts in her chair.

"And little wonder, poor lady…"

"It is no more than other, lesser women suffer…"

"Yes, but it is one thing to acknowledge him, but to bring him to court? The king is rubbing the queen's nose in his indiscretion…"

Their voices dip lower. I want to scream at them to speak up, to stop mumbling, but I know that if they suspect I am not asleep, their conversation will lapse into trivia.

"I've heard the boy is to be made Duke of Richmond and Somerset – that makes him equal in rank to…"

What boy? I wonder. *Who are they talking about?*

"He might even go so far as to name him heir … if the queen should fail..."

One of them, I can't see which, leans forward to poke the fire and smoke wafts into the room. Hetty coughs.

"Oh, we both know the queen is no longer fertile. She will never bear another child. The king can either let his legitimate daughter inherit … or his bastard son."

It is as if I have been struck. My eyes open wide again, and a sharp frantic ringing begins in my ears. *A son? My father has no son. What do they mean? How can my father have a son when my mother does not?*

Since I am not supposed to know of his existence, there is no one I can ask about this so-called son of my father's but I keep my ears open, my mind attuned to learning more. For the first time I realise I am not the centre of the universe and my parents have secrets that they do not share with me. Sometimes I think everyone is keeping secrets.

Whenever I can, I listen at doors, pretending indifference to adult conversations and concerns, but all the while I am alert, desperate to learn the identity of this mysterious boy – the rival for my father's affection.

A year passes. I grow up fast. I am no longer allowed to soil my clothes or waste my leisure time in trivial things. I must not sit on the floor. I must learn Latin; I must practise my lute. Mother insists I must learn to dance and to carry myself like a future queen.

It is from the lips of my dancing master that I finally discover the boy's name. *Henry Fitzroi* is the son of Bessie Blount, a former lady in my mother's household. I frown, thinking back, and can just recall Bessie's plump pretty face, her merry laughter.

The king's court has always been dominated by pageants, feasts and tournaments. I cannot pinpoint when Bessie ceased to be part of it, but I am sure I was quite young. It seems that her son is now four years old, three years my junior.

After Mass, I crawl beneath a table, pull the cloth down to hide me and pretend I am an anchorite bricked up behind a church wall. I close my eyes, place my hands together and think saintly thoughts.

Someone enters the chamber. I can tell by her voice that it is Mother's friend, Maria de Salinas and my aunt Mary, Father's sister who used to be queen of France.

"He will not inherit, of course," she says. "Fitzroi is of *bastard* stock."

That word again. *Bastard.* I am not sure but I think it means he was born to a woman who was not my father's wife: a *strumpet* according to Aunt Mary, but I'm not sure what that word means either.

With each passing day the world grows more complex, more confusing and uncertain. While my mother spends increasing time at prayer and I spend more in the company of my tutors, I see Father less and less. But when he does visit me in private, I push aside my books and run into his arms, a thing I am not permitted to do when we meet formally before the court.

He pulls me onto his knee and I feel like an infant again, playing with the jewels on his doublet, trying to prise the rings from his great fingers, tugging at his beard. Sometimes I ask him to sing me the old songs he sang when I was in my cradle, and he strokes my cheek before indulging me, his clear tones filling

13

the chamber. Tentatively, I begin to sing along, and without pausing he smiles encouragingly, and our voices entwine like two butterflies dancing in a garden.

At times like these, it is as though there are just the two of us in the world. The rest do not exist. There is no court, no kingdom, no bastard sibling to steal him away – there is just me and my father; Henry Tudor and me.

While Father seems to grow in vigour every day, Mother shrivels. She tries not to let me know of it. Her chin is high, her bearing as proud as it has always been, and a gentle smile plays upon her lips, but I sense her misery. It is eating her up. She seems to be shrinking; her face grows sallow and her step lacks its former energy. There is little I can offer her but love.

Often, when I come upon her unawares, I notice the trace of tears on her cheeks, but I pretend I haven't seen them. She is proud and it would hurt her to know that I see through the shield she erects around herself.

We are sewing together in her chamber. Her exquisite black stitches increase rapidly while mine are slow to form and resemble the path of a drunken bee … a bee that has fallen into an inkpot and stumbled across my strip of grubby linen.

She leans across and takes it from me, her brow quirking.

"Oh dear, Mary. You will have to unpick it and begin again. Try to keep your lines straight – perhaps we should ask one of the women to draw a route for you to follow – would that make it easier?"

"No, thank you, Mother." I retrieve my work. "I will learn. I want to get it right." This is not true, I'd rather be outside, but I want to please her and nothing satisfies my parents more than trying my very best.

"Good girl." She beams at me and I bask in her approval. I may lack skill at the needle, but I have inherited her pride and resolve. I am determined to do this.

"You will be in charge of your own household when you go to Ludlow."

Her words clang like a great bell in my head, ringing out doom. I drop my needlework.

"Ludlow? Where is that? When am I going there? Why am I going there?"

"Because you are precious, my child, and must do your duty as the king's daughter ... his probable heir."

It is the first time I have heard her admit that she is losing hope of bearing further children. The workings of the human body are a mystery to me but I assume it has something to do with the growing gulf between Mother and the king. I frown at the soiled linen in my hand. If I am sent away, the gulf between them will only increase without me to pull them closer.

"I have no wish to leave ... not yet. I think I am too young."

She continues to sew, the needle slipping in and out of the fabric, her chin lowered, the light from the window shining on her forehead, glinting on the jewels of her headdress.

"It won't be for a year or so yet, you must first be prepared. I think you will like Ludlow; I lived there with my first husband, Arthur, when I was the Princess of Wales."

I try to imagine Mother as a little girl but can only manage to shrink her form to a dwarfish, pious figure. I cannot picture her carefree and bright as she must once have been.

"He died there, didn't he? My tutor said Ludlow was a place of contagion."

She laughs. "No; his death had nothing to do with the castle. It was misfortune; the pestilence came upon us with no warning, just as it did elsewhere. My apartments were large and luxurious. I have ordered them to be refurbished for your comfort. As I said, I am quite certain you will come to love it there, as much as I did."

I don't want to go. The Welsh border is far from court. I will be alone … I will miss my father, miss my mother.

"Will Lady Margaret accompany me?"

Margaret Pole is my father's cousin and has been in charge of my household since I was an infant. Putting aside her sewing for a moment, Mother tilts her head to one side and places a calming hand on mine.

"Of course, all of your present household will go with you, and more besides. You will have every luxury and a whole wardrobe of new clothes, as well as new plate and goods. I will sew your linen myself, so you can feel close to me when you wear it. If you work hard at neatening your stitches, you can help…"

My answering smile is tremulous. I lower my head and try as hard as I can to keep my stitches straight but the thought of Ludlow is like a terrible cloud. Tears well up. I try to blink them away but blindly stab the needle into my finger. I squeal, hold my finger aloft and watch as a bead of blood forms, runs down my wrist and drips onto the cloth. Mother drops her work.

"Mary!"

Her women come running and the chamber descends into chaos as they vie to tend me. Maria wraps my finger in a strip of fabric and wraps her arm about my shoulders.

"There, there," she croons. "It will soon stop smarting."

They make as much fuss as if my hand has been severed at the wrist. I retrieve it, bury it in my skirts and scowl at them.

"I think that is enough sewing for one day," the queen says, and while they scurry around clearing away the skeins of silk, I droop at my mother's side, my face against her sleeve as I suck my sore finger and think fearfully of a future without her.

The dread of leaving court for the strangeness of my own establishment is leavened by the heaps of new garments that arrive daily: gowns and sleeves; shoes; new hoods; fine jewellery; furs and plate.

For the first time, I am given the luxury of choosing which shade of velvet I prefer, which style of hood is more pleasing. Although I am not yet ten, I am no longer regarded as a child. I am Princess Mary of England, my father's heir, and one day I will be the wife of the emperor.

But just as I am becoming accustomed to the idea of Ludlow, I learn that while I am preparing to leave court, Henry Fitzroi is preparing to join it.

He too is to be given a vast household but he will be installed at Bridwell Palace, just a short trip along the Thames from Greenwich. He will be closer to the king while I am sent away. The news lodges in the base of my throat like an unshed tear.

The blazing light of my infant days fades and is replaced by the dimness of age. The figure of the girl is a dark shadow against the blazing fire.

"You can imagine how that felt. I was being replaced. My position usurped by some *bastard* boy."

The child gapes at me, shakes her head and picks up her bucket, dipping a curtsey before turning toward the door. As she goes, I notice her wipe her cheek as if she has been weeping and, to my surprise, I notice moisture on my own. I dash it away with the back of my hand and call after her. "Of course, had I known what was to come, and how much worse things would get, I would have saved my tears."

She turns slowly. I sense her discomfort, her lack of ease in my presence, and I despise her for wanting to leave me.

"But I was a child, do you see? I had no notion of the cruelties of this world and I had been brought up to believe I was special. Irreplaceable. Favoured by God. I thought it didn't matter that I was a girl because the king loved me ... and he *did* love me, you know, better than the others - despite everything that came after ... I *do* know that. I haven't ever forgotten."

She makes a nervous sound. I try to win her over with a soft laugh, gain her friendship, but the sound that emerges is more like a cough. I fumble for my kerchief and spit blood into the fine Flemish lace. When I look up, I sense that all I have gained is her pity.

She steps forward, offers me a cup that I take from her with trembling hands. The wine is welcome. It fills my mouth with flavour before flowing down my throat and warming my belly. When I give her the empty vessel, I sense she is holding back comment.

Narrowing my eyes, I peer at her grubby face. "What is it? What do you want to say? You can speak freely."

"I – I was going to say ... perhaps it would help you to remember that at least you had a father ... at least you know how it feels to be loved. My father died while I was still in the womb..."

"And you think it is better to know what you're missing, do you? Better to suffer a lifetime of wondering what it was you did wrong? Sometimes I wish I'd died in the womb like my siblings ... then I'd have avoided the agony of watching the father I loved destroy the mother I adored."

My throat closes painfully. Self-pity swamps me. I bite my lower lip to prevent myself from weeping, so this lowly person will not witness my pain. It is better that she sees only my anger, but ... I should explain the injustice, the suffering, and perhaps she will understand the battles I have faced.

She clutches the handle of her bucket so hard her knuckles turn white, and I feel a glimmer of admiration for her courage. She is, after all, a nobody debating with a queen. She thinks for a while and when she finally speaks, her words gush like water from a breached dam.

"Perhaps he loved the queen too, but perhaps he put his obedience to God first. It was all long before I was born but … didn't King Henry claim to believe the marriage to be a - a sin against God?"

I glare at her.

"A sin against God? Are you a fool? Of course there was no sin, or do you believe his lies like the rest of them, and think me a bastard too?"

"Oh no, Your Majesty!"

She wags her head in denial, falling to her knees. "I did not mean to offend. I merely tried to offer you comfort." Her voice is a whisper. I turn away and stare moodily into an empty corner.

"There is no comfort. Not on this earth. I wait impatiently for God to take me and put an end to this misery … although…"

She looks up, her eyes dark, but the fear in them is no match for the bleakness in mine.

"What do you think will happen to my realm when I am gone? I have worked so hard to undo the damage my brother Edward inflicted on the church. When I am gone, Elizabeth will have it all. She will take apart all I have done to reverse Edward's heresies, and the bastard daughter of a whore will hold the reins of England."

She swallows, wagging her head from side to side as she searches for and fails to find an answer.

"I suppose you know very little of the real Elizabeth, do you? Yet her day will come. She will be queen and there is nothing I can do to prevent it now. If *only* I had birthed a child, a fat healthy boy. That would have taken the wind from my sister's sails.

"She was ill-gotten, you know, born of sin, to a sinner. I knew it as soon as I saw her just as I knew her mother for my enemy on the day I first laid eyes on her. It took my own mother a little longer to realise that the younger of the Boleyn sisters was a very different kettle of fish to her sister Mary, or to Fitzroi's mother. Mary Boleyn and Bessie were good sorts, they knew their place, but *Anne* Boleyn refused to be kept down. She continually bobbed to the surface of my life, like a rotting corpse in a river."

The door opens and Susan pokes her head into the room. Quickly, I close my eyes, pretending to sleep. When she sees the girl, Susan bustles forward. "What are you doing?" she hisses. "Why are you taking so long?"

"Her Majesty was talking to me."

"Nonsense. She's spoken to no one for days. And why are you tending the fires when it isn't your job to do so?"

"Her Majesty asked me to. It was cold, the queen was..."

"Go and see if Her Majesty's supper is prepared..."

"Get someone else to do it," I raise my head and snarl, not bothering to open my eyes. They are all so tiresome, so ... infuriating. I prefer the company of this half-grown girl to the

21

forced pleasantries of my women. Susan may be my dearest friend but I cannot speak so plainly to her. She is too close and I would hate to see her disappointment in me. But this child, even if she judges me ... her opinion is nothing.

Unable to hide her disillusionment, Susan withdraws, and I open my eyes, smile conspiratorially at my new friend.

"Now, where was I? Oh yes ... Ludlow..."

Ludlow – 1527

My humiliation at being ousted from court is cast into shadow when my cousin breaks our betrothal and marries Isabel of Portugal instead. I am forced to put away the idea of myself as Queen of Spain and instead I bury myself in study, determined to hone my knowledge until I am as learned as any boy, as good as any prince in Europe. Better than Fitzroi.

My time is not restricted to Ludlow; I travel from palace to palace up and down the border. Sometimes at Thornbury, sometimes at Tewkesbury. I visit shrines and religious houses and, on several occasions, I act as my father's representative.

For the first time, I go out among the common people without my parents. Everywhere I go they line the streets, toss their caps in the air and call my name. Their adulation is like a warm wave, an embrace, and I am so far from home, so starved of affection that I fall passionately in love with them in return.

The long dark hours of winter are spent playing cards and dice with my women and, during this time, I grow closer to Margaret Pole than ever before. When we learn that my marriage to Spain has come to nothing, she assures me that a better husband will soon be found. But there is little comfort in her words for no marriage will be as welcome to me as one with Spain. So, when a proposal is put forward for a union with France instead, I confess to weeping a little in the privacy of my bed.

Francis is quite old, of an age with my father, and his reputation is so bad it has even reached my tender ears. I heard one of the women whisper that he has bedded half the French court.

I am growing up and no longer the naïve child I was before. Although I am short on detail, I realise that the conception of a child involves some sort of intimacy between a man and a woman. What I cannot quite decide is why Francis would want children with so many different women; surely a court full of bastards would only cause trouble.

As I understand it, a king requires sons but not so many as to cause conflict within the family. An heir and one to follow after should the eldest perish is a safe number of royal princes – my grandfather was fortunate to have my father to step into Prince Arthur's shoes when he died. The country would have fallen into chaos had Father not been born, although my aunt Mary would probably not agree.

Although the thought of joining with the King of France does not bring me joy, I must accept it with good will while privately hoping that, like my marriage to the emperor, it will come to nothing.

The only positive thing about the whole affair is that I receive a summons to return to court. As soon as preparations are made, I ride joyfully east to be reunited with my parents.

I expect everything to be as it was before. I envisage intimate dinners with my mother and father, walks in the privy garden, feasts and pageants in the great hall, but within hours of our reunion, I realise that nothing is the same.

Mother is pinched and tense, while Father's suppressed anger rumbles like a subterranean river. He is not skilled at concealing irritation. If all is not well, he makes sure everyone is aware of it; he rages and storms like a boy. But this time he struggles to contain it so it simmers just beneath the surface. Everyone walks on tenterhooks, fearful of igniting the royal rage.

My aunt Mary, the dowager queen of France, joins us for the St George's Day celebration, and a dozen or so French dignitaries and ambassadors also attend from Venice and Milan. We feast on crane, heron and peacock, and I am delighted by the royal confectioner's creation of a huge tower of marzipan and two delightful chessboards with real gold pieces. When it is laid before us, I clap my hands with glee and turn to my mother to draw her attention toward it. But both my parents have turned their faces away. They are so wrapped up in their joint misery that they cannot share my joy.

They are pleasant and courteous with the company but their private conversation is clipped and chilly. Where once Father would have reached out for Mother's hand to ensure she was enjoying the entertainments, now he keeps his eyes on his plate. Like him, I turn to food in times of trouble and we both eat too much. He washes his fingers; an usher dries them on a linen towel. I notice the sheen of perspiration on his forehead, the way he constantly dabs it away with a napkin. Pushing my half-empty plate to one side, I feel deeply unhappy.

Afterwards, when the meal has subsided and my belly is no longer straining against my gown, I am

24

conducted into the revel house where I am to show off my skill at the virginals. The company take their seats, gossiping and fidgeting as we make ready to begin. This performance has been long in the planning and I should be confident of my skill, but now that the prospect is upon me, I am filled with nerves. My palms grow moist; my heart leaps and dances with fear.

For the first time, I am to lead the masque. I wear a jewel-covered gown that dazzles the eye and, as we sweep onto the floor, Lady Exeter gives me a bracing smile. I smile back.

At our entrance, Father stands up, his applause loud, encouraging everyone to follow his lead. I see Mother, her face full of pride at my debut. Lady Exeter takes a bow and I do likewise. The dance begins. For a moment, I hesitate. *I have forgotten the steps!* But then, just in time, some inner Mary takes over.

As if I am being guided by invisible strings, I weave in and out of the company, the music sending waves of delight across the back of my neck. My feet are light, my heart is sunny again, and I am sure I could dance all night.

My worries of the future float away, the fear that something obscure and horrible awaits me in the darkness of tomorrow dissipates. My soft slippered feet seem to grow wings and I float on a cloud of joy until, all too quickly, the strains of music fade and I find we are taking our final bow. Lady Exeter and I exchange glances; she embraces me and, with great relief that it is over and I haven't spoiled it, I burst out laughing.

Father, who injured his foot in a wrestling match the day before, limps toward me and I seem to grow taller when I note the pride in his eyes. I look up at him as he rests a hand heavily on my shoulder and gives it a little squeeze. Then, as if by accident, he tugs the strings of my cap and my hair falls free in a golden wave across my shoulders, cascading like water down my back. The gathered courtiers gasp, and murmurs of appreciation spread across the room as they do homage to their perfect princess.

With burning cheeks, I beam at the company, aflame with joy. When the applause dies down, the king pushes me in the direction of the queen.

"A fine performance, Mary," she says, drawing me into her embrace. "You are so light on your feet. I am very proud. All England is proud."

At Mother's right hand, I lean forward, applauding loudly as more dancers trip lightly onto the floor. The performance that follows is fierce, the troupe leaping high into the air, setting the atmosphere in the hall alight. The flame from the torches catches on their spangled clothing, the jewels in their hair. When it is over, I turn to exclaim in wonder, but my words die in my throat when I see Mother's expression.

Dislike and disdain is splashed across her face. Her hands are clasped in her lap, her knuckles white, and her lips are pinched, the lines around them revealing her age. Following her stony gaze, I see that Father has apparently forgotten his injured foot and has taken the hand of a woman I've not seen before.

She is entrancing, beautiful, yet … *not* beautiful. Her ebony curtain of hair gleams in the candlelight and her bold, laughing eyes coupled with her strange, almost foreign mannerisms, somehow mark her from the rest. A newcomer to court.

As I watch her graceful stance, her delight as the king presses his lips against her wrist and prepares to lead her into the dance, I wonder who she is. When the music begins and they start to sway, I am captivated by their practised movements, their shared grace, and mesmerising harmony. Dragging my eyes from the mysteries of their dance, I turn to my mother - my ageing, grey-faced mother.

"Mother," I whisper. "Who is that woman?"

They fill my days with lessons, leaving me no time to think, to ponder on the changes that are taking place within my life. I am used to living apart from my parents yet the separation at court is new and highlights how different things are. There used to be unity, there used to be respect, and it makes me miserable to watch the rift grow daily wider between them.

"What is happening?" I ask Margaret Pole. "My mother and father are acting like strangers." As if they are crumbs on her skirt, she brushes my questions aside and hands me a thread and needle.

"These sleeves will never be finished if you don't apply yourself," she says with an uneasy smile.

I am supposed to be adorning the cuffs of my father's nightshirt with flowers and vines, but it is dull stuff and I would far rather be out on the chase.

"I need some fresh air," I complain. "Why must I keep to my apartments while Fitzroi rides out at the king's side? It isn't fair."

"No, my lady, life isn't fair. While we must stay indoors by the warm fireside, our menfolk must ride out in all weathers. In times of unrest, while we stay here, they ride to war. I am sure they too must envy us our leisurely days."

Lady Margaret has a way of turning my words around, making wisdom from my infantile petulance. I stab the linen with my needle and insert a few ugly stitches.

"I am so bored."

"It will soon be time to go to the great hall. Remember, the master of revels is preparing a pageant for the king's feast. I am sure you will have a part in it."

Putting my sewing aside, I rise to my feet and begin to practise the steps I learned last week.

"I had almost forgotten the pageant practise was today," I say. "Come, Alice, and the rest of you, come dance with me. I want to see if I can remember what we practised before."

Gladly my ladies put away their embroidery and join me in the centre of the room. I join hands with Alice, the other ladies do likewise and line up behind. Slowly, we begin to move, our chins high, our linked fingers at shoulder level. Every fourth step we are obliged to hop, but the chamber is far too small for such formal dances and Alice stumbles into a low stool, squealing when she barks her shins. The ladies following behind bump into us, and it ends in chaos. We all collapse into giggles.

"It will be easier in the hall," Lady Margaret laughs from her seat at the hearth and, as we give up the frolic and re-join her, she sends a girl to fetch the soft shoes that I wear for dancing lessons.

Once ready, we follow Lady Margaret, who sets a stately pace, to the great hall. As we come closer, I feel excitement building up inside me and can barely wait until the music begins and I can release it.

Nobody pays attention to our entrance when the doors are thrown open. The large assembly already gathered buzzes with excitement. Young men and women, eager to show off their skills before the king, have formed small groups to practise their steps. When they notice me, the company parts to allow me passage, but as I draw close to the master of revels, a small knot of people close to the dais continue to gossip.

I stop, glancing up at my lady governess with a question on my brow. The sudden blanket of silence draws the group's attention to my arrival and they turn, break apart and make a knee to me … all but one.

One woman stands defiantly. She looks me briefly in the eye before tossing her head and making a reluctant and very tardy bob of deference. The dancing master bustles forward and bows low in greeting as, from the corner of my eye, I see her spin away. She laughs behind her hand as she is swallowed by her friends.

"I didn't realise *children* were going to be involved," I hear her remark. I turn my head sharply but she has her back toward me. I open my mouth, ready with a reprimand, but Lady Margaret's fingers grow tighter on my arm and, taking her silent advice, I decide to say nothing … this time.

Throughout the afternoon, I keep an unobtrusive eye on the woman. She is graceful, elegant, making me feel clumsy in comparison. I find myself envying the tilt of her head, the way she places her feet just so … beside her, I am like a performing bear.

Her laugh rings out across the hall; her voice is light, intelligent and touched with the faintest of accents. I know from Alice that her name is Anne, and she is the youngest of the Boleyn sisters, recently returned from the French court. I can see from her clothes and her exotic manner that this is true.

Her presence spoils the afternoon for me; somehow she undermines my position although I don't know why. When I complain of it to Margaret, she dismisses her as a fool to risk offending the king's daughter. But she doesn't look like a fool. I make a note to ask my aunt Mary about her when I see her next.

Turning my attention to the last few turns about the floor, I try to forget the Boleyn girl with the mocking eyes, but as the steps of the dance lead me past her, I pray fervently I will not stumble. I cannot bear the thought of her laughter turned against me.

In truth, although I'd admit it to no one, I'd like to be part of her elegant group. I'd like to enquire who sewed her gowns, how she manages to achieve such a sheen upon her hair, how she moves as though she is walking on air. But I know without being told that there is no place in her circle of friends for a gauche, dumpy child … princess or not.

On the morning of the masque, I wake full of anticipation for the coming evening. *Is the gown I selected clean?* I ask. *Have my new slippers been brushed and perfumed?*

I am all smiles as my lengthy toilette is carried out and the day stretches like a spotless carpet before me. But on our way to Mass, one of my attendants tugs at my sleeve.

"Did you hear, my lady? The king has cancelled the entertainments."

I stop dead in my tracks and turn frowning upon her.

"No; you are mistaken, Margery. Surely, I would have been informed…"

But I can see from her face and the gloomy expressions of those gathered about me that it is true. My heart plummets. Disappointment washes over me. I have practised so hard, waited so long, and my steps are now perfect.

"Are you sure? Why? Perhaps I can beg an audience with the king and persuade him to change his mind…"

She leans forward, her hand on my arm, to whisper in my ear. "They say it was at the request of Anne Boleyn."

I frown. "But why … what does she gain from cancelling the pageant? She is as involved as anyone!"

As I speak, the chapel begins to fill with people and the rustle of anticipation, the murmur of deference informs me that the king has arrived to hear Mass. Turning to greet him, I prepare to make a deep curtsey but … my jaw slackens for, as if she is the queen herself, the Lady Anne follows closely in the wake of my father.

As they pass me, my eyes clash with Anne's. Hers are full of triumph and I know beyond a shadow of doubt that her intention is to injure me.

I recognise my enemy and I know that she is not only behind the cancellation of the pageant, but also the cause of the breach between my parents.

Anne Boleyn intends to steal my father, and undermine my position as his heir. Loathing unfurls deep within my belly; hatred that is bitter and cold, and futile.

I beg leave to spend an hour with my mother who is closeted with Chapuys in her privy chamber. Her women, who dote on me, greet me cordially and I am forced to linger with them while they praise the colour of my gown, the shade of my eyes and the hue of my cheeks. It is Lucy Talbot who eventually remembers to make my request known to the queen. As she opens the door, Mother's voice floats from within, her accents strained and upset.

"They tell me nothing …nothing…"

Ignoring etiquette, I glide through the portal, spread my skirts and sink into a curtsey. She halts mid-sentence, pastes a smile on her face and holds out a hand.

"Mary," she says and relief floods through me when I hear the affection in her tone. Mother will always love me, no matter what. There is no one and nothing that can come between us, but it is very evident that something is wrong.

She pats the window seat and I hurry to sit beside her. I listen as the ambassador takes his leave and we are alone.

She quizzes me on my progress in the schoolroom, passes me her lute that I might show her the latest tunes I have learned. As my fingers stumble across the strings, she taps her foot, pretending gaiety, and when I reach the end of my repertoire, I let the lute drop to the ground.

Her happiness is feigned. I wish she would speak to me of her troubles, ease her burden, but I recognise her pride and understand her refusal to reveal her concerns, even to me. She smiles brightly.

"And how is your needlework coming along?" she asks. "Are your stitches smaller, are you managing to keep the lines straight?"

She smiles as she speaks so I know she is not displeased with me. I just wish I could erase the two deep lines above her nose and hear her merry laughter once again. Reaching out, she takes my fingers in her palm. Her hand is cold and I notice her thumbnail has been bitten almost to the quick.

I want to hang on to that hand. I close my eyes and pray hard for God to bring back the days of my infancy when everything was sunny, and I felt safe. *Oh God,* I pray silently, *make the king send that woman back to France.*

"What is it, Mary? Are you not well?" Her voice breaks through my prayer. I blink and look up at her.

"I am well in body, Madam, but I am … troubled."

"Troubled? Is it the marriage with France? I have told your father I do not approve of it. You should have been joined with Spain. Spain is in your blood, part of your history – a union with Spain would please … all of us."

She dashes her cheek, shakes herself as if to dispel a surge of unhappiness.

"It isn't my marriage, Madam. It is…" I drop my voice to a whisper, "… it is that *woman*…"

Our eyes meet and this time she makes no attempt to disguise her pain. She doesn't pretend not to know to whom I refer. She squeezes my fingers gently.

"Do not worry. As soon as his eyes fall upon a prettier face, she will be gone. It was the same with her sister, and Bessie Blount, and countless others I cannot name."

Mother has never spoken to me so openly before. I feel adult, the few years I've spent on this earth inflated to nineteen or even twenty. I lift my chin and tighten my lips, her face blurring slightly when I narrow my eyes.

"I don't think she is at all like Bessie and Mary. I don't think she has any intention of letting the king go. She made him cancel the entertainments just to spite me. Next time one is arranged, I know she will ensure I am left out, and Father will do nothing to prevent it. I have seen the way she goes about court, her band of followers treating her as if she were the queen and not you! She means to…"

"Mary!"

Mother's sharp voice cuts my tirade short but her displeasure is tempered by the light touch of her hand. "I understand how you feel but we must never, never let our disquiet show. We must conceal our feelings behind a mask of dignity. It is beneath us to be troubled by a woman of such low birth – her grandfather was a mercer, did you know that?"

I shake my head, uncertain what difference that makes. I lower my head, frowning with confusion at our entwined fingers. Mother is queen, I am heir to the throne – nothing but death can change that. Why then are we so unhappy?

But, as the weeks pass and my household staff behave more and more strangely, I know they are keeping something from me. As soon as I enter the room, they draw apart and paint rigid smiles upon their faces. When they address me, their voices are light and high, as if they are humouring a small child. Like a thief, unease creeps upon me and steals my peace of mind. My security is shattered and I live each day with uncertainty until, toward the end of August, I hear the word for the first time.

Annulment.

And when I hear that word, although its meaning is unclear, I know for certain the end is very near.

St James' Palace – October 1558

I open my eyes to find they have put me to bed. I have no memory of it. *Did I say my prayers?* I grope for my rosary and mumble a few lines before the cough rips at my lungs again. As I struggle to sit, hands appear from nowhere to assist me. A pillow is tucked at my back, a cup pressed into my palms. I blink at the white face floating in the darkness. I do not recognise it. It is featureless; terrifying.

The past looms back again, more powerful than the present. The past in which I was lusty with youth, not broken by the years.

"I didn't believe it at first. It was unthinkable, do you see? *Unthinkable* that the king should put my mother aside for the sake of some lowborn concubine. I was sure they must be mistaken. Gossips take things, don't they, and blow them up, inflate the smallest details into outrageous lies and present them as truth. I don't know why. I don't know what satisfaction that gives them."

When nobody answers me, I fall silent. The crackle of the flames in the hearth is loud but my thoughts are louder. They scream at me, the turmoil of that far away world as raw as if it were yesterday.

"I dismissed it all as lies but when I eventually questioned Margaret Pole, she wouldn't answer at first. It wasn't until I saw the tears swimming in her eyes that I knew it was more than that. Father was losing his mind."

Sensing someone close beside me, I grab the woman's wrist, draw her close and peer into her face again.

"Margery. Why are you here? Where's that girl I was talking to just now? Who said she could leave? I didn't dismiss her."

"Your Majesty, that was yesterday. The physician says you must rest today. You must not excite yourself."

"Why not? Scared I will die on your watch? Go now and fetch that girl ... I forget her name but she listens. She doesn't fuss and order me about as if I were the servant and she the mistress. Go and get her now."

"It is two in the morning. Everyone is abed, Your Majesty."

"I don't care. Fetch her."

Darkness encroaches again and, despite the fire in the hearth and the warming stone at my feet, I feel alone and cold. I must speak to her now. I cannot be sure I will be alive come morning and there are things I need to say. My head lolls on the pillow and as the past pushes in again, a tear begins a convoluted journey down my cheek.

He loved my mother. I knew he did, I saw it first-hand. He loved her and he loved me too – it was *that* woman, the Boleyn woman, who poisoned him against us. She made him no longer see his wife of twenty years and his beloved daughter – his 'Pearl' – he saw only a barrier preventing him from getting a son. He raged at us, called us stubborn, and I suppose we were stubborn ... but we were in the *right*. It was the king and his whore who were wrong ... and he knew it.

The door opens again and a small figure creeps in; a taller shadow following just behind melts into a dark corner. I reach out an arm.

"Come here, girl, sit on that stool. Where've you been? It was wrong of you to sneak off mid-conversation."

"I am sorry, Your Majesty. I thought, when you fell asleep, you had finished with me."

I sniff. Why do they always accuse me of falling asleep when all I am doing is closing my eyes for a few moments?

"Hmmph, well, where was I? Can you remember?"

She scrapes her stool on the floor, clears her throat and clasps her hands tightly in her lap. Her face is slick with perspiration.

"The annulment, Your Majesty. You had just discovered the king believed the marriage to be invalid because of your mother's previous marriage to his brother, Arthur of Wales."

"Phwah, invalid my foot! Had my mother provided him with a stable of sons the king's conscience would have been just fine. It was Boleyn; she persuaded him that only *she* could provide him with a son. He was easy prey."

"It must have been a hard time for you, Your Majesty..."

"Hard? It was hell. My tender years were stolen. I was in constant torment. Kept away from court, away from my mother ... and Father refused to acknowledge my letters..." My voice breaks. I take a deep breath and exhale so furiously the candles on the nightstand dip.

"At the time, the future was a closed book. I couldn't see beyond the next hour. I expected the worst to happen at any minute. I knew hardly a moment's peace at that time. News filtered through to me ... oh yes, there were those loyal to us, people who hated the Boleyn woman as much as I did – although little good it did them, or us. My mother refused to retire from court, declaring God never called her to a nunnery and she'd be damned if she'd go to one to suit the king.

'I am the king's true and legitimate wife,' she cried over and over, and refused to budge from that. For years she kept Father and his advisors at bay, fending off every attack on us, even in the face of the king's fury ... and I tell you, his fury was something to behold.

"In the end, he sent to Rome, and still my mother stood firm. There were times I wanted to give in, just for the sake of a little peace, hold up my hands and admit to being a bastard. I'd have given anything just to bask in his smile again, but how could I when Mother was so insistent she went to my father's bed a maid? She denied her marriage with Arthur was ever consummated because it was true. She was the king's honest wife, and had he tied her to the rack and tightened the ropes himself, she'd still have sworn she went to his bed a virgin.

My mother was strong and honest and godly, the wisest woman I have ever known. She would never lie, especially not before God."

Our eyes meet. Anne's are sorrowful and, irritated by her pity, I scowl at her until she looks away.

"Perhaps you should sleep now, Your Majesty," she says at last.

"I have no need of sleep. Do my tales bore you?"

"Oh no, Your Majesty, indeed, I am enthralled."

"Well, be quiet then and let me think."

1530

Hard years follow. My childhood is all but forgotten. I drift miserably into young womanhood. My parents are torn apart, my security is in tatters, but the world goes on. The players continue to play, the mummers continue to prance, and while Christendom rocks beneath her feet, Anne Boleyn sits in my mother's chair and applauds.

I learned young to heed my father's displeasure. I have felt his ire, his rage has rung furiously in my ears, but I had never expected him to turn his anger so openly against the Pope. As a young man, the king had been proud of his title 'Defender of the Faith' for his argument against Luther, *Assertio septem sacramentorum adversus Martinum Lutherum*. But now, he scorns it. He strikes out at the Pope when he refuses to sever the king's ties to my mother. He breaks with Rome – for the sake of Anne Boleyn, he cuts England adrift from the mother church, and assumes the title himself.

Father is now the *Supreme Head on Earth of the Church in England*. I had never dreamed he would go this far. The people of England, afraid to protest too loudly, mutter among themselves and only the bravest in the land dare speak out against it.

The church, like the queen, is a victim of Anne's ambition, yet my mother has no champion. Although a few of the old families – the Staffords, the Nevilles, the Courtenays – are firmly on her side, their own influence is waning as the friends of Anne Boleyn wax.

My governess, Margaret Pole, stands with us, as do Elizabeth Stafford and Gertrude Courtenay, but they have no power, no real *influence* over the king. They are soon as far out of favour as my mother and me.

The gossip reaches me in my sick bed at Alton. As womanhood encroaches, I am afflicted with great monthly suffering. For one week a month it feels as if demons are prodding me with red-hot forks. My belly is bloated, wracked with pain, and my mood is as deep and dark as Hell itself. I look into my glass and see my hair hanging limply either side of a pale face; my pores are enlarged, and a pustule the size of a quail's egg is lodged in the crease of my nose.

I might as well be dead.

My women offer what comfort they can but I burrow beneath the covers and give way to despair, mourning the dainty princess I once was. Everything is ruined. I want my mother, but her company is denied me. From time to time her letters are smuggled in. They are my single source of comfort. And that is fleeting.

Why does my mother's cousin, the king of Spain, not come to our aid? He could invade our shores, set his assassins on the Boleyn woman, and force my father to reinstate us! My mother is close kin to them and so am I. Why do they sit by and allow our rights to be stolen from us? There is so little I understand.

But at last, because I have been so ill, I am permitted to return to court where everyone is talking about the *king's great matter*.

In every parlour across Europe, the details of my parents' marriage are being discussed. *I* am being discussed. Did my mother lie with Prince Arthur? Was she a virgin at the time of her marriage to my father? Am I the legitimate heir, or just a bastard? That word again ... *Bastard*.

It haunts me.

At court, close to the leading players in this marital farce, the conversation ceases when I enter a room; the silence makes my ears burn with humiliation. People are hesitant, afraid to show kindness toward me for fear it will put them out of favour with the king, or with his whore. As their backs turn slowly away from me, I ache with loneliness.

Gradually, the pain turns to resentment, resentment to bitterness. I suspect everyone of spying for *the great goggle-eyed whore* as I have begun to think of her. She makes no secret of her hatred. Because of this, fearful of everyone's motives, I rebuff those who do run the risk of befriending me. I go about court in fear of my life, terrified that the next person I meet may conceal a dagger, or a phial of poison in their sleeve.

I have no doubt she is wicked. I have heard how she goes against God's teaching and embraces the new religion that is creeping across the channel from Europe. She supports Tyndale and his heretical scribblings, and I have no doubt that, in the privacy of his chambers, she dribbles her heresy into my father's ear.

Like a bear in a trap, chained to a woman he does not love, the king grows more furious by the day.

Angered by Wolsey's failure to win the annulment of the marriage, he turns against his erstwhile friend. When he is taken, I know beyond doubt that the best the Cardinal can hope for is a lengthy stay in the Tower, for once my father turns against a man his fate is sealed.

I can't remember a time when the great Thomas Wolsey was not prominent at court. All my life, his red skirts and his soft sandaled feet have licked at the corners of my consciousness. I recall Father slinging an arm around the Cardinal's shoulders while they laughed together at some secret jest. I remember my resentment of the long hours they spent closeted away from me. Wolsey was always the first man the king turned to, the scholar whose wisdom Father sought, and now he is naught but a felon.

In truth, although he has great pity for us and has done his best, the Cardinal managed to do very little for the cause of Mother and me yet … what could he do against the will of the king? He is trapped, the king on one side, the Pope on the other, and it is impossible for him to please both masters.

Deprived of his offices, accused of treason, his goods confiscated, Wolsey is placed under arrest, but dies, broken-hearted some say, on his way to the trial. In his absence, his assistant steps forward to take his place: Thomas Cromwell, a toad of a man whose careful tread and sombre expression makes the blood go cold in my veins.

Mother is obliged to leave the court and retire to Windsor where, to my great delight, I am granted leave to join her for a few days. She looks older now, her step has slowed and there is little sign of the girl who was once hailed as the fairest princess in Christendom. Her brow is furrowed, her cheeks sallow and deeply cut with lines.

At first, we speak of innocuous things and she strives to smile but, as the afternoon wanes, her grief seeps through the veneer. It is the most uncomfortable time I have ever spent in her company. Her speech is spotted with snippets of prayer and bouts of outrage. I sit close beside her, my hand in hers and, even when our palms grow slick with sweat, she does not release me. We sit so close our skin seems to act as a conduit for her anger, and we tremble with mutual rage and disappointment.

While her women sit a short distance away, sewing quietly, a musician plays a sad song. The fire that crackles and dances in the grate is the liveliest thing in the room. Her chamber is a dead place, a place of lost hopes, of unrequited love.

I brace myself and clench my fingers tightly as I prepare to ask the question. I have to ask it of her because I can bear to speak of it to no other, but the words burn my tongue.

"Mother … if the annulment is granted, what will become of me? Will I be named a *bastard*?"

That hated word issues like a gob of spittle, my mouth turns down at the corners and my chin begins to wobble. It is shame that makes me feel like this. She grips my hand tighter, her Spanish accent thick with emotion.

"That will *never* happen," she says, "not as long as we have strength to fight it. I will write again to the Pope."

But Mother is wrong. She is so very wrong.

The king cares nothing for the cost of separating from his queen and installing a whore in her place. He would not mind were the world to burn. He risks war with Spain, with the whole of Christendom, and the people of England are resentful. They love my mother and detest the woman who means to replace her. They despise her for a commoner, a heretic and an adulterer.

Stifled by the treachery of court, Mother and I seek an escape and steal an afternoon to ride together in the Great Park. It is a bright day with a buffeting breeze tossing small white clouds across a brilliant blue sky. My favourite weather.

For a few hours we are able to forget our troubles. For a little while we forget we are a besieged queen and a princess of nebulous status – we are mother and daughter and our talk is of nothing but the weather, a clump of primroses beneath the hedge, the shade of the grass that is the exact hue of my skirts.

My horse is young and full of vigour. She lifts her nose and whinnies to her companions and, after turning to request Mother's unspoken consent, I dig in my heels and canter on ahead. With my groom at my side, our mounts thunder across the turf; the ground speeds below me, the scenery blurring and the laughter of the queen's ladies like far-off birdsong. I give the horse her head, crouching low between her ears, my skirts flying, my breath high in my chest. I am still Mary, and I am alive!

As we approach the greenwood, I do not enter but haul on the reins and our pace slows. I pat the mare's neck and ride with a long rein while my palfrey and I recover both our breath and our dignity. The mare snorts and green foam from her bit spatters across my skirts, her sides vibrate beneath me. I raise my arm and wave to Mother who is waiting with her companions near a stand of trees. We return slowly and when I grow close, Mother leans forward and gives her horse a friendly smack.

"You rode too fast, Mary. My heart was in my mouth…"

"I was safe enough, Mother. The fresh air is invigorating."

She laughs, reluctant to scold me on such a lovely day, and we continue on together, side by side. Today we are happy, but who knows what awaits us tomorrow.

St James' Palace – October 1558

"And that was the last day we spent together. I try to always remember her like that; laughing in the face of her destruction. Loving me, in spite of everything. Had she been childless she would probably have obeyed my father and gone quietly into a nunnery, but she had to fight for me; do you see? For my rights; for my inheritance. The throne was my due and she would settle for nothing less. Some people criticise her for that; some say she should have gone gracefully into a convent as others have before, but my mother was proud. Had she bowed to the king's will she'd have hated herself. Instead, we fought the great whore that we hated, and she hated us in return.

"Mother's very existence angered Anne Boleyn. Even after Mother was sent away and I'd been exiled from court, she still detested us. They were long aching years. I was lonely and afraid, terrified of what might happen next. For

45

once you've suffered an unthinkable event, anything seems possible, do you see?

"Mother and I both knew it was only a matter of time. Without the protection of the Pope we felt *naked;* we were bereft and vulnerable.

"But the strange thing is, I never stopped loving the king. In those years I came to realise that whatever he did to me, I would always love him. I would spend the rest of my days yearning for the golden man who once played with me in the garden, because he was my father.

"One by one, atrocities were heaped upon us. The break with Rome, exile from Mother, the brash triumph of Anne Boleyn ... and then the country began to crumble. Bishop Fisher was taken, and Thomas More resigned as Lord Chancellor. I remember my women weeping, mourning his loss before it even occurred. He was a good man ... a proud and righteous man. If he'd only had the foresight to realise the sort of king my father would become. He'd known him since he was a child, you see – had a part in his education. He probably came to wish it had been Father who died instead of his brother, Arthur. Arthur might have made the better king."

"Just one more mouthful, Your Majesty..."

I jerk my head. Margery is holding a spoon beneath my chin, urging me to eat. A napkin has been tied about my neck and my mouth tastes of broth. I clench my lips tight and glare at her until she lowers the spoon. Warily, she dabs my lips with a napkin.

"You've eaten much more than you usually do, Your Majesty; I suppose you must be quite full."

I have no memory of eating anything. My last recollection is of talking to that child ... we were speaking of Father, of those long-ago days that seem much more relevant than the here and now.

"We must get you up and dressed; the ambassador is coming today."

"Ambassador?" I sink into my pillows and tug the covers to my chest.

"Yes, Your Majesty, don't you remember? From your husband; the Duke of Feria will be attending you at noon."

She speaks loudly, enunciating the words as if I am deaf ... or stupid. Philip should come himself. I have had little news from him, and no acknowledgement of my last letter when I confided that there would be no child this time ... no heir.

I sigh gustily, aghast at the woman's cheeriness as she helps me from bed. Every bone in my body aches. As my attendants wash me, I stare into a corner, pliant beneath their attentions, sick of the ritual and tedium of the long process of dressing.

Layer after beastly layer: shift, petticoats, a farthingale so heavy I can barely stand. Lastly, they attach the fore sleeves and hook on my girdle. My knees slump a little beneath the weight. Someone hands me my Bible and I cling to it so hard the jewelled cover digs into my fingers.

I am so tired I could fall.

"Let me sit," I gasp, and they produce a chair. I sink into it, closing my eyes against the pain that surges though my head, my joints that squeal in resentment.

When I next open them again, I am in my state apartments. The sun casts long shadows across the floor and I realise it is late afternoon. I wonder where the last few hours went, passed by in an ebbing tide of faces and voices. A door is thrown open.

"I apologise for the lateness of the hour, Your Majesty. I met with an unexpected delay on the road."

Feria bends over my hand; I feel his breath on my knuckles. I stare at him and force my mind to focus through the fog. I have forgotten what he is here to discuss.

"How is Philip? Is he well?"

"Hale and hearty, Madam. He sends regret that he could not accompany me on this occasion, but next time...."

His lies are loud in my ears. I notice with sudden clarity the way the younger women smirk behind their hands. They think my husband has abandoned me; they think he will never return.

"I deeply regret finding you are still ailing, Your Majesty. I had hoped to find you recovered. Perhaps you will rally once the fine weather returns in the spring."

I will be dead by then and he knows it; they all know it but it must not be spoken aloud. His voice drones on. My mind drifts. Behind the figures and faces of my attendants I see shadows; shades of people I lost long ago – beloved faces of my mother, my father, Lady Margaret. I hear the laughter of long dead courtiers, watch them dance to music that withered a lifetime since. The torchlight glints on their jewels, their perspiring faces. I hear the chink of coin and smothered laughter; inhale the aroma of deceit. I catch the bellow of my father's laughter, an amused gentle response from my mother – the scent of happiness. But then, a face looms forward, a curtain of dark hair, a glint of wickedness and the strain of cruel laughter.

"BOLEYN!"

A sudden silence pulls me back to the present and I realise I have spoken the name aloud. Feria smiles uncertainly, showing his yellow teeth.

"Your Majesty, my master feels it may be prudent to ... to..."

I peer at him, watching as he scrabbles for courage. He takes a deep breath and speaks the words quickly before he can change his mind, "... to name the Lady Elizabeth as heir, Your Majesty ... in the event of ... should the worst happen..."

He has spoken aloud of my death. Nobody breathes; nobody utters a word in the screaming silence as they wait for my reaction. I stare at him, reluctant to break the tension. *Let them*

49

suffer. I gaze over his shoulder, far beyond him as the past drifts closer. A hand falls upon my arm and I look up to find Jane Dormer; her face is blurred. I blink at it, trying to clear my vision.

"Are you feeling quite well, Your Majesty? Would you like to withdraw?"

I cover her fingers with my own and nod; my voice, when I find it, is hoarse.

"Yes, yes. Take me back to my quarters please, Jane."

As she assists me from the room, I glance over my shoulder to scowl at Feria, who sweeps a deep apologetic bow.

They walk me slowly along the corridor to my privy apartments. It takes so much effort. My heart leaps and dances beneath my bodice; a loud ringing has begun in my ears and I am finding it hard to breathe.

"Where is Lady Pole? I want Margaret."

Jane squeezes my fingers. *Why don't they fetch Margaret?*

"Calm yourself, Your Majesty. Don't let him upset you..."

"Name an heir indeed..." I gasp as the guards throw open the doors and we pass into my chamber. My favourite chair opens its arms and I fall into it, someone thrusts a footstool beneath my heels. One of the maids vigorously flaps her fan beside my head, creating a hurricane. Perspiration erupts on my brow. I put up a hand to massage my temple.

"Elizabeth ... she ..."

"Yes, Your Majesty. Don't think of it now. You are tired, close your eyes while I fetch you a posset."

A flick of skirts and she is gone, leaving me to the mercies of my other women. The buzz of their concern fades; like wasps, my worries bump and blunder against the window of my thoughts where Elizabeth has taken up residence. My sister is clever and beautiful and above all young ... everything I am not.

I close my eyes against the memory of our last meeting, the image dissolving before reforming into a picture of her in my place, sitting on my throne, ruling over my people, desecrating *my* church.

I refuse to let her have it.

September 1533

I am at Beaulieu, watching from the window as the heath turns pink beneath the setting sun. I hear the door open but do not move straight away. It is only when Margaret Douglas clears her throat to attract my attention that I turn.

"I was watching the sun set..." I pause when I see her face and realise she has some news.

"What is it?" I beckon her forward and she moves toward me across the floor, then hesitates, her cheeks as rosy as the evening sky.

"News from Greenwich, my lady."

I know what news she speaks of. The whole country has been on edge, waiting for the birth of the concubine's son. I lift my chin, bracing myself for evil tidings.

"And…?"

She wets her lips, visibly swallows before answering.

"A girl, Madam. The queen has given birth to a girl."

I had expected to feel despair. I had expected grief. I had expected a boy – a prince to replace me in my father's affection. But a girl! I had not expected that.

Delight floods through me. I put my hand across my mouth to smother my laughter. A stupid, useless girl! How sharp Boleyn's disappointment must be. How ungoverned my father's rage. Triumph is a heady thing. I click my fingers at a servant.

"Bring me a pen and parchment, I must write to my mother."

This is forbidden, of course, but Mother and I still manage to exchange secret letters, to share our sorrow, our love and our fears. It is the one thing that keeps me going. She must hear this news from no one but myself. It will gladden her sorrow.

The nib of the pen scratches across the parchment. I know that for once she will excuse my untidy scrawl. She will understand the upheaval of my emotions at such a time. But slowly, as I write, the fierce joy is replaced by nudging regret – and I am surprised to feel some pity for my father who has given up all his worldly joys in the hopes of a son.

God has denied him again.

But my pity does not last. As I seal the letter, I see in my mind's eye my father plucking his newborn daughter from her cradle and holding her high. I see her clasp his great finger in her tiny fist and squint up at him with a blue-hued eye. *She will steal him from me.*

I know beyond doubt that even though she is not the son he longs for, he will love her anyway while I will remain forgotten, tucked away like an old plaything – tainted and soiled, and undeserving of his affection. She, *Elizabeth,* will take my place as Princess of Wales, as Father's heir … until a boy is begotten.

Sorrow drowns my brief joy at Boleyn's failure. I drop my pen and bury my face in my hands as the carcass of my former status is cast up and broken.

I think I am in the deepest pit of sorrow but further miseries soon fall upon me, thick and fast. As soon as Elizabeth is proclaimed the High and Mighty Princess of England, my own titles are stripped away. I am no longer to be named 'princess' and must immediately cease to use the title. My own household's badge is cut from my servants' clothes and replaced with the king's arms. I am now merely the Lady Mary, the king's daughter – a *bastard* and a servant. Lower than Fiztroi, because he at least has the benefit of being a boy.

I write straight away to my father, striving to conceal my pain behind dignity and reason.

...when I heard, I could not a little marvel, trusting verily that your Grace was not privy to the same letter, as concerning the leaving out of the name of princess, forasmuch as I doubt not in your goodness but that your Grace doth take me for his lawful daughter, born in true matrimony. Wherefore, I were to say to the contrary, I should assuredly your Grace would not that I should...

I sign it *Your most humble daughter, Mary, Princess* knowing full well the onslaught of royal displeasure this will bring. I am not surprised when, a few days later, the Earl of Oxford leads a deputation to Beaulieu with a clear message from the king as to his expectations.

At first, they are polite, but when it becomes apparent that I will not concede, they rail at me and make the folly and danger of my conduct quite clear. My knees shake and my voice is tremulous as I attempt to refute their words. These men are tall, they are broad and they fill my chambers with contempt when by rights they should kneel to me as the princess of this realm.

It takes all my strength to quell the fury that rages within me. I close my lips so firmly over my teeth that it makes my jaws ache. My eyes sting with tears and my chest is so constricted I can scarcely draw breath. For hours they harangue me with the king's expectations, demanding that I do my duty and adhere to his wishes. It takes all my reserve to repel them.

At last, when they ride away, I watch from the window, glad to see the dust from their hooves settle, leaving the bailey empty and Beaulieu Abbey in peace again. But for how long? I tilt my head back and call down the vengeance of Heaven upon them.

Still trembling with rage, I turn on my heel and return to my chambers, sit down to write a letter to my father. He may be the king but even kings must answer to the law, and to God.

As long as I live, I will be obedient to his rule but I will never, *NEVER* renounce the titles, rights and privileges with which God has endowed me. I will *never* cast doubt upon the validity of my mother's marriage, or upon her virtue, by acknowledging illegitimacy. They can kill me if they want to.

Shortly afterwards, I learn I am to be evicted from Beaulieu and must attend upon the 'Princess' Elizabeth at Hatfield … as her servant. While humiliation clangs like a great bell in my ear, I stare at the letter. This cannot be happening. I want to hide myself away in my rooms, lock myself in and refuse to see anyone, refuse to eat, refuse to pray, refuse to live – but I do not. All I can do is write again to the king, informing him of my unhappiness, begging that he take pity.

In response, he sends Thomas Howard, the great whore's uncle, to force my compliance. I am not yet fully grown but while I wait for him to speak first, I clench my fists tight and stand as tall as I can.

"My lady," he says, his lips twitching at the glee of using the reduced address. "The king demands that you attend the Princess Elizabeth at Hatfield."

I clear bile from my throat and look down my Tudor nose.

"Sir." I curl my lip at the word. "Pray inform my father that the title 'Princess of England' belongs to myself and no other. By rights it should be *she* who serves *me*, when she is of an age to do so."

His cheek twitches, but not from any sense of humour; it is disdain I see in his eye. Were it not for fear of the consequences, it is clear he would take a rod to my back.

"I am not here to debate but to do my master's will," he growls, "no matter what it takes."

I stand silently before him and wonder that a man with so much nasal hair can still draw breath. He is a brute and a bully, and I am at a loss as to how to breach such coldheartedness. I realise there is nothing I can do but comply.

Refusing to look at him, I keep my gaze fixed on a rich tapestry hanging behind him; a blur of gold and red, with a splash of green.

"I cannot just leave. I need time to prepare myself, my servants…"

"You'll not be taking servants with you." He cuts rudely through my speech and mentally I vow that if I am ever in the position to revenge this day, he shall receive no mercy.

"I must have servants." I speak through clenched teeth. "My cousin, Lady Pole, must accompany…"

He cuts me again.

"My orders are that Lady Pole will no longer be required in this household…"

I stand up, clench my fists and shout in his face.

"Lady Pole has been with me my entire life!"

"Until now."

A movement beside me. I had forgotten Margaret's presence. She clutches my wrist and holds out her other hand beseechingly to Howard.

"Sir, show mercy. I ask no payment but will gladly serve the … the Lady Mary … at no expense to the king."

Norfolk turns his back. The guards at the door snap to attention. "Make arrangements, Lady Mary," he snaps rudely over his shoulder. "You depart for Hatfield tomorrow."

With the sound of his footsteps still echoing along the corridor, I turn to Margaret and find my own hopelessness mirrored in her face. We have been together for so long she has become a second mother to me. I will never be happy without her. It is hard, cruel, to be separated from the queen, but from Margaret too? She is my Godmother, my friend…

"Oh Margaret," I whimper. "How am I to endure this?"

Her fingers wrap about my wrist and she squeezes reassuringly, her nose close to mine.

"You shall endure it, my lady. You are stronger than you know. Look how you have borne the brunt of the king's displeasure thus far."

"Because I had you. You made me feel safe. Your love … gave me hope and courage. Without you, I am just a girl … a weak and feeble child…"

"Just as I was, my dear *Princess*. There have been times when I too have been close to despair. When my father was killed, and later when my brother was put to death … when my husband died and left me a widow with children to raise. There are times in everyone's life when we feel we can't go on, but we *do* …we can … *you* can."

I sniff and wipe a drip from the end of my nose.

"Can I? Without you to care for me, I shall be all alone – vulnerable. Who will look after me? Who shall guard me against the hatred of that woman? She means to poison me, you know…"

Somehow, we have come to be kneeling on the floor. She leans forward and takes me in her arms; my head is tucked beneath her chin and her hands are soft on my hair. As we drown in the pool of our spreading skirts, she does not deny my last statement as I had hoped she would. She too has heard the whispers and believes them as I do. The Boleyn woman sees me as a rival to her daughter's throne and means to eliminate me from the game.

When night falls and my eyes are still sore from weeping, Margaret agrees to share my bed. For a long time, I lie upon her bosom and soon her night rail is damp with the tears that will not stop.

Miserable nights are always the longest. While she drifts into uneasy sleep, I stare unseeing at the canopy while a pageant of pictures floats across my mind. The past is bright, shining like a bauble, while the present is dank and chill – but the future is impenetrably bleak. Tomorrow I must ride into hell and feast with the child of the devil.

Hatred for the infant lodges in my chest, sickening me, filling my soul with so much resentment that I can neither see nor taste a single drop of goodness. It eradicates every ounce of my kindness. I blink blindly and whisper into the night.

"I swear by Heaven that I will *not* serve the little bastard. I may be forced to tolerate her, to live beneath her roof and call her 'princess', but I shall *never* look on her as a sister, or her mother as my father's wife."

When I wake in the morning there is blood on the sheets, and I realise my monthly megrim has begun. Usually at such times I would take to my bed, weep into my pillow for a few days until the cramps have eased and I can hold my head high again, but today … I must get up or bear the brunt of Norfolk's fury.

This is the last morning I shall spend with Margaret, and the rest of the household who have served me for so long. Sorrow tears at my heart as I wish them goodbye. The women weep and the men avert their eyes, hoping I shall not notice the tears they hold back. It is the last time I shall be treated as a royal princess – by this evening I shall be nothing but Mary, the king's illegitimate daughter.

It is not until my dressers are tying on my sleeves that I realise my jewels have been taken. By order of the king, they tell me. I absorb this with less sorrow than I bore the removal of my servants, my friends, but I do miss the comfort of my pearls, and my bodice seems bare without them. The only embellishment I am allowed is my rosary. I clutch it tightly beneath my cloak and pray desperately for the strength to bear the trials that lie ahead.

When it is time to leave, the palace yard is deserted. Nobody comes to see me off, there is no pageantry, no one to call out and wish me a safe journey. I am helped into the saddle and jolt as we begin to move. I grab the pommel and slump over the horse's neck. My mood is as dejected and as cold as the dreary day, but just before we clatter beneath the outer gate we pass a small girl driving a gaggle of geese to slaughter. She lifts her head and our eyes meet. When she recognises me, her face lights up and she smiles, curtseying low in the mire.

I manage to smile in return and then I grit my teeth, tighten the reins and dig in my heels. If I must take this journey, then I shall do so in a manner that would make my mother proud. I must never forget that I share the blood of Spanish queens.

But my determination is soon thwarted. The road is long and the weather is bitter, a hint of snow in the air. Norfolk allows me little rest. By the time we embark upon the last stage of the journey, my body is screaming with pain. My menses are always cruel but travelling makes it harder. My lower back aches; my knees, despite the thick layers of skirts and petticoats, throb with cold. I hold on to the reins as desperately as a drowning man to a rope, and long for the journey to end.

The Great North Road is interminable, the hamlets we pass through are small and mean, yet I'd give all I own for an hour to sup pottage before one of their humble hearths. Norfolk ignores each request I make to rest a while.

"It's not much farther now," he barks rudely over his shoulder. "Potters Bar is ahead and Hatfield lies just beyond."

Just beyond. The words give me hope. I pull myself up in the saddle and blink into the wind, expecting to see the lights of the town around the next bend.

The dwellings we pass are sparse and down at heel; a dog leaps barking, straining his chain as we ride by. My eyes linger on his slobbering teeth; I can almost feel the bite of them on my ankle. Nudging my mount sideways, I draw closer to a man-at-arms and he turns his head, smiles encouragingly before looking away again. Somehow I manage to draw a small amount of comfort from his rebuttal, the small quick smile would have been wider had he not been afraid of drawing his master's displeasure.

With no friend beside me I am grateful for his fleeting warmth, but as soon as he turns away, I grow cold again. I shiver and try not to think of roaring fires or warming cups of frumenty. I push away memories of thick blankets, gentle arms, and clutch my fur-lined cloak tighter to my throat, lowering my head against the freezing rain.

Slowly, the eternity of road unreels beneath the hooves of my mount. My head is so heavy I can scarce hold it erect and I can barely keep my eyes open. I long for a soft mattress, a hot drink, for sleep and oblivion.

"Take care, my lady, lest you fall." A rough male voice jerks me awake. I blink blearily at the man-at-arms. His hand is clutching my rein and he smiles tightly. "Not much farther now, my lady."

I am so grateful for his solicitation that I cannot find my voice. Ahead, the broad expanse of Norfolk's back rises and falls with his horse's gait. I smile wryly at the man but he does not return it. I understand that he dare not and make do with the cold comfort of his unspoken empathy.

Not long now, I tell myself. Dusk is falling. Ahead, I imagine I see a glimmer of light, a yellow speck of suggested destination. I blink into the gloom.

"Is that…?"

"I believe so, my lady."

The lights of the inn grow brighter as we draw closer. An ostler looks up as we ride by and tugs his forelock, but that is the only greeting I receive. Usually my arrival is hailed ceremoniously with a fanfare and great pomp, but today I could be anyone. My arrival passes unnoticed. I turn regretfully in the saddle as the brightness of the inn diminishes behind us, and with it the hope of warm drinks and a lively fire. We climb uphill, my horse's head nodding at the effort. Then a church looms from the dusk, the stocky bell tower solid and reassuring against the dark sky. A cry goes up and the gates of the house start opening.

I have been here before, of course. I have stayed here, slept in the best chambers, walked in the softness of the gardens, sheltered from the rain beneath wide gnarled oaks. In those days, everyone did my bidding, striving one against the other to please me. Today, the palace yard is empty; only a stable boy comes forward to help me dismount and lead the horse away.

I stand hunched and hungry and wait for someone to appear to greet me, but nobody comes. Jane Browne, the only woman permitted to accompany me, hobbles forward as stiff as I from the saddle, and together we move beneath the arch toward the great hall.

As we near the door I hear footsteps behind me, and Norfolk pushes ahead, causing me to step aside to allow him passage. I tighten my lips, making note of the incident. One day, I vow, I will be in the position to repay him for the slight.

We follow into the bright hall and I head straight for the hearth, holding out my hands to the flames, wincing at the devilish lick of pain as my fingers begin to thaw.

A light step behind. I turn to find a woman, a lady by her dress, and at first I fail to recognise her until she moves forward from the shadow.

"Lady Shelton." I extend my hand but she doesn't take it and neither does she curtsey as she once would have. Instead, she inclines her head.

"Lady Mary," she replies indifferently … and then she catches sight of Norfolk. "My lord…" She holds out a hand in greeting and he swoops upon it. I recall they are some sort of kin. My gaolers have been chosen well, for she is another cousin of the great whore.

I watch as he greets her, marvelling at his warmth when he has shown me nothing but malice. Ignoring my presence, they rudely exchange news and tidings from court while I am forced to swallow the slight. Just as I am about to snap, Lady Shelton turns and casts a derisive eye over my soiled skirts.

"I suppose I should show you to your room," she sniffs.

Turning on her heel, she hurries before me along twisting corridors, up a flight of stairs. Then she halts, fumbles with her keys and throws open a chamber door. I duck my head beneath the lintel and look around. Jane Browne shakes her head, her eyes wide. "Oh, my lady," she whispers.

"It isn't the worst room in the house," I say, as much to convince myself as anyone else. "At least there is a window and … and a brazier."

But it isn't lit. I crane my neck to peer across the rooftops and discover my room looks down upon the barnyard where pigs no doubt root all day in the manure pile, and the cockerels shriek in the dawn from the stable roof.

"It is not fit for you though, my lady. It is an outrage you should be housed here. You should write to the king."

I sit down on the bed and find the ropes loose beneath my weight.

"He will not care, Jane, it would be a waste of ink and paper."

"Come, let me help you out of these wet clothes."

As I submit to her gentle persuasion, I am overwhelmed with a sense of isolation. I am no better than a servant, and there is no one who can help me now. A tear trickles from my eye, drips onto my bodice.

"Ahh, my lady, come here, come here…"

She stands on tiptoe, puts her arms about my neck, and I give way to the tears I have been stifling for so long. While my body heaves, her hands are gentle on my hair, and she rocks me to and fro as if I were an infant. At length, I pull away, wiping my wet cheeks with my fingers. She hands me a kerchief and smiles ruefully, tempting me to smile in return.

My mouth wobbles and goes out of shape as I try not to cry again.

"Really, Jane, you must not be so kind, it will be my undoing."

"Tears are necessary sometimes, my lady. My mother says they are healing, a gift from God to help us cope with sorrow."

I sniff inelegantly and firm my mouth, clenching my weak chin and pushing the raw pain deep, deep inside.

"I suppose I should put in an appearance downstairs in the hall."

"Anne Shelton is not so bad, my lady, and you must agree her job is not an easy one. She has nothing against you, I'm sure, but probably feels obliged to not disobey the k … her orders."

I look at her from the side of my eyes as we return to the hall. At the top of the stairs, I hesitate, unsure of the way we took before.

"I think it is this way…"

I stride ahead and she follows in my wake, and on entering the hall I find Lady Shelton and my lord of Norfolk in deep conversation. No doubt they are concocting further methods of torment.

"Lady Mary." Anne Shelton's smile is like a serpent's. "Would you like me to convey you to the Princess Elizabeth so you may pay your respects?"

Norfolk smirks, stroking his malicious beard. I cannot restrain myself any longer. I have been stripped of my title, my assets, my status, and I will not be further humiliated by these people. I raise my chin, looking down my Tudor nose.

"I know of no other princess in England other than myself but … I will greet Elizabeth and treat her as a sister, just as I treat my father's other bastard, Henry Fitzroi, as my brother. Please, Lady Shelton, take me to her."

Norfolk snorts, his face purpling in fury, while Lady Shelton opens one arm and ushers me from the room. We pass through fine corridors, sumptuously appointed with tapestries and plate. At the far end of the passage men are standing guard; at our approach they throw open the heavy doors and I am escorted inside. The murmur of conversation hushes, mouths drop open, but no one bows as they once would have done. Lady Shelton touches my elbow.

"Come, Lady Mary, you must meet the Princess Elizabeth of England."

I hesitate. I want to run away, to quit this palace for the solace of my mother's arms, but I cannot. I am a prisoner. Held as fast here as the meanest traitor in the Tower. I take a reluctant step toward the cradle, halting when I hear a gurgle of infant glee.

"Come, Mary, the nurse has loosened the princess' bands to let her limbs free for a while."

I peer into the nest of satin and lace and a pair of wide blue eyes meets mine. Something stabs me, like grit in the eye. I blink rapidly and grip the edge of the cradle before reaching inside. She stops kicking, bubbles of spittle at her lips, and grabs my finger, clings to it and tries to bite it. Despite myself, I smile, and she smiles back, her pink gums gaping. I waggle my hand, making her arm dance, and she emits a crow of laughter that pierces my heart like a lover's dart.

St James' Palace – October 1558

"I've not been free of her since..." My voice echoes around the empty chamber. I look up from the pillow, remember where I am, who I am.

Night has fallen, the fire slumbers in the grate, and a woman is sleeping at the hearth. Susan ... *I was rude to her earlier*. That was cruel of me; she has been with me for so long, served me faithfully, through thick and thin.

When she wakes, I will try to rouse myself from this megrim and tell her I'm sorry. Her attendance on me this night is out of love, not duty. As my mistress of robes, it is far beneath her station to watch me sleep. The quietest of my women, her services often go unnoticed and unrewarded. I make a note to remedy that when day breaks. I watch the flames' shadows dance about her face, deepening the lines and pouches that time has painted there. We were both young women when we met. What must it be like to spend one's whole life in the service of another? It was hard when I served Elizabeth but ... that was forced upon me. Susan serves me from love ... devotion. I had her support when all others were turned against me – while I fought for my throne, while I struggled with my marriage and ... the babies.

Susan believed in my babies as much as I did.

My hand delves beneath the coverlet, coming to rest on my flaccid stomach – my empty, barren womb. I close my eyes against a sudden griping pain. I had wanted a child so much. A brave boy with flame-red hair and the determination of ... of a *Tudor*, to rule in my stead when I am gone.

Elizabeth is a Tudor, she is strong and staunch, but how can I name her my heir when, despite her pretensions, I know where her heart truly lies? If she inherits my throne, it will condemn my loyal subjects to her heresy, the realm will once more be thrown into religious turmoil. Yet ... who else is there? Who else can I trust? There are no Catholic Tudors to follow when I am gone.

Susan stirs, wipes a trickle of drool from her chin and blinks about the room.

"Your Majesty." She runs her hands across her face, rises and moves toward me, the knee that always causes trouble making her hobble. She looks into my eyes and I remember my resolution to let her see her worth.

"Susan, you must be so tired, you should have gone to your bed."

"Oh, Your Majesty, you are feeling better! Do you know me now?" She clasps my hand, holding it to her bosom.

"Was I rambling before?"

"A little," she confesses with the suggestion of a laugh. "You had us worried."

"I was thinking of my father ... it was as if he were right here with me. And I was with my mother and my sister too, when she was little. I tried so hard to hate her, you know, but she is kin, do you see?"

"She is, Your Majesty. You could not hate her."

She smoothes the coverlet and tucks it so firmly beneath the mattress that my arms are trapped. I struggle against the restraint and throw the coverlet back. As she turns from the bed, I grab her sleeve, and she sinks back onto the mattress beside me, lowering her face close to mine.

"Oh Susan, I fear I have no choice but to name her my heir."

"Yes, Your Majesty." Her expression is unreadable.

"But she is a heretic, I know she is. How can I be responsible for the hell she will unleash upon the realm?"

Her hands cover mine.

"It is your duty to name an heir. If you fail to do so, there will be unrest, if you name Elizabeth there will be unrest also. You wouldn't want her to have to go through what you did when King Edward died. Perhaps you could send word to her, instil in her the importance of maintaining the true religion, both for the sake of her soul *and* the welfare of the people."

A vision of my sister's face rises before me. Inscrutable, intelligent and, I suspect, intractable. If I implore her for the sake of England, she will ostensibly comply but inwardly she will be laughing at me, knowing that she has the victory at last.

Oh, Elizabeth has always won. One toss of her head and all men do her bidding; it has always been so, since she was knee-high. She usurped my place in my father's heart and stole the love of the people from me and now ... now she thinks to take my throne. I will not have it! The crown of England will *never* sit on her head, not while I breathe!

I struggle to sit up; Susan's hands are on my shoulders. "Hush, Your Majesty, hush; lie down, please. You must be calm."

I clutch her wrists. "What shall I do, Susan? What *can* I do?"

"Send her word, Your Majesty. Send Jane with a loving letter, entreating her to stay true to the Roman Church. It is all you can do, and then, when it is done, we will pray. God will instruct us. It is one last trial he places in your path; you must not fail now."

I gasp into her face, my heart racing as if I have been running. I nod and gently push her hands away. I must act quickly before the darkness ... the madness descends again.

"Fetch me a pen and parchment. I will write to her now while you rouse Jane from her bed."

She runs to do my bidding and I fall backward onto the pillows. It is not an answer for there is none, but it is action and once it is done, the matter will be out of my hands and I can concentrate on dying.

Hatfield – January 1534

A cockerel shrieks outside my window, shattering my dreams. I roll over and burrow beneath the blankets, dreading another day. As soon as it grew dark last evening I took to my bed, but no matter how early I retire, the noise from the kitchens drifts up to hinder my slumber. Now, before the day has properly dawned, I am woken again, and now face another day of humiliation and bullying.

Although Anne Shelton is not physically cruel, her manner and lack of respect toward me is wearing. Yesterday she ordered me to carry a basket of Elizabeth's soiled linen to the laundry, a task that is far below my station. Every action, every order, is designed to remind me that my status is nothing, that even she is better than I because *she* was not born a bastard. *But neither was I.* I am a princess of this realm and I will not forget it.

One day, one day soon, I will free myself from this; I will rally those loyal to me, call on Spain for help and restore my rightful place. When that day comes, I shall have the Boleyn woman, Anne Shelton, and her uncle, Norfolk, thrown into the Tower and Elizabeth shall be made to wait on *me*! But that is just a dream and … it isn't her fault, is it? She is just a babe, as innocent as I in all of this. She might be the barrier between me and all I desire but at the same time, she is the only soul in this place who has any affection for me.

When nobody is looking, I take her on my knee to let her tug my hair, pull my nose and dribble on my gown. She is as fat and warm as a tabby cat and in my greatest torment, I find my only comfort. Whenever she sees me, she holds up her fat arms to be held. I think Elizabeth is the only person in the house who likes me.

"Lady Mary!"

I jump, swing my legs over the mattress.

"I am up."

The serving girl ducks her head in tenuous allegiance and my heart soars. I think I have found a friend. "I am up," I repeat.

"Lady Shelton bids you attend her in the parlour."

There is no one to help me dress and it takes a long time to wriggle into my kirtle and tie up my own sleeves. There used to be half a dozen women to help me dress but now I must do it myself and, as a result, I am often late, appearing halfway through breakfast with my gown crumpled and my hair snarled at the back of my head. Thank goodness I can hide it beneath my cap.

Thrusting my feet into threadbare slippers, I hurry along the twisting corridors to the chamber that Lady Shelton has taken as her own.

When I scratch upon the door, she swivels in her seat and looks up coldly. "Ah, Lady Mary." I take two steps forward but she holds up her hand and bids me come no closer. "The king will be visiting the Princess Elizabeth today and I have been instructed that you are to remain in your chamber until he has departed."

"But ... surely my father will not ride so far without wishing to bid me good day. I will wait in my chamber but he will send for me when he is done with…"

"Those are the orders I have been given, and you *will* do as you are bid. Good morning, Lady Mary."

She turns her back and I long to strike out, tear the hood from her head and rip out a handful of her glossy hair. I shake with rage but there is nothing I can do. I clench my fist; the pain as my nails dig deep into my palms is almost a pleasure. When I do not take my leave at once, she picks up her pen and continues to write – black marks upon the page. "You may go."

It is an order not a request and, with a growl of impotence, I turn on my heel and wrench open the door. I slam it so hard behind me that I twist my shoulder; pain shoots through me and tears smart my eyes.

There is nothing I can do. I am powerless. I am nobody, the least important member of this household. Deprived of breakfast, my belly growling, I walk as fast as I can back to my lonely chamber. I sit on a hard stool and take up a book, staring blankly at it while the sunlight tracks across the room. I do not see the words.

The muffled sounds of the household drift up from below, setting me apart, segregating me from the rest of the company. I hear running footsteps, a strain of laughter, Elizabeth crying in her nursery demanding her nurse. It is almost noon when a clamour breaks out in the palace yard, hailing the arrival of the royal party. My heart leaps and then quickly sinks again. The royal party – how strange to have no part in it.

Putting my book down, I crane from the window, hearing the jingle of fine harness as the groom leads my father's horse to the stable. I daresay even the horse will receive better care than I; he will get the best stall, the sweetest hay, the fattest oats and, when it is time to leave, he will be given the honour of a royal scratch behind the ears.

My throat closes and tears gather as I imagine the king sweeping into the royal nursery, picking up my sister, making much of her, kissing her fingers and remarking on the wonder of her development. I expect he has brought her a gift, but he will have none for me. I doubt if he will even think of me, or even remember that I am here. I must remain hidden from his sight, a blot on his happiness, a blemish on his perfect life.

A knock comes on the chamber door and hurriedly I knuckle the tears from my cheek. It is the girl again.

"Does the king wish to see me?" I blurt, but her expression answers clearer than any words.

"Madam." She bobs a sort of curtsey. I must tell her not to do that; if anyone sees it will only bring her trouble. I smile as winningly as I can.

"Lady Shelton and Lord Cromwell wish to speak to you."

"Indeed." I raise my brows in surprise. I had thought I was to remain here in my chamber but I do not contradict her. Hastily, I straighten my hood and arrange my tired gown as best I can. The girl leads me downstairs to a dark antechamber in a little used part of the house. They are so determined that my father shall not see me that they keep me hidden. I feel like a dirty secret.

The chamber is chilly and ill lit. Cromwell and another man wait at the hearth where a sulky fire has been lit. Neither man bows when I enter. I firm my chin, lift my head and look down my nose at them. *I am Mary Tudor.* I am not some lowborn girl to be so rudely used.

"I hope you are in good health, Lady Mary."

How extraordinarily easily the lies trip from this man's tongue. I can scarcely prevent my lip from curling into a snarl when I make reply.

"I am not, sir. I am most rudely treated and grieving for the company of my mother, as well you know. My chamber does not befit my station and my gowns are too small; some are threadbare and need replacing. The servants here are rude. Anne Shelton treats me as an underling."

Cromwell's face creases into furrows. He clasps his hands as if he is about to pray … to the devil, I presume.

"Lady Mary, you are disobedient to the king's wishes. If you wish your circumstances to improve then you must denounce your title and acknowledge that the king's union with your mother was illegal. Then and only then will you be taken again into your father's favour…"

"As his *bastard*."

He inclines his head.

"The marriage was no marriage, your birth no different to that of your brother Fitzroi, yet look at the benefits he receives. Your father honours him as his son, as he would honour you as his daughter if you would only cease to be so stubborn."

"I was born *within* wedlock, sir, I am no *bastard*! My mother is a God-fearing woman; she would never stoop to immorality. She is a princess of Spain and the rightful Queen of England and she *never* lies!"

He throws open his hands, revealing red work-worn palms, and I remember he is the son of a blacksmith. What times are we living in when the son of a farrier can grind a princess of the realm into the dust?

I stand a little straighter.

"You waste your time, sir, with your bullying and bombast. You do not frighten me. You can mistreat me all you like; you can send me to the Tower and threaten me with death, but I will never renounce my title or my position as the true born princess of the realm and my father's legitimate heir."

His face pales, his lips a slash of bitterness, and I know he silently curses me. I curse him in return. As he opens his mouth to speak again, I forestall him, stepping forward and looking directly into his shifty eye.

"I wish to greet my father, the king, sir. Pray inform him that the *Princess* Mary awaits his convenience."

He smirks and thrusts his face closer, his tainted breath blasting directly into mine.

"Oh no, Lady Mary. You shall not see the king. You will remain here at Hatfield and see nobody until you decide to be obedient. You will serve the infant princess and I shall instruct Lady Shelton to heap any humiliation she pleases onto your head. Until you realise that you have no claim on your father, you will be kept away from him. I am confident that he will neither miss you nor even enquire as to your health. He has a new daughter now and every expectation that a male heir will follow."

He pushes past me so violently that I almost lose my footing. The chamber door crashes closed behind him, the sound of it reverberating through the floor, through my body, to lodge deep in the darkest places of my mind. I clench my trembling hands. *He will pay for this, one day. As God is my witness, he will pay.*

When the sound of their footsteps has faded, I pick up my skirts and run from the chamber. Skimming swiftly through the dark corridors to the upper floor, I tumble out onto the terrace where I sometimes like to take the air. They might refuse to convey to the king my entreaty for a meeting but he *shall* see me. I shall make sure of it.

This terrace overlooks the front of the house. If I stand on my toes I can just about see the steps to the main hall. I need only linger here until it is time for him to leave, and then…

Hours pass and I am quite cold before the doors finally open and the household spills down the steps to wave the king on his way. His horse is brought round and it sidesteps, tossing its head and chomping on the bit. Idleness in the stable has made it eager for the road and the groom struggles to keep it steady. Father will enjoy a heady gallop back to court.

A babble of fawning conversation floats up to me, high-pitched women's voices mingling with the deeper chorus of male laughter. I lean as far as I dare over the edge, but all I can see is the fluttering feather on the king's cap. And then I hear his voice, louder than the rest. I close my eyes and glory in the sound of it.

Clinging to the balustrade, I stand on tiptoe to gain an even better view. He seems smaller from my vantage point, shrunken somehow, yet his hair is as bright, his shoulders just as wide as I remember. The big golden laughing man of my childhood. Despite everything, the sight of him makes me smile.

He has one arm thrown around Cromwell's shoulders, listening as the obnoxious toad spits poison into his ear. Father nods and smiles again, then he turns his attention to Lady Shelton, who falls into a deep curtsey of farewell, her black skirts pooling like oil. My heart leaps as he moves away, seizes the pommel and takes a last look round. He is leaving! He cannot leave!

I lean further forward, call out and frantically wave both my arms. "Father! Father!"

At the last second, either my voice or the movement catches his eye and he hesitates, letting go of the saddle. For a few moments, as if frozen to the spot, he looks at me.

Our eyes lock and his face droops into a thousand sorrows. As my heart breaks, my mouth turns upside down and my grief and longing for him emerge in a wail of misery. I blink to clear my eyes and, lifting my fingers, I trap a kiss within them and let it fly toward him. It is an old game we used to play and, unable to help himself, he reaches out … and catches it.

After he has left, everything is so much worse. I had hoped that having seen me, he would reconsider. I imagined he would write and welcome me back to court, and force his concubine treat me with due courtesy. But days pass and there is no word from him and, as my monthly megrim approaches, I fall again into deep despair.

"For Heaven's sake, girl, will you cease your weeping!" Lady Shelton complains when she bothers to notice me. What does she expect? If her sole purpose in this household is to subject me to humiliation and misery, does she not expect me to weep? Am I supposed to welcome it?

I cannot rouse myself and, as my misery deepens, so my fears grow. I have spent most of the morning crying in my chamber, avoiding the other members of the household. And then the serving girl creeps in whispering my name, and I sit up, knuckling away my tears.

"What is it?"

She steps forward, holding out her hand.

"A letter, but please, your, your … my lady. You must tell no one or I will be punished."

I look down at the salutation, scrawled and unreadable. I tear it open and discover a letter inside. It is *a letter from the queen.*

What stealth my mother must have gone to in order for this letter to reach me. I read aloud, drinking in her words, words that speak of a misery that matches mine. She exhorts me to be brave, to be vigilant for those who wish for my death. I long to see her. I miss her wisdom, her strength of purpose. Her Spanish blood may run thickly through my veins but I lack her resolve. I would give what little I own for an hour in her company. If I could only see her, she would boost my spirits and help me to be strong.

Loneliness. I sink to the floor and wipe my dripping nose on the sleeve of my shift. The girl steps forward, hovering a few feet away. I, who was once courted by kings and emperors, am driven to keeping company with serving maids. I look up at her and she casts a glance at the door, fearful of discovery.

"What is your name?"

She shakes off surprise at my question and smiles fleetingly.

"Nellie. My mother calls me Eleanor but to everyone else I am Nellie, or Nell."

I reach out my hand.

"Thank you, Nell. I am in your debt."

Her palm touches mine and my fingers wrap around hers.

"You should let me destroy the letter, my lady. If they discover it, the punishment will not be mine alone."

I clutch the parchment to my chest and feel that my heart will break to part with it.

"Read it once more," she says, "and then let me destroy it."

It is my last link with my mother. She has touched it; the words are stained from the tears she shed as she penned them. I shake my head, my mouth agape. Nell steps closer, her face dark with fear.

"You *cannot* keep it. Doesn't the queen beseech you to have care? Isn't she warning you that your enemies are gathering? She would want you to burn it."

She is right. I nod miserably.

"Let me read it just one more time…"

As Nell closes the door and stealthily takes her leave of me, I commit Mother's warning words to memory. She warns me to be vigilant of assassins and, in the days that follow, I come to suspect every morsel I am offered. I walk in fear, starting each time the arras stirs in the draughty corridor, barely able to partake of a hearty meal for fear of poison.

At my request, Nell now prepares my breakfast, and I take to eating it alone in my chamber. She piles my plate high and I eat every morsel to fill my belly so completely that I can plead no appetite and escape dinner later on in the hall.

But fear and worry take their toll and I grow wan and weak, constantly ailing, a shadow of the girl I was before. We are moving to Hertford while the apartments at Hatfield are thoroughly cleaned. On the morning of our departure, I wake to the now familiar cramps in my belly. I cannot bear the thought of the jolting nightmare of travelling by litter and bury my head beneath the pillow. When they come to rouse me, I groan, barely lifting my head from the mattress.

"I am too sick to travel. I will follow on after, when I am recovered."

Footsteps patter away and I sink gratefully back into the feather-stuffed mattress. A short while later, the chamber door is thrown open and Lady Shelton's voice cuts through my slumber.

"You will get up now, Lady Mary, and prepare for the journey. It is the king's desire that you accompany us. If you do not wish to offend him, you would be better to do as I say."

Father's face floats before my mind's eye. I see his beaming smile, a look of love, a kindling humour, but … it melts again. His lips tighten, his button mouth disappearing in fury, his eyes narrowing into contempt.

I cannot bring myself to displease him. Throwing the pillow across the room, I thrust my legs from beneath the covers and, cradling my griping stomach with both hands, I stagger to the close stool.

The screen that offers privacy from the bedchamber is faded now but once it was a rich tapestry of colour. While I attend myself as best I can, the grey faces of ancient huntsmen and washed out maidens of yore stare back at me. The hind they have slaughtered pours dark brown blood onto a bleached sward. I pull down my shift and creep, weak-limbed, back into the chamber. Lady Shelton watches me intently, unsure if I am shamming, but one look at my face and she softens, just a little.

"I will send someone to help you dress," she says, "but do not tarry. We leave at noon."

I am tugging at my tangled hair when Nell arrives. She is carrying a large covered ewer that she sets on the nightstand. "The water is still warm," she says. "I brought it from the princess' chamber."

I smile widely, grateful for her small kindness. Softly and tentatively, for it is far outside the requirements of her usual duties, she wipes my face with a soft cloth, dabs my fingers and the back of my neck.

"At least the sun is with us today, my lady. Your journey will not be so dour in this weather."

Although it is barred, I look instinctively toward the shuttered window. I cannot see out and even if I could, the chamber is north facing and subject to the coldest winds. It will be pleasant to see the sun.

"I hate it here," I whisper, "but I am loath to leave."

"It's only for a short while, my lady, and I will be among the company. Should you feel … uneasy, look for me. I will try not to be too far away."

Once, I was served by only the grandest in the land. It was regarded an honour to sit at my side at dinner or walk with me in the gardens. Even to comb my hair and wash my linen was a sought-after appointment, but now I am grateful to this lowly servant for she goes beyond duty and shows me friendship. The first true friendship I have ever known. She gains nothing from it and likely never will. Grateful tears well in my eyes but I do my best to smile. My cheeks are so taut I feel they will crack; my face crumples and I drop my head into my hands.

"Now, now my lady," Nell says. "Tears never helped no one."

I dash them away with the back of my hand. She is right. Tears won't help but I am damned if I will be pushed around. I am a Tudor princess and it is I who should be doing the pushing.

I stand up, momentarily forgetting my indisposition. My head swims. I grab Nell's shoulder and wait for my equilibrium to return. When the room has righted itself, I pick up my prayer book and look around to see if I have left anything behind. For a moment, I have forgotten that I have few possessions now.

"Come along, Nell," I say as if she was the one reluctant to leave. "I'd better not keep them waiting."

I make my way downstairs as swiftly as I can manage but, on reaching the door, I find the travelling party almost ready to depart. Elizabeth has been settled in the first litter with the foremost ladies of the household comfortably installed around her. The lesser ladies have mounted the second litter, and I suppose I am expected to take my place with them.

It is an insult. I should have my own litter, attended by the grandest women at court! The very least I should expect is to travel with Elizabeth. My former resolve to be obedient dwindles away and the old fury raises its head again. I clutch my prayer book and when Lady Shelton leans from her litter and urges me to hurry up, I stick out my chin and stubbornly refuse.

Her face freezes.

"Do as I say, Mary. You will make us late."

I shake my head, just once, and glare defiantly at her.

"I will not ride behind. I am a princess of this land and should be given precedence."

She sighs and begins to clamber from her seat; a servant rushes forward to assist her. My heart almost fails as she strides toward me, no longer even trying to conceal her contempt. Her face is white, her eyes slit with fury.

"Get in the litter," she spits through her teeth, pointing toward the waiting vehicle.

I shake my head again and our eyes clash – this is a battle of wits that I am determined not to lose, but my courage is flagging.

I am Mary Tudor, I tell myself. *I am Mary Tudor!*

There is nothing she can do to force me to her will. Let her tell the concubine. Let her send for the king. Let him throw me into the Tower if he wishes. They cannot make me submit to their orders.

Her eye shifts from mine to focus on something to my rear. I turn my head and catch sight of Norfolk, accompanied by a household guard. Before I comprehend what is happening, he grabs me rudely from behind, constricting my arms so I cannot fight. As he lifts me from the ground I feel the warm gush of blood between my thighs, and pain shoots through my body, but the humiliation of his manhandling hurts me far more.

I kick out and struggle against him but he is broad and strong, and I am just a girl. Letting loose a torrent of abuse, I fling words at him that would destroy my mother if she heard them. With my body held firmly against his, he carries me forward and drops me onto the floor of the litter with my skirts about my knees. I sit up, straining forward, the tight bodice cutting into my ribs.

"You benighted whoreson!" I scream above the pounding of my heart. "I will have your *head* for this! Do you hear me? You will burn in *hell* for what you have done!"

My curses are not meant for Norfolk alone but for the concubine and all her cohorts, for Cromwell, and even for the king himself.

1535

And so it goes on. Year after year of humiliation and misery. I miss my mother, I miss my father, I miss Margaret Pole, I miss my aunt Mary – all who were so dear to me, so vital to my happiness, have been taken away. I have only Nell and, to some degree … Elizabeth who, although the cause of most of my pain, is only a baby and cannot be held responsible. Her mother, on the other hand, is solely to blame.

Far too frequently, the concubine visits Hatfield to spend an afternoon with her daughter. I keep to my chambers; I have even less desire of her company than she has of mine. When the coast is clear, I go quietly to the nursery and take my sister onto my lap. I recall the way she sat so happily on her mother's knee and tugged at her jewelled bodice, dislodged her splendid cap. I realise I've been imagining some bond between us, a fantasy in which Elizabeth loved me. I'd played a game where she was mine alone, and witnessing her affection for the woman I hate taints our time together. Ignoring her playfulness, I pass her back to the nurse and quit the chamber to seek the solace of the gardens.

The years I have spent here have been long and irksome. Sometimes I wonder how I have withstood it all. Nobody cares how miserable I am, or how ill I become for a few days each month. Sometimes, it takes me a week to recover from the megrim and then, as soon as I am recovered, it is almost time for the next month's bleed. In the privacy of my chamber I give way to tears, but in the company of the household or when Norfolk comes to bully me into agreeing my parents' marriage was no marriage, I maintain a grim and steely demeanour.

They think me hard and intractable but since the day I was thrust bodily into the litter, I have concealed every hint of personal pain. My misery is tucked away, out of sight, but inside I am broken, my heart as tangled and torn as a bunch of discarded ribbons.

They try every trick they can think of to break my resolve. They make false promises; they make false threats. The concubine wheedles, pretending friendship and preference at court if I agree to her demands, but I see straight through to her vile black heart. I refuse to look at her and will never acknowledge her as my queen.

In the end, the king sends Cromwell to deal with me, but still I refuse to concede. He doesn't shout and storm like Norfolk but speaks in whispers. He is too wise to bawl at me; he employs the stealth and duplicity of a snake.

"I have tried to intercede with the king, Lady Mary, but since you refuse to do his bidding, I must support my king. I cannot stand against him, not even for you."

His sneering words appear to wash over me as water washes from a duck's back but, in truth, they hit every mark. I am terrified he will carry out his threat to throw me in the Tower. When it is over, and I am safely back in my chambers, my body starts to shake. I can do nothing to control it. As the tears come, I fall to my knees. *Dear God, provide me with the strength to endure this.*

The noose around me has drawn so tight that there is no way even for Chapuys to find a way to get Mother's letters through. Nell brings me news but it is second or third hand and I cannot rely on it. There really is very little for me to live for. Nothing but endless misery. I wonder if the world has forgotten me; if perhaps, sometimes, one of my old friends remembers me and asks: *Whatever happened to Mary?*

Afraid to eat and denied the liberty of the park where I might take exercise, I soon become so sick that Shelton is alarmed enough to inform the king. He does not come himself, of course; Father is fearful of any contagion. Instead, he sends Dr Butts, the royal physician, straight from court. I am abed when he arrives. He enters my chamber, a ghost from the days of my childhood, and places his cool fingers on my brow. His smile is so kind it almost breaks my steely reserve.

I grasp his wrist.

"Have you seen my lady mother, sir?" I whisper, to avoid the keen ear of Lady Shelton, who waits a little way off by the window. His eyes meet mine and he shakes his head.

"Stick out your tongue, Lady Mary," he says loudly, and I do as he bids. He frowns at it and asks about my diet. I open my mouth to answer but Lady Shelton breaks through my words, afraid I will damn her.

"She is stubborn and refuses proper food. It is no wonder she is frail. She has brought this on herself. I do my best, but she is defiant and stubborn."

"Hmm."

He presses my stomach, making me wince, and we both stare at the tight bloated belly protruding like a huge boil beneath my shift. My torso is thin, my arms and legs like sticks, but at this time of the month when the curse is upon me, my belly swells and every part of me is scourged by growling pain.

"You must eat, Lady Mary. Light meals will be best, particularly during menses, and ensure you take some gentle exercise in the park or gardens. No riding, no hunting at these times though, mark you."

I want to tell him I am not permitted access to the garden. I want to explain my fear of poison. I know the great whore wishes me harm; if she cannot get what she wants she *will* resort to murder.

I snort rudely and turn my face away. It will not do to speak of such fears now, so I focus on his misapprehension that I am allowed the liberty of the park.

Although I had once loved to be out on the chase with Mother and Father, I am now forbidden the freedom of the hunt. When the household makes up a party, I am left behind. As they ride out, I make sure Lady Shelton notes my wan expression but, as soon as they have gone, I hurry to the nursery. It is the only room in the house where I find one small consolation to being left indoors. When the household rides out, Elizabeth remains behind with me.

The women left in charge of my sister are less hostile than Anne Shelton and Lady Clere. When I creep into the nursery they smile and bid me welcome, sometimes offer me wine and draw me into conversation. Words do not flow from my tongue as they once did. Nowadays I am wary, afraid of condemning myself, afraid of spies.

On this particular day, I refuse their offer of refreshment and show them a plate of sweetmeats that I've brought for Elizabeth's treat. There is nothing she likes better.

"Is she awake?" I ask.

"Yes, she is, my lady. She woke a half hour ago; her linen is being changed. She will be here soon. Please, sit with us."

Unaccustomed to kindness, I take the stool beside them. The chamber is warm, gaily decorated with tapestries and cushions, and a scattering of toys lies on the floor. It is a far cry from my own apartment. It is the chamber of a princess, an heir to the English throne.

I smile nervously and the nurse begins to talk of the weather, the litter of kittens that was found behind the settle. Friendly welcomes seem so strange; surely any moment someone will disparage me, call me a bastard.

I take so long thinking up a safe reply that the door opens before I have time to speak. Elizabeth enters, clutching the finger of her nurse, her tiny steps light and unsteady. I stand up and when she sees me her face lights up, her tiny teeth glinting like a necklet of pearls.

She is like my father, golden-haired and determined, a fat, merry, lively child. She totters forward and tries to clamber onto my lap.

"Mary," she says, and the way she pronounces the word makes it sound like 'merry'. I scoff at the irony for I am the least merry person in all England. Even contact with my infant sister, whom I have come to love, does not fill me with joy. Instead, the battle between my affection and resentment of her steals the pleasure we might have had.

I love her, but how I wish I didn't. I begrudge her usurpation of my position but I hope she never knows the pain I live with every day. I admire her fine Tudor looks but also despise the spirit of her mother that sometimes lurks behind her eyes. I hold her close, both loving and hating her as her fine red hair tickles my nose. I pray the future will be kind to her … but not at my expense.

For a moment she tolerates the embrace, but soon grows tired of it and pulls away. She glares up at me with eyes that have become exactly like her mother's. Hastily, I let her slip to the floor. Once more, her whore of a mother has spoiled what should have been a good day. Elizabeth is Tudor and Boleyn in equal parts – I imagine the love I bear her will always be conflicted.

January 1536

"Lady Mary?"

I am in the garden when the voice intrudes on my thoughts. I turn and raise a hand to shield my eyes from the low-lying winter sun. Anne Shelton is standing at the junction of the dissecting paths; I cannot properly see her face for she is obscured by the brightness of the day. I move closer and see she is not scowling for once. When she speaks again, her voice lacks its usual impatience.

Suspicion creeps upon me and I know beyond doubt that she brings me news that is bad indeed. My heart sets up a low and heavy beat as a feeling of dread spreads in a swathe of goosebumps. I take a hesitant step but stop when she holds out a letter. I stare at it and notice her hand is trembling.

I take the parchment between finger and thumb, as if I fear it is poisoned. I cannot read it. I shake my head and hand it back, scarcely able to find the words to ask her to read it.

"Tell me," I say, and wait like one condemned for her words to slay me.

Mother has been ailing for weeks, both she and I begged the king to allow me to visit her for one last time but … it seems it is not to be. Long before Anne begins reading, I am wincing. I know what she is going to say.

"It is your mother, the dowager Princess of Wales. I regret to tell you that she has passed…"

Her words drop away and the garden spins. The skies above my head, so blue and bright and promising a few moments before, are now filled with storm clouds. I really am alone now. A great tempest gathers, it builds in my heart and inflates my lungs; my belly churns and I vomit the grief from me.

The world spins; I lose my mind and fall. The gravel is sharp beneath my cheek. A dozen pairs of hands lift me and bear me back to the house, to the detested solitude of my chamber. Someone is sobbing.

The mattress is soft, the air musty with damp, and all around me I hear voices, as if in a dream. They murmur of her death and the consequences it may bear upon the king and his…. The concubine's hated face floats before me.

"Whore!"

I sit bolt upright, screaming the word at the ring of white, frightened faces. I see my own madness reflected in their eyes but I cannot stop it.

How can she be gone? How can the world still be turning? I tilt back my head, open my mouth and wail like a lost infant, howl like an abandoned puppy. I want my mother. I *need* my mother.

I am alone. I have lost the fight and am fatally wounded. I will never be the victor now. My resistance against the king is futile. With her gone, there is no point in continuing to stand against him and claim the marriage was false. It will serve no purpose. Mother will not come back; my father and she will never be reconciled. Whether I admit to it or not, I *am* a bastard, and Elizabeth is the princess now. I can never win.

The only refuge I find is in my bed. I refuse to let them draw back the heavy curtains or open the shutters. I merge into the darkness until it becomes part of me. The bed hangings screen me from unkind prying eyes and in a small way, the blackness soothes the pain that daylight makes unbearable. The darkness helps me see clearly.

A miserable year. While the king and his concubine celebrate my mother's death and the courtiers kneel to their every wish, I am left at Hatfield while Elizabeth is summoned to court.

Cruel as ever, Anne Shelton ensures the stories of Father's contentment filter back to me. I battle to conceal my hurt but when Chapuys tells me how the king paraded my sister before the company while Anne Boleyn, fat with child again, looked on as smugly as a cat, I feel my heart will break. Nothing will ever be right again.

While the court dances and the Boleyn woman grows larger, preparation for my mother's interment is carried out.

I am forbidden to attend.

With her gone, I no longer belong here. I have no place in England. I need to escape. This land is not safe. It is the domain of Boleyn, not Spanish princesses. I have no place here among them and I never will. Chapuys promises to write to my kin in Spain and urge them to help me escape. I prepare for a life of exile.

"If this fails, sir, then you must help me to a nunnery where I might take the veil, but even then I will not be safe from the concubine. She will not rest until I am dead. She will get me in the end."

I hear the hysteria in my own voice and breathe deep and slow in an attempt to calm myself. His cool dark eyes look into mine.

"Have peace, my princess. I will do all in my power to free you from this place. In the meantime, very soon you are to be moved to Hunsdon; perhaps things will be better there."

"I pray it is so, Chapuys. I pray that is so."

The twenty-sixth day of January dawns bright and cold. I have left my chamber and crept to the terrace where I once waved farewell to my father. With a shawl clutched tightly about my shoulders, I watch the sun rise. Slowly, the park lightens. I see an owl flap silently home, and I am still standing there when the first rabbits emerge to dance in the pink mist. The household is just beginning to stir when I turn away and make the stealthy journey through the corridors to my chamber.

Today, my mother is to be interred at Peterborough Cathedral; the name that marks the grave will make no mention of the twenty or more years she spent as Queen of England, no mention of her victory at Flodden, or the proud day she sent the head of the defeated Scottish king to my father in France. No mention of her unfaltering devotion to a country that mistreated her in youth, and again in age and sickness. No mention of me.

For the first time, revulsion for my father consumes me. He could have stopped this any time he desired. He could, even now, curb the actions of his detested wife and reconcile himself with me. I close my eyes and, as I picture my mother's coffin lowering into the eternal darkness of her tomb, I feel I am buried with her. If only I had the power to curse the name of Boleyn, and cast a hex of misery upon the king.

The very next morning, a messenger arrives from court. He slides from his mount and hurries into the great hall where Anne Shelton has been haranguing me over some small misdemeanour. She snatches the letter. I see her face turn white and her hand creeps to cover her mouth. The message falls to the floor and I pick it up.

Father has fallen from his horse. His life is despaired of and his whore, for fear of losing him, has miscarried of a son.

I turn stunned eyes upon the messenger. He grows discomforted beneath my glazed stare but cannot seem to look away. It is as if I have been turned to stone. Last night I wished misfortune on them both and now it has come to pass, but … I am no *witch*.

"The – the king will live?"

I mean it as a question but it emerges as a statement. The messenger shuffles his feet.

"I understand so. His physician is hopeful, and my lord of Norfolk is furious that word of the accident was taken to the queen without his leave. She lost the child, but her…"

"I have no interest in the state of *her* health unless…"

I want to add 'unless she should die' but I know my words will be carried to the king, so I allow the sentence to trail away.

My mouth turns up at the corner. The king has been spared and the heir *she* carried, the hub of all her hopes, is dead. I remember again my bad-wishing of her yesterday and bite my lip, momentarily fearful of my own powers, but then I shake my shoulders and emit a puff of breath. If I were a sorceress, the concubine would not merely be bereaved of a son. *She'd be dead.*

In the weeks that follow I feel as if God, who was certainly deaf to my entreaties before, can suddenly hear my prayers. It is as if Mother is sitting at His right hand, whispering directly into His ear.

Rumour reaches me from court that the king is tiring of the great whore. I hear that his eye has fallen upon another and Anne Boleyn, unschooled in queenly manners, scolds him for it. Their relationship that once simmered with desire is now ripe with rancour and recrimination. I am glad of it and keep my ears perked for further gossip.

Anne Shelton goes about her day with a worried frown and although her manner toward me remains cool, it lacks its former venom. My life becomes subtly easier. The household continues to shun me but I keep within hearing distance, eavesdropping on their conversation which is usually very dull.

Something in my bones tells me that change is imminent and I am eaten up with curiosity about events at court. If I am not praying for my mother's soul, I pray for the concubine's rapid decline. She belongs in Hell. I long for her to fall completely from Father's favour and suffer such torment as I have known, exiled from his heart for so long.

Sensing change, my supporters creep from the shadows and work against her, and her status suffers. At last, God is showing His disfavour of her and all her ilk. I am sure that soon, all those who flirt with the new learning will face the consequences. One day soon, things will be as before.

I wish the changes would come swifter. There are many days when nothing happens, days when I doubt it will ever come to pass. I am impatient for the end. I act out scenarios in my mind in which the whore is shut away in a house of nuns, shut off from the world, away from Father, away from Elizabeth, away from me!

At last, Chapuys is allowed to visit me. I greet him warmly and retire with him to an antechamber. He brings assurances of affection from the king. Father loves me still. His desire for the concubine is waning. Her days are numbered; soon she will know the ignominy of displacement. She will be exiled from court and forced to live out the remainder of her days in misery … as I have done. I cannot wait to forget her existence and wipe her from the record.

The new apple of Father's eye, Chapuys informs me, is one Mistress Seymour, a pious, kindly woman and a lover of the true church. I sigh with relief, a light in the everlasting darkness winks at me. With the witch out of the way, Mistress Seymour will lure the king back to the true faith and the equilibrium will be restored in the realm.

Justice, it seems, is not dead after all.

St James' Palace – October 1558

"They took the concubine's head, didn't they? Do you think she was guilty or was it a plot of Cromwell's?"

"Eh?"

I turn stiffly. Anne is at my bedside, her arms linked about her raised knees, her eyes enraptured. She has forgotten to whom she is speaking but I can't blame her for that ... for a while, I too had forgotten who I am. For a brief moment, I'd been Princess Mary again, young and vigorous, full of lost hope. I am surprised to find myself back in this weary old body.

I look down at my age-stained hands, the veins standing proud, the skin marred by rusty spots and wrinkles. I rub them, trying to erase the damage of years, and the skin moves beneath my touch, loose and dry.

"What did you say?"

"Oh." She lowers her eyes. "I – I asked if she was guilty but of course she was. She was found so – and paid for it justly ... with her life."

"Yes."

I pause and travel back along the years. Most of my old emotions have faded away with the passage of time. Sometimes I can scarce recall the deeds that evoked them, but the hatred I felt for Anne Boleyn is unchanging. It rises on the back of my neck like hackles and rage makes me feel young again. My heart skips and jumps. I cough, clearing my throat of phlegm.

"Yes, she deserved to die. She lied. She stole my father, killed my mother and turned me into her daughter's slave, and all the while she was making my father a laughing stock and sleeping with half the court. That was the main reason she had to die, of course. No one mocked my father and lived to tell the tale – oh no."

I laugh as I knuckle away a tear. It is not a sign of emotion, just a weakness of age. "I was surprised though."

"Surprised? At her lewd behaviour? I thought she was a ... you know ... a w...."

"A whore? Oh, she was, but she was intelligent too. I'd have thought she'd be wiser than that. To give in to lust was weak and it was foolish, and that was out of character somehow, but I lost no sleep over it. I was just glad she was gone. Out of my father's hair once and forever. There's no coming back from the scaffold."

That is the greatest lesson I learned from my father. *If thine eye offend thee, pluck it out.* Anne Boleyn dominated his life for many years but when her spell weakened and he was finally able to see her for what she truly was, he eliminated her, without hesitation or regret. Or if he did regret it, he never let it show.

In the years that followed, when someone offended me I would remember how my father dealt with Anne. He didn't hesitate. As soon as he realised her duplicity, her *evil*, he had her dealt with. From their first offence, I always picture my enemies dancing on the end of a rope. Often as not, that is how they end up, leaving me able to move forward. The past is the past, move on, assume the new, don't look back.

"Ha!" My sudden bark of laughter makes the girl jump. She leaps to her feet.

"What is it, Your Majesty?"

I wave a hand for her to sit again.

"Nothing, I was laughing at myself."

It seems I didn't learn that last lesson too well; all I've done these past weeks is look back and regret. She breathes out, smiles at me like an intimate friend, and retakes her seat.

"Were things better after that? After the concubine was dead?"

"I expected things to be better. For a while I thought I'd never know trouble again, but I was young, do you see? For all I'd been through I couldn't imagine fortune would not turn the full strength of her smile on me at once, but ... the wheel turns, and then it turns again. One day sunshine, the next it comes on to rain."

Hunsdon – May-June 1536

We are at Hunsdon when we hear the news about the concubine's death. The May sunshine streams through the windows, echoing the joy in my heart that I am finally free of her. The surprising thing is that with the

97

concubine gone from my life, everything remains the same. I walk the same corridors, brush aside the same servants, eat the same food, play the same lute…

Elizabeth is miserable with a back tooth, her cheeks red and her eyes wet from weeping. As I watch her knuckle her eye and snuffle in pain, I realise *she* is the royal bastard now. Her status is as nebulous as mine. I should feel triumphant but instead the only emotion I hold in my heart is pity. I know exactly how she feels, for her life has become an echo of my own. We have both lost our mothers and our father hates us.

I sweep her into my arms, kiss her sweaty forehead and begin to sing discordantly to distract her from her woe. One day she will be old enough to understand that she is the product of a king's lust for a concubine, and nothing more. I close my eyes, squeezing her so tightly she squeaks in surprise.

Her nurse looks up from the fire and frowns. I suddenly realise that the nursery is unusually quiet; the attendants who habitually fawn upon Elizabeth's every whimper are no longer here.

"Where are the princess' women?" I ask, and the nurse shrugs, bending her head back over her darning needle.

"We are instructed to address her as Lady Elizabeth now," she sniffs. I turn away with my sister in my arms. My poor little bastard sister. She is no better than I. Her former title is counterfeit. The best she can hope for is a place at court as 'My Lady Bastard'. We are a pathetic pair.

My heart jolts as I picture the next time she sees Father. She is too young to understand what has happened and will run to him as she always does. She will hug his knees and beg to be taken into his arms, and he will push her aside, turn away and break her heart ... as he has mine.

When she is finally sleeping, I hurry to my chamber and write again to the king. Since his marriage to Jane Seymour, I have written to wish him happiness and to request a meeting with my new lady stepmother. There has been no reply. Surely he has forgiven my stubbornness; surely, he understands it now. He will welcome me back to court and into his heart. Surely my reinstatement is imminent.

Instead of the expected loving letter welcoming me back to court, the king sends Norfolk. With a sinking heart, I watch his arrival from the turn in the stairs.

His displeasure is clear from the manner in which he leaves his companions outside and bursts unceremoniously through the door. He sweeps off his hat and throws his riding gauntlets on a chair. "Send for the Lady Mary."

I pull back into the shadows and begin to creep backward up the stairs. Once at the top, I lift my skirts and race along the corridor and into my chamber. I sit on the bed, heart thumping, and wait for the summons. There is no reason for me to feel such alarm, yet I know without doubt that I am in imminent danger. Norfolk cannot hurt me, I reassure myself. Bastard or not, I am still the king's daughter! He cannot hurt me.

A short time later, a servant scratches at the door and summons me below. Gathering my resolve, I stand up, tidy my sleeves, straighten my cap and, with my chin as high as I can lift it, I follow her downstairs. A ring of greybeards awaits me, Norfolk at their centre.

He does not look up when I enter. His delegation shuffles papers; a servant enters with a tray of wine and places it at Norfolk's side. He fills a cup, the liquid as thick and red as bastard blood. The eye he turns toward me is jaundiced and full of contempt.

"I will dispense with pleasantries, Lady Mary. Your refusal to obey the king displays a freakish departure from the natural obedience of a daughter toward her father."

I open my mouth to reply but he cuts across my words. "The king could banish you, remove the comforts that now ease you but ... he is merciful, he is kind and is willing to withhold his displeasure if you will now submit to him."

He places both hands on the table and leans threateningly toward me.

"Will you accept the laws and statutes of the realm and accept King Henry as Supreme Head of the Church and repudiate the jurisdiction of the Bishop of Rome? Will you acknowledge your mother's marriage was invalid and accept all the king's laws and statutes?"

My heart skips around my chest, thumping loudly in my ears. Summoning all my courage, evoking the memory of my sweet mother, the love and blessing of sweet Jesus Christ and His Father in Heaven, I swallow my fear and whisper,

"No."

"NO?"

He thumps the table. The wine cups rattle. I flinch from his roar as if he is the lion and not the messenger. I clench my fists, my nostrils flare. I am a princess of England, a daughter of Spain.

"I will obey my father in all matters save those that injure my mother, or my present honour and faith."

Norfolk stalks like a preying wolf around the edge of the table, his head thrust forward, the fur on his collar raised like hackles.

"You are an unnatural, traitorous jade! I can scarce believe you are the king's daughter at all and if you were mine..." He is on his toes, his chest inflated as he towers over me. I cannot help but cringe away as his spittle blasts into my face. "... I would knock your head so hard against the wall it would turn as soft as a baked apple."

How dare he! I straighten up and glare into his face but have the sense to keep my lips tight. I do not speak, but my thoughts are eloquent. They must be blazing from my eyes. I have no doubt he understands them.

One day, I scream internally, *one day I shall take my revenge on you for this ... and your henchmen. I will hang you from the highest tower in the land and unravel your sorry innards before the nation. I shall bring you down and Norfolk will be NO MORE!*

My courage lasts only as long as it takes for them to gather their things and ride away. Then I collapse on the floor, a girl again, stricken with terrified tears. Try as I might, I am unable to compose myself and lie limp in the arms of the servants who take pity and carry me to my chamber.

Afterwards, I am kept under constant surveillance. I am allowed no privacy, no peace, and letters from my friends and supporters are confiscated. Cromwell, who lately spoke in my support, now backtracks and advises me to sign the required articles or I shall be the most vain, ungrateful, unnatural and obstinate person living. But there is something inside me, something I cannot control, and I refuse to obey. I cannot and will not concede defeat and so ... my father names me traitor.

The king then turns his attention to my friends, starts to target my supporters. Anyone with sympathy for either me or my dead mother is removed from office. Sir William Fitzwilliam and the Marquess of Exeter are dismissed from the Privy Council, and sometime later Sir Anthony Browne and Sir Francis Bryan are arrested and interrogated in the Tower. Sir Nicholas Carew, who has long been sending me letters of encouragement, is also arrested, along with Thomas Cheyney and John Russell, who is thrown into the Tower along with Lady Anne Hussey, the wife of my chamberlain.

It will be my turn next, I know it will.

Sometimes my fear is so great it steals my breath away. There is only God, yet when I fall to my knees, gasping for air, afraid of the walls, afraid of the sky, afraid of the very world, I am not sure He is listening.

There is to be an enquiry into my treachery. I am to be questioned and judged. I know they will find me guilty. They will say I am wilfully defiant of the king's authority and must die by the sword. I imagine climbing the steps to the scaffold, speaking bravely to the people, but the picture is washed away by my tears. They say Anne Boleyn died bravely. Will I be so courageous? I do not think so. I think I will die a screaming craven.

Lower than I have ever been, I write with terror in my heart to Chapuys, beseeching aid from Spain. I can wait no longer. I must escape the country now!

When at last his reply arrives, I greet his words with both relief and disappointment. If my life is in peril, he urges me to consent to the king's will. My safety is paramount, and I must sign whatever damn paper the king wishes in order to preserve my life.

With the threat of imminent death hanging heavily over my head, I take up the pen and peruse the despised papers.

First, I confess and acknowledge the king's majesty to be my sovereign lord and King, in the imperial Crown of this realm of England, and do submit myself to his Highness, and to all and singular laws and statutes of this realm, as becometh a true and faithful subject to do...

I inhale sharply and, before I breathe again, I sign it: "Mary."

I do recognise, accept, take and repute and acknowledge the King's Highness to be supreme head on earth under Christ of the Church in England, and do utterly refuse the Bishop of Rome's pretended authority, power and jurisdiction within this realm heretofore usurped...

I sign it: "Mary."

I do freely, frankly recognise and acknowledge that the marriage, heretofore had between his Majesty and my mother, the late Princess dowager, was, by God's law and Man's law, incestuous and unlawful.

I hesitate; close my eyes and beg my mother's forgiveness before signing it: "Mary."

I throw the pen aside and slump forward onto the table, my head in my arms. I have betrayed everything I believe in, all that is dear to me. I have named my mother a whore, and myself a bastard, and offended not only the Pope in denying him but my dear God in Heaven too.

There is not a person on this earth whom I despise more than I despise myself.

Within weeks, I am summoned by the king to a private audience. Full of trepidation, I wait for admittance, walking on wooden legs through the door where he holds out his arms and invites me into his embrace.

It is as if all my prayers have been answered. Instantly, I forget the years of neglect, the nights of weeping, the cruel separation from my mother. His vast chest pillows me, his lips are warm on my forehead, and when he pulls away and looks into my face, I see there are tears standing in his eyes … as there are in mine.

"Mary," he says. "My own sweet daughter, how glad I am that you are obedient once more."

I smile uncertainly, piqued by his sentiment, but I say nothing for my attention has been drawn to the quiet presence of a woman waiting a discreet distance away. This must be his new wife, Jane. I release the king's hand, turn toward her and curtsey low, but she moves swiftly forward and raises me up, kissing my cheeks.

"My dear Mary, you are most welcome. I am glad to have you home, where you belong."

She presses something into my hand, something that digs sharply into my palm and, when I look down, I see it is a diamond ring.

My own jewellery was taken when I was sent to Hatfield, and I gave it little thought during my years of want, but the thoughtfulness of the gift, together with the warmth of her welcome, is almost my undoing. I swallow grateful tears, slide the ring onto my finger and offer up a watery smile.

<u>St James' Palace – October 1558</u>

"What was she like, Queen Jane? I've only ever heard good things."

Jane's face fades from my memory. I blink at Anne, rubbing a dry hand across my face as I readjust to the present.

"She was a good woman, mild but not so meek as some would have it. She was subtle, worked her wiles on the king without him even knowing she was doing it. Where the concubine roared and stamped her foot to get her own way, Jane smiled and complimented him, or if circumstance demanded it, she wept a little and won him round that way. She was like a mother to me ... until she was taken."

The girl fetches a cup. As she holds it to my lips, a door opens and Susan enters. I have been unkind to poor Susan lately. It isn't her fault. She misunderstands my terror at leaving the country to the whim of my sister. As she nears the bed, I send her a smile and she relaxes visibly.

"Are you feeling better, Your Majesty? We have all been so worried."

Anne moves aside to allow the older woman to approach. I flap my hand dismissively, although I am grateful for her concern.

"You worry too much, Susan; you always have."

She leans forward to adjust the bolster behind my back and hauls me higher in the bed.

"I will send for your supper. You must eat to conserve your strength."

"I will die anyway, whether I eat or not. I have been supping on the past, with the help of this child."

I wave a finger at Anne, who is standing in the shadow of the bed canopy, clutching the hanging with one hand.

"The child has whetted my appetite for conversation. She is not dull or fawning as so many are these days. She listens and doesn't deny me when I speak the truth of my miserable life."

"She knows no better, Your Majesty..."

Susan's face is close to mine, the light of the candle deepening the lines on her face quite unkindly.

"Perhaps she does, Susan; perhaps she knows better than all of us. Anyway, whatever the case may be, she pleases me. She hasn't once accused me of rambling. I will reward her well, before I take my leave of you all..."

"Your Majesty must not speak so..."

"There you go again; denying me the right to speak the plain truth. Deny it all you like, Susan; I will die soon, and Elizabeth will have the throne and turn the realm topsy turvy again."

I wave a finger in Anne's direction. "Go take your ease, girl, but come back in the morning. Your company soothes me."

She looks pleased, bobs a curtsey and quits the room, leaving me alone with Susan.

"Where does she come from?"

"Who?" Susan stands back clasping her hands, a frown on her face.

"The child. Anne – I misremember her other name."

"Oh, she is the … youngest daughter of Thomas Wren. The family fell into hardship when he was taken up for treason, Your Majesty. Do you not recall? After his death, you took pity on the mother and instructed that the offspring be found work. She is a good girl, so I am told."

I had forgotten.

"Gently born then. I thought her conversation too pronounced for a serving girl." I recall her fine eyes, the smooth brow beneath her shabby cap. "Find her other, less arduous employment and give her a bath and some decent clothes. She is too good for servitude."

Susan bows her head in acquiescence. "I will see it is done, Your Majesty."

"Ahh, Susan…"

I lower my head to my hand, squeezing my temples to ease the bite of an encroaching headache.

"What is it, Your Majesty?"

"She is so young, so naïve. I hope life is kinder to her than it has been to me."

She moves closer with a waft of fragrance, and gently touches my arm.

"There have been times when fate has dealt you a harsh hand but … you are strong.

107

Stronger than anyone I've ever known. You have always risen above it."

I place my hand on hers.

"I always intended to be kind."

"And so you have!"

"Have I? Perhaps God would have preferred me to be more merciful."

"With your enemies? The enemies of His church? Why so? What would that gain?"

I shrug, wincing at the memory of the people who have perished on my order – the tortures, the burnings. If only they had listened to reason and followed my direction. If only they had not strayed from the true path, the true church. I was forced to wreak justice on God's foe. It was my duty as head of the church. My hands, as they say, were tied. Maybe there is no reason for guilt.

Perhaps Susan is right. My mother always stood against heresy and lies, and so did my grandmother, Isabella of Spain. I very much doubt they spent their last days regretting the justice they dealt. Even my grandmother, Margaret Beaufort, would turn in her grave at the desertion of the old ways, her grandson's father's treatment of the monasteries. All those monks – good men of God tortured and burned – and those who tried to stand against it; Robert Aske, hung in chains to die a slow and shameful death. I shake my head over the misguided laws of my father's England.

In those days, I was newly welcomed back at court and lacked sufficient courage to speak against it, but Jane did, or at least she tried to.

But Father was difficult to persuade. Cromwell had convinced him that monkish duplicity was rife in England, and once Father realised the riches he could reap from the fall of the church, the great abbeys of England were doomed. Now their ruins blight England, the great carcasses of a dying faith, and a world that has been tumbled and pillaged.

By the time I finally came to the throne, I wanted to make restitution, but how could I? Most of the property had been gifted to the very people I required to help me restore order. The abbey lands were now in the possession of the greatest lords of the realm, men whom I needed on my side. They had supported my claim, and helped me fight my cousin to win back my crown. How could I possibly demand the return of the church's property that they regarded as theirs?

But I cannot worry about that now. The days remaining to me on this earth are dwindling. Death comes to us all but there are matters I must address. I must prepare myself.

I would welcome Philip today, wish he would come for one last goodbye, but I know he will not. He has no love for me. Ours was a marriage of politics only, and now he is king of Spain, his country occupies his thoughts. He will not spare more than a passing thought on the loss of a wife he never cared for.

Life has always treated me harshly but leaving it is harsher. There are matters I have failed to deal with. I lower my chin. The weight of my head puts pressure on the nape of my neck but I ignore it. I probably deserve it. Why should my end be any more comfortable than my life has been? I close my eyes. I will sleep now; perhaps I will not wake again.

Whispering voices are sometimes more disturbing than normal tones. Instantly, I am on the alert. *Are they plotting? Are they speaking gossip behind my back?* It is treason to speak ill of the queen. I jerk my head, squinting into the gloom. Why have they not lit the torches?

"Who's there?" A flurry of skirts, a pattering of feet, and Susan is standing before me.

"Good morning, Your Majesty. I hope we didn't wake you."

"Of course you did. All that foolish muttering and giggling. What's to do?"

"I did as you asked, Your Majesty, and bathed young Anne and furnished her with a new gown. Unfortunately, her feet are quite ... large, and we can find no slippers to fit her."

My laughter sounds like a wheeze. I cough and splutter. My own feet are small and dainty, something I am proud of. When I was a girl, I excelled at the dance, and Mother always said it was because I had such dainty feet. A memory stirs of Father bending low over my hand before leading me in a reel, his benign smile, his sparkling blue eyes. A happy day, when he was godly and kind, and all men loved him.

I loved him.

My humour diminishes.

110

I crook a finger.

"Bring her forward, I would see how she looks now you've given her a scrub."

The ring of women parts. I peer through the gloom, blinking at the blurred figure before me. I wave a hand in irritation. "Light the damn lights!" and one by one the torches are lit, a candle is brought forward, and Susan throws open the shutters.

The girl steps forward to stand self-consciously before me. I wrinkle my nose, squinting my eyes.

They've given her a gown of buttermilk yellow that emphasises the blue of her eye, the clarity of her cheek. She is younger than I'd thought, balanced like a promise on the cusp of womanhood.

She must be the same age I was when my parents' marriage was torn apart by Boleyn. Exiled at Hatfield, the unhappiest girl in the land, I had little time for fine gowns and sleeves. Lady Shelton did not care or even notice when my bodices grew too tight and my skirts too short, and her mistress cared even less. Resentment and envy snatches at me but I cast it away. I want to be kind in my final days. I smile at the girl.

"By Heaven, child, we may wed you to a prince yet."

She cannot help but giggle and my women laugh too, casting fond glances on Anne, whose existence they'd not noticed a few days before.

"Come," I wave her forward. "Join me for breakfast. The rest of you have work to do, no doubt. I will see you all when it is time to prepare for Mass."

Momentarily they pause, their smiles frozen, insulted by the strangeness of my order. As they file reluctantly from the room, the girl moves closer, a trifle clumsy in her finery but she will learn. Her skirts rustle as she takes a seat.

"You know about the atrocities Cromwell inflicted on the monks, I suppose."

I blame it all on Cromwell because I cannot bear to criticise my father, an anointed king. Kings can do no wrong, after all.

She nods and I hand her an orange from the nightstand. Raising it to her nose, she inhales the exotic scent before plunging her fingernail into the thick peel.

"They were sorry days in England, but I had just returned to court and I had only recently been accepted back into my father's favour once more … there was little I could do about it."

Hampton Court – July 1536

Now I am back in the king's good graces, people who formerly shunned me begin to smile again, trying to court my friendship. Outwardly, I return it, but secretly I mark those who did not lift a finger to aid me in my time of need. False friends are worse than open enemies; I have no need of them.

I accept their homage and kind words but it means nothing. My true supporters, those who worked tirelessly for my reinstatement, are a different matter. I trust them implicitly, especially those who suffered imprisonment or worse. It is a relief to laugh and look about my chambers and see friendly faces. I have missed the pageantry and celebration of court as much as I have missed my father.

When I dine in the great hall on the first evening after my reinstatement, I cannot help but glance in the king's direction from time to time to ensure he is really there. He is solid enough but the huge figure of merriment that I remember from childhood has become tarnished.

At first, I do not notice the change. He is clad head to foot in gold, his laugh is as loud, his voice just as dominating as it ever was yet ... he isn't the same. I frown at the sudden narrowing of his eye; suspicion seems to perch like a devil on his shoulder, his small mouth is compressed into a bitter slash of scarlet. One moment he laughs, louder than any of us, but then, just as suddenly, he lashes out without warning into temper. The court treads carefully, as if walking on glass around him. Once his closest companions, the men of his privy chamber used to tease the king as roundly as they do each other; now they think before they speak. Nobody questions his decisions, and everyone compliments him whether it is deserved or not. Their real opinions are kept close – at least those who disagree.

In late July comes news that, after ailing for half a year, my half-brother, Henry Fitzroi – *that boy* as I used to call him – is on the point of death. Since the arrival and the impact of the great whore on my life I have come to look on Fitzroi with rather more tolerance than I once did, so I am sorry to hear a few weeks later

113

that he has lost his fight. He leaves an unloved widow, Norfolk's daughter. I smirk a little at the blow it will have dealt him.

Father is morose but, although I pray for Fitzroi's passing, I am not deeply affected. For as long as I can recall, Fitzroi has been my rival. While I was pushed aside, named a bastard and forced to live in penury, Henry – the *real* bastard – was raised up and made much of by the king. Even lately there has been speculation that, should Jane not bear a son, my father would name him heir.

Part of me, the wicked Mary, is glad of his death; the other side, the pious Mary, is sorry for it. It is the latter side of me I allow the public to see. When I offer Father my condolences, he doesn't notice the quiet triumph in my face but weeps pathetically on my shoulder. I stand coldly in his suffocating embrace and speculate as to whether he'd display such sorrow if it were me.

The death of a bastard does not usually create much upheaval but Fitzroi, wed to Norfolk's daughter, owned riches that Father needs to reclaim. Since the marriage was never consummated, Mary Howard is left with nothing. There are matters to be sorted out in Ireland too since Fitzroi was Lord Lieutenant there. While Father is occupied with this business, my supporters begin to whisper of hopes of the reinstatement of my legitimacy, a possible return of my status as heir to the throne.

I dare not hope this will be so. If fortune ever smiles on me and makes me Queen of England, I will repair our relations with Rome, reopen the monasteries and champion the monks and abbots who have been so sorely used.

Since the closure of the monasteries, the north has been up in arms. They call for a return to the old ways, for my reinstatement, for justice in England. When some 40,000 men and women, many of them monks, take to the roads and begin a perilous march south, Father is furious. I should be outraged too at such treasonous actions, but secretly I agree with their demands, and so does the queen.

I visit Jane privately from time to time. We spend pleasant afternoons working our needles, discussing the latest fashions and sometimes, when we are alone, we talk of other things. Keeping our voices low so no spies can overhear, we discover we are kindred, the queen and I. She is of the old faith, unshakeable in her devotion, and there is nothing Jane desires more than the reinstatement of the church … unless it be a son.

She would have to be a fool not to be aware of the fate of Father's wives who've failed to give him an heir. It is little wonder she prays for a son. I am torn. I want her to be happy. I want the marriage to be a success, for my father's sake as well as my own. But the birth of a prince will see me ousted from my father's favour again. My chance to inherit will be lessened but I also know that if Jane gives the king his longed-for boy, he will be like butter in her hands. As the mother of his son, the king would deny Jane nothing. It would be a simple task to persuade him to allow the true church to rise again.

The question of my unborn brother prompts me to examine myself closely. There is just one question I find difficult to answer: What is of more import to me, the crown of England or the reinstatement of my beloved church?

With the preparations for Christmas underway, winter falls hard. The country is rimed with heavy frost and at Westminster it is so thick upon the window panes that I can scarcely see out. Even inside, when I sit as close to the hearty fire as I can bear, my nose and the tips of my fingers feel cold. I request an extra layer and my women lay out a fur-lined gown and sleeves, but others are not so fortunate.

Reports reach me of common folk freezing in their homes, without a stick for the fire. Yet they are the lucky ones, with a roof to shelter them. It is always colder in the north and when I think of the pilgrims, still determinedly marching for the reinstatement of the church, I cannot imagine their misery.

Three days before Christmas, I ride with Father and Jane to Greenwich for the celebrations. Usually the journey would be taken by barge but today the river is frozen, so we travel on horseback instead. The city is gaily decorated and despite the cold people come out to line the streets. They call down blessings upon us; I hear Jane's name coupled with my father's, and it warms my heart to see him glad again.

Jane Seymour is a worthy woman, a good Catholic who will make him happy, unite our family and lead the king gently back to his former grace. On this frigid day I am warmed when the people call my name. "God bless you!" they cry and I raise my hand in acknowledgement, blinking away tears. I have missed them sorely and it seems they have missed me too. I wave and smile at their cold, pinched faces. The people have always loved me, even in my absence. If only I'd realised it then, my trials would have been so much easier to bear.

The service at St Paul's marks the beginning of the festivities and Father dispenses with solemnity as soon as we leave the church. While the crowd roar appreciation in our ears, we ride toward the Thames that has become a wide white serpent of ice so thick that we are able to ride across to the opposite shore. Clinging to the saddle, I laugh aloud as my horse's hooves slip and slide. We struggle up the sloping bank, and my cheeks are stung by the biting wind as I follow Father's broad back to Greenwich Palace.

Darkness is falling as we arrive, the lighted windows blaze in the winter gloom, promising gaiety and mulled wine. Grooms come running and we climb stiffly from the saddle in the frozen yard.

"Brrrr!" Father claps his hands together and stamps his feet, his breath floating like a dragon's around his head.

"Come, ladies," he cries, holding out his elbows. Jane takes his right and I his left arm, and together we mount the steps to the great hall.

A blast of welcoming trumpets, a blaze of torches that makes me squint my eyes after the darkness. The warmth of the hall is smothering after the bitter chill outside. An excited company greets us. Someone removes my cloak and I turn to thank them, but as I do I notice the queen accepting a letter from a messenger. She frowns and excuses herself from the company, slipping from the hall. After a few moments, in which I notice that Father has not seen the exchange, I follow her. I find her in an antechamber; she is seated at a table, weeping quietly. She starts when she hears my footstep, visibly relieved that it is only me. She tucks the letter into her pocket and dabs at her eyes with her kerchief.

Surely she does not have a sweetheart. I frown, turn my head questioningly, and raise my eyebrows.

"What ails you, dear Jane?"

"Oh, Mary." She dries her eyes again but the tears quickly return. Her attempt at a brave smile fails.

"You can confide in me, Jane. Anything … I can keep a secret."

"It isn't a secret. It is a letter from home; my father…" She clears her throat and forces her voice not to quaver. "It seems he was taken from us … yesterday. I – I – they hadn't even informed me he was ill."

I cannot imagine losing my father. With a smothered whine of sympathy, I slide to the floor at her knee and take her hands in mine.

"Oh, Jane! Shall I fetch the king? The celebrations must be cancelled. I will go and find him now…"

I attempt to rise but she detains me.

"No. Please, Mary. Let there be no fuss. My father was not a figure of the court. I would not spoil the king's enjoyment. He has been looking forward to the festivities and has had such trouble of late. I will inform him later, when we are alone. His pleasure in the season must not be marred."

She wipes her eyes, tucks her kerchief back inside her sleeve and smiles determinedly. "There, how do I look?" She smiles gaily and it is only by looking carefully that I can detect she is concealing something.

Jane knows how to dissemble. Throughout the days that follow there is no sign of the unhappiness she must be feeling. I wonder what other emotions she hides from us all.

But in April there comes a joy she cannot disguise. She is pregnant and the king is certain that God smiles upon him at last and will bless him with an heir. While Father struts about the court, talking of the son that will soon be born, Jane tries her best not to be sick and I, torn between delight and despair, battle to

118

hide my disappointment that the king has once more declined to reinstate my legitimacy.

I try not to blame the unborn prince but Father was on the cusp of agreeing to my request. My supporters have long been searching for a way to persuade the king that my nebulous status is detrimental both to him and to me. If our position at court were made clearer, both Elizabeth and I would have more political value. No prince in Christendom will consider either of us as potential brides while we are tainted with bastardy.

But, as usual, I bury my disappointment and begin to sew small garments for the forthcoming prince; I show off my efforts to all and sundry, eager not to be seen as resentful of this new usurper of my father's affections.

Hampton Court – October 1537

My struggle to be recognised as the king's heir is finally at an end. It is all over. There is no point to it now. I look down at the child cradled in my arms and despite the fact that he stands between me and my greatest ambition, love creeps into my heart. Another sibling. Another rival for my father's affection yet … he is so tiny. As he sleeps, he makes sucking motions with his lips, his blue-veined eyelids moving rapidly. I wonder what he dreams of. What can a child of a few days old be dreaming of when he knows nothing yet, beyond the nourishment of his nurse's teat?

What sort of man will he make?

Unaware of the trials in store, the Tudor prince sleeps peacefully. I lift him, close my eyes as I inhale the fragrance of his fine, red hair, and gently kiss his forehead. Jane stirs in the bed, blinking up at me.

"Mary…" She tries to pull herself up on the pillows but lacks the strength. One of her ladies steps forward to assist her. "Are the preparations for the christening all in place?"

"Yes, of course."

I pass the child back to his nurse. "You must not worry about anything. He is beautiful, Jane. I am so glad you have birthed a son at last; Father is quite beside himself with joy."

To my amazement there is no bitterness in my voice. It is gratifying to see the king restored to his old self. It is what I have always wanted and if I am envious of the delight he displays in his son, well, I am a woman grown and should know better. I refuse to submit to such a vile emotion as envy, and vow to say a few extra beads on the rosary this evening.

Mother instilled in me the importance of always striving to be a better human being, a kinder, sweeter girl. She never once, even at the end, rebuked my father for his treatment and I must endeavour to be as forgiving as she. Edward and Elizabeth have taken no active part in the misfortunes that have befallen me, and now that I am restored to court and in Father's favour again, there is no need for rancour. I must forget the past and move into the future with a kinder, warmer heart. I will be the richer for it.

As midnight approaches on the fifteenth day of October, my women help me into a richly embroidered kirtle of cloth of silver. Lady Kingston bears my train as, with some three hundred other courtiers and envoys, we process from Jane's bedchamber to the chapel royal for the prince's christening ceremony.

A huge structure has been built to allow all those attending the best possible view. Brandon, Norfolk and Cranmer have been given the honour of standing as God-fathers while I am given the blessing of being named God-mother. Proudly, I take my position at the font and watch as Archbishop Cranmer anoints the head of the heir to the throne. The child squirms, opens his mouth in a silent mew of protest before falling asleep again. After the confirmation, the heralds announce the new prince, his name echoing out across the chapel.

"Edward, son and heir to the King of England, Duke of Cornwall, Earl of Chester."

The sudden boom of the announcer's voice wakes the child and he opens his mouth and screams for the duration of the ceremony.

"We can be certain there is nothing amiss with his lungs," I remark to nobody in particular, and those closest to me titter. When the prayers are at an end, taking Elizabeth's hand, I lead her back to the queen's chamber to offer up our baptismal gifts.

As I urge her along the corridor, Elizabeth yawns widely, and I jerk her wrist to gently remind her of her manners. She smirks unapologetically. "I'm tired," she explains. "Why am I up so late?"

I am unsure if it is late or early but, stifling a yawn of my own, I swing our joined hands.

"It will be over soon. You did well carrying the chrisom-cloth; Father will be very pleased with you. Once we have given the queen our gifts for the prince, you can return to your bed. You can lie like a slugabed all day if you wish."

"Slugabed," she repeats. "I like that word," and to demonstrate her love of it she repeats it like a mantra all the way to the queen's chamber. I wish I'd chosen a word less appealing.

I have commissioned a gold cup for the christening gift and, as a gesture of appreciation, I offer

Edward's nurse and rockers each a gift of £30. While we gather in the queen's chamber, outside the palace the city celebrates with great bonfires on every corner, and the night comes alive with the sound of church bells celebrating the birth of the boy who will continue the Tudor line.

Everyone in the kingdom is joyful.

Father's voice rises above the clamour, hailing his son as a miracle incarnate. He has the bluest eyes, the sweetest nature and the heartiest lungs in all England. I concur with Father's last claim, as the child can still be heard adding to the din.

Amid this hubbub, the queen wilts on her pillow and tries to look as if she is enjoying herself. But I notice a sheen of perspiration on her forehead, and the deep shadows beneath her eyes. She should be allowed to rest but … it is the obligation of queens to suffer such things. Personal comfort must always be put aside for the sake of duty.

Elizabeth begins to tug at my hand and I see her attention has been drawn by Thomas Seymour, the queen's brother. Since the king deigned to wed his sister, Seymour seems to see himself as an uncle to all the king's children. He is a handsome man with a playful manner that I find overbearing. I never know how to respond to his jests but Elizabeth adores him. She delights in his teasing while I am never sure how to react. I try to ignore him while he loudly discovers a few coins hidden in Elizabeth's ear, but when he goes so far as to draw a silver sixpence from mine, I step back sharply and scowl at him.

Elizabeth roars with delight and, unhindered by my disapproval, he laughs with her and proceeds to lift her onto his shoulder so she can see the queen, who now has the infant prince cradled in her arms.

Elizabeth's skirt has become caught, and I bite my lip and tug the hem down to hide her chubby ankles.

Rising on tiptoe, I peer over a gentleman's shoulder. I am concerned that Jane seems to be in danger of dropping the prince.

"Oh," I cry and the gentleman before me turns around. I discover myself face to face with Norfolk.

"My Lady Mary."

He bows politely, as if there has never been a cross word between us.

"My lord," I reply, scowling at him before pushing through the crowd to make my curtsey to the queen.

"Let me take him, Jane. Are you feeling quite well? Shall I try to get the company to disperse?"

"Oh no," she smiles whitely. "Thank you, Mary, but it is such a happy crowd, such a happy day. It would be a shame to spoil it."

Doubtfully, I withdraw, find a quiet seat at the perimeter of the room and observe the celebration. Even in my mother's day I never saw such lavish joy. England finally has a male heir. Everyone is relieved.

Things will be easier now, I reflect, watching my father fling an arm about Brandon's neck. He laughs loudly, his mouth wide, cheeks stretched. He is a different man now he has fulfilled his duty of fathering an heir and soon, God willing, others will follow. The royal nursery will be replete with princes, Father's anger will fade for ever and, with Jane's help, the country will return to Rome. It will be a glad day when the true church thrives again in England.

But, just a week later, I open my eyes to see a lighted candle bobbing across my chamber. A figure bends over the bed.

"Margery?"

"Yes, my lady. It is me. I have some news … ill news, I am afraid."

I sit up and fumble for my prayer beads while she lights another candle.

"What is it? What has happened?"

"Oh, my lady. It is the queen … she has gone. God has seen fit to take her from us."

The candle dips and dances as the breath is forced from my body. I put my hands to my head.

"No, not that! Not that!"

I knew she was taking a long time to recover. I heard only yesterday that the physicians had been called in again. But she cannot be dead. Jane *cannot* be dead.

Margery and I cling together. We pray for Queen Jane's passing soul. We pray for my father, for the poor motherless prince, and for all of us. When will we ever be merry in England again?

St James' Palace – October 1558

"Poor sweet lady…"

I blink into the gloom, clear my throat and fumble at the neck of my bedgown.

"Yes, she was. Life has a way of striking the best people down when you least expect it. We were all grief-stricken. It was as if God was denying our right to be joyful, as if even after all we'd suffered, we still needed a lesson in humility. Perhaps we did. Perhaps we deserved it. Perhaps I have deserved all the misfortunes that have been strewn in my path."

"Oh, no, Your Majesty. Do not say such things. You have suffered but you will be rewarded in Heaven."

"I hope so. Would you call for Susan? I have a need for the close stool. What time is it, anyway? Earlier, I thought I heard music. Is that daylight I see beneath the shutter? Am I late for Mass?"

Susan comes bustling in; from the hoarseness of her voice I can sense she has been weeping. I hang on to her arm as she hauls me from the mattress and assists me to the screen in the corner of the chamber.

"What are the tears for?" I pull her close, searching her face and, seeing the lines engraved upon it, I know she was weeping for my passing. "I am not dead yet, Susan. I am still here. It is too soon for grief. Save it for when I've gone."

"Yes, Your Majesty," she says, hastily wiping away a stray tear. Turning discreetly aside while I go about my business, she lowers her head, rubbing her arms.

"I've left instructions for you all when I go," I call from the close stool, "all save that child, Anne. Can I rely on you to look after her, secure her a good place?"

"Yes, of course, Your Majesty. I will be glad to."

She helps me to stand and pulls my bed gown down to cover my knees. With me clinging to her arm, we totter back to the bed.

As the morning wears on, I sense activity in the outer chamber and cock my ear to the low buzz of voices and hasty footsteps.

"What is amiss?" I ask as I am helped to a chair while the maids remake the bed. "Has something happened?"

"No, Your Majesty. Nothing has happened – people have come to enquire after your health, that is all. I will order them to be quiet."

"They can't wait for me to go, can they? Before my eyes have closed for the last time, they will be calling for their horses and high-tailing it up the Great North Road to Elizabeth."

I picture them fawning at her feet, wishing her long life and pledging their loyalty – loyalty that used to be mine. Her joy at laying hands on my crown will overshadow any fleeting grief she may feel at my passing. *God rot her shallow soul.* Men will fall at her feet as they never did mine; even at Kennilworth when they flocked to my banner, it was not due to the beauty of my person but only to the power of my name. Mary Tudor.

They will love Elizabeth as they never have me. She will look the part of a queen, resplendent in the same royal finery that has never sat well on me. She will marry, she will have sons. Her body is healthy and strong, where mine was ageing and sick. I was kept too long a maid. I know that, had I been allowed to wed sooner, I'd have borne many healthy sons, and she would never have come to wear my crown.

Who will she marry? I wonder. There will be no lack of suitors. Half of Europe will come courting, and our own nobles will already be polishing their plate in an attempt to impress her. Even my Philip will gamble his chance on her. I've seen him admiring her golden good looks, her light step on the dance floor.

On their first meeting, he laughed each time she made some sharp witty comment. How I hated him for it. On one occasion, he snubbed me by offering her his arm on the way to the great hall. I had to make do with the ambassador.

Oh God, I will not bear it if Philip makes her an offer of marriage. Although, by then, I suppose I will be past caring. My preferences will be irrelevant. *I will be irrelevant.* Me, my church, my rule will be in the hands of a heretic!

A screech of frustration escapes my lips and instantly my women come running. "Do not fret yourself, Your Majesty." "Can I fetch you anything, Your Majesty?" "Shall I call the physician back, Your Majesty?"

I wish they'd leave me alone. I wish Philip would come.

I picture him throwing open the chamber door, his handsome face alight with the pleasure of seeing me again. Perhaps he will fall to his knee at my side, take up my hands and kiss my fingers, declare his love for me has never wavered...

And what would I do? Would I believe him? I shake my head. No; the scales have long since fallen from my eyes. I can only see our marriage for what it is. Where once I had hopes of it being a union of love, I now admit it was political, nothing more than that, at least on his side.

I was smitten at first, of course. He was the man I had dreamed of as a girl, and a Spaniard at that. Tall, handsome, powerful – I imagined our bedding would touch the part of me that had never been breached, a part of me I longed to discover. I dreamed of being able to give myself to someone at last but ... I was wrong about that too.

Our first joining was embarrassing and painful but mercifully quick. My only consolation was the hope that I would bear a child, but I was mistaken in that too. I search my mind for a time in my life when I have taken the right decision or been right about anything.

Philip is a cold fish, and arrogant too. His lack of consideration grew to such proportions that I was actually glad of the respite the last time he returned to Spain.

"Tell those children to either sing louder so I can hear properly, or to shut up."

"Children singing, Your Majesty? What do you mean?"

"Surely you can hear them. They've been singing all night. If I could only catch the tune..."

I thrust my ear toward the outer chamber but the sound dwindles, then fades away altogether. I straighten up, feeling a little ridiculous. "They've stopped now. No doubt they will start up again when it is time to sleep."

Susan squeezes a small sponge over a bowl of water and gently dabs my skin, washes the crust of sleep from my eyes, makes certain my nose is clean. The linen towel is soft and fragrant. I bury my face in it for a moment before it is taken away.

"Just a loose gown," I say. "I will not be leaving the chamber today."

In fact, I doubt I will leave the chamber ever again, not until the day they place me in a casket.

"I am not ready…"

"Not yet, Your Majesty. Just your cap to fit now…"

"I meant, I am not ready for the grave."

I pull my cap about my ears and turn the collar of the gown up to screen my neck from draughts. "I suppose none of us ever are."

She lowers her head and I see something glistening on her cheek.

"There's no need for sentiment, Susan. We both know God will call me soon. He, or the devil, comes for all of us in the end."

From her stricken face I see my words offer no comfort, so I flap my hand at her and change the subject.

"That girl, Anne. She's an interesting little thing."

"What did she speak to you about, Your Majesty?" Susan takes a stool beside me and begins to clean my nails. I think back on my conversation with the child and realise she said very little. I was the one who did all the talking.

129

"Well, she listens well anyway," I concede grudgingly.

"I hope we all listen, Your Majesty. I have been at your side for..."

"Oh, don't count the years, for goodness sake, or you'll remind us we are in our dotage."

She laughs, the merriness of the sound belying the lines and wrinkles on her cheek, the dullness of her eye. It seems just days since we both enjoyed the full flush of youth. Life passes so swiftly but we don't realise it until it is done. Until it is too late.

"Perhaps it just pleases me to have a new audience. It seems to me that if I can explain it all to her, make her see what my life has been like, she will speak well of me when others may not. I would hate to be disparaged once I am gone."

"Who would do so?"

She is offended at the suggestion, but I know better.

"Those who abhor the true church, and those who would undo my good work. They will not hesitate to speak ill of me. They will twist things, distort the truth. There are many who resent the deaths ... the burnings of the heretics."

She sniffs and flaps her hand.

"They knew the risks of flirting with the devil, it was their choice. The law is written plain for all men to see."

I beckon a hovering servant. "Fetch the girl, Anne, back again. Let us see what she thinks of it all."

When I ask her, astonishment erupts on her neat features and her cheeks burn ruddily.

"I am not fit to judge, Your Majesty. I am unschooled in politics and the law."

"Well, those two things have never been honest bed partners." My laughter cackles about the chamber. Then I sober abruptly and rub my hands over my face, eradicating the fleeting mirth.

"Imagine yourself a heretic. Imagine you deny the true church, the sacrament ... would you then believe you deserve to die by the flame?"

She is pale now, her chin wagging up and down as she searches for the right answer. She is loath to offend me. I place my hand over hers to still the rising panic.

"I don't require the right answer; I want the true answer, the one that is in your heart. There will be no punishment."

She blinks at me. I watch a pulse beating in her pretty neck. She swallows and, at first, her voice comes hoarsely.

"I imagine I would not like it, Your Majesty, but it is the law. Everyone who acts against the law of the land knows the risks. Obedience to the monarch and to God is paramount, we all know that."

"So they deserved a roasting, you think?"

"If they were guilty then yes, if taken up in error then ... no."

The last is but a whisper. I have never considered that a heretic may have been taken in error. I suppose she is thinking of the common folk, the women and children who perished at Smithfield. Now that it is too late, I see that the children could have been spared. It is damned rude of her to point that out.

Anger stirs in my old bones and my heart begins to race. I put a hand to my chest as if I can slow my heart, squeeze it into compliance. *How many of them think this way, and believe my punishments too harsh?*

If the people had only been more obedient I'd have cherished them all, but they were the devil's creatures. Sent to try me. All I did was chase them back to Hell where they belonged. Anne notices my frown and shuffles her feet.

"I am sorry to displease you, Your Majesty, but you did order me to speak truthfully."

"You don't understand how hard it was. The things I'd suffered. When ... Queen Jane's death came just as I'd begun to think all would be well again. It wasn't just an end to my hopes of happiness, it was the beginning of hell on earth."

"Why?"

"Why? *Why?* Because my father was almost mad with grief. Because he would look at none of us, speak to none of us. He closeted himself away, lost faith in his own self. He ceased to believe that God would ever smile upon him and that made him increasingly mean; increasingly dangerous.

"He said things to me that still burn in my memory to this day. His only comfort was

Edward and even though I was glad he had that small comfort, it stung as fiercely as a thousand wasps that he didn't choose to turn to me … and there was no balm, do you see? Nothing to soothe any of us."

Hampton Court Palace – 1537 - 40

I spend as much time as I am able with my infant brother and sister. Now that her mother is dead and Edward is heir, the resentment I felt toward Elizabeth transforms into love. I may be far above them both in age, but in my heart I am a motherless child … just as they are. It is a bond, and knowing as I do the unpredictability of our father, I try to offer them some form of stability.

Cromwell assists me in forming a new, and very restricted household. Where I once had three hundred people in my service, now I have just forty-two. But at least I am free to come and go and am no longer given the lowly status of servant.

To my great delight, Susan Clarencius joins me and so does Margery Baynton, and it feels good to be among friends again. Away from the cloying grief of my father, I wish I could live the lavish life I'd once been accustomed to. Unfortunately, my purse is short and I find it almost impossible to live within my means. I resume my studies in Latin and music and endeavour to be content with the company of my household women, to practise my lute and the latest dance steps, but it isn't easy.

Those who have missed me during my travail come calling almost straight away, and I welcome their friendship, realising that there was nothing they could have done to assist me when I was out of favour.

I throw away my old worn clothes and spend far too much of my income on replenishing my wardrobe. I have a great weakness for finery and jewels, and indulge my passion until my coffers are almost empty and I must apply to Father for extra coin. It is impossible to be scrupulous in my spending but one day, I tell myself, one day I will have all the coin I could wish for.

Father continues in his search for a husband for me but I still hanker for a union with Spain. The king and council prefer the suit of Dom Luis of Portugal or the Duke of Orléans. But I have received so many offers of marriage in my life that I no longer waste my time fearing, or even expecting, it to take place.

Relations between Father and I are still uncertain. As my household expands and my friends are no longer afraid to show affection for me, I come to realise that the king greatly dislikes them. I suppose he imagines we are working against him, plotting to usurp his throne and his hold on the church.

Of course, the dream of restoring Catholicism is never entirely out of my mind but I love my father and would never work against him, or do anything that might risk his favour any further.

He seeks to drive a wedge between the emperor and I, and I am as torn now between Spain and my father as I was in my youth. Chapuys continues to urge me to escape England and seek the safety of the emperor's protection but … although he is unpredictable, the king is my father and I cannot let go of that fact. No matter what dangers I face, I am loath to quit his kingdom because I know that to do so would be to lose his love forever.

While I live in bodily comfort, ostensibly in my father's favour once more, outside the palace walls there are stirrings of unrest. Cromwell, in his attempt to put an end to the old ways once and for all, persuades the king to move against the old Catholic families.

Since my grandfather's day, those of Plantagenet blood have never wholly been trusted. One by one, members of the Pole family, and the Nevilles and the Courtenays who were so supportive of my mother, are targeted. They are arrested for treason, interrogated and found guilty of conspiracy against the crown.

Father knows best, I tell myself. He is the king. I am powerless to stop him, but my heart breaks for my old friends. The Poles never failed us in the past and showed unwavering support for my mother's plight. If I was brave I would speak out, risk my own life for theirs, but Chapuys warns me that to do so would be suicide.

"You must say nothing, Princess, say nothing that might appear to go against the king."

I nod reluctantly, wishing I was made of sterner stuff, but when I hear that my dearest friend and cousin, Margaret Pole, has been taken, I fear my heart will crack in two.

"He will not harm her," I whisper to Chapuys who brings me the news. "She is his mother's cousin, her lifelong friend. Margaret Pole dandled my father on her knee when he was an infant. It is unthinkable that he should…"

My mind drifts to my childhood, when Mother and I walked with Margaret in the gardens. I can still hear their merry laughter as they related tales of when Mother was married to Prince Arthur … long before she ever dreamed of me. Margaret had been with them at Ludlow – they shared memories of a time that the rest of the court had forgotten.

And later, after Mother was queen, I recall Margaret soothing my nightmares in the dead of night, helping me with my first crumpled attempts at embroidery, instructing me how to shoot an arrow, how to daintily follow the steps of the dance... Father *loves* Margaret just as Mother did, just as I do; she is *family*.

I frown at Chapuys. "He just means to frighten her," I whisper with a shudder of fear. He shrugs his shoulders, his sad face crumpling with regret.

"I think not, my lady. The countess's son, Geoffrey, has implicated them all quite damningly in his confession, and as long as the exiled Reginald Pole continues to speak out against the king, he puts his entire family in peril."

"Then you must urge him to stop. He will listen to you. Tell him I urge him to think what it might mean..."

He splays his hands, his head sinking into his shoulders. "I have no influence, my lady. The rumour is that he plans to unseat the king and marry you."

"But I would never agree to that!"

Chapuys tilts his head and pulls a wry expression.

"But the king fears it and, as harsh as it sounds, these old families have plagued your father and his father before him for years. Once they are fallen, his position – the position of the Tudor line – will be more secure..."

"And the king's soul will be in peril. Has he thought of that? Perhaps I should speak to him, try to reason..."

"No!" He forgets himself and places a restraining hand on my arm. "You must never do that, my princess," he says earnestly. "Promise me, you will never do that."

"If only Jane were still alive. She could dissuade him."

But Jane isn't here, and as my friends continue to fall it is as if someone has thrust a dagger between my ribs. Their plight is killing me too. The old families are shamed and ruined, tainted by treason, their property confiscated by the crown. Early in December, Lord Montague, Lord Neville and Henry Courtenay go to the scaffold, while Courtenay's son is sentenced to a lengthy stay in the Tower. I look out at the cold grey skies above London and see the ravens fly up from Tower Hill. Perhaps it is as well Mother has not lived to see this day.

I summon Chapuys, beg him to implore Reginald Pole to desist with his treasonous talk but, even with his elderly mother, my beloved Margaret, held fast in the Tower, Pole continues his attempt to rally the Catholic powers of Europe to move against the king. In January, France and Spain agree to cease dealing with England. There will be no further trade. Our kingdom now stands alone, isolated, and while Father sets the country in readiness for war, Cromwell makes overtures of friendship to the Protestant German princes.

My relief is great when a proposed match between me and the Duke of Cleves comes to nothing. I could never ally myself to a Protestant. Cromwell, never one to be distracted from a goal, manages instead to arrange a match between the king and the duke's sister.

With a sigh, I prepare to meet another stepmother. This one is called Anne, which may bode ill, but I reassure myself she will not be like Anne

Boleyn. No, this one will be like Jane – a friend, a champion and hopefully a confidant.

Above all, I pray she has a calming influence over Father. I must befriend her at my earliest convenience and urge her that my friends should be spared. I sit down to write her a letter of welcome, expressing my joy at the coming union, while Anne of Cleves begins her perilous journey to England.

The winter sun will not be with us long and I write so fast that my words are a hasty scrawl. I am just blotting and sealing it when the door opens and a visitor is announced.

I have no love for Wriothesley, who is Cromwell's man. My spirits drop when he enters my presence, snatches off his cap at the last minute and makes a sketchy bow. I do not get up but I lift my chin to look down my nose at him, although he stands a deal taller than I.

"Ah, Lady Mary," he says, as if he is surprised to find me ensconced in my own apartments. "I have news."

He leaves a rather wet kiss upon my knuckle, which I surreptitiously wipe on my gown. I smile but do not speak, preferring to let him do the talking. He remarks first upon the weather, as if his errand is a social one. Suspicion erupts from somewhere deep within, foreboding creeping up the back of my neck.

I signal to Susan for wine and indicate that Wriothesley should sit. He sweeps his cloak from beneath his buttocks and takes the nearest chair, knees akimbo, feet spread far apart. I wait for him to speak.

"Lady Mary," he says again, although I have it on good authority that in the many marriage negotiations recently undertaken on my behalf, they have officially allowed me the title of 'princess.'

"In spite of the misfortune of your previous alliance with the Duke of Cleves coming to nothing, we have news that will surely bring a smile to those wan cheeks."

He is a condescending fool but I do not show my contempt. I also keep a tight rein on my alarm.

"Indeed."

I cannot like this man. He is a Lutheran and a traitor to my mother, and he was a supporter of Boleyn before he and his butcher-son master turned on her. "I am all ears."

He smiles a quick, tight smile that does not reach his eyes, and I realise our dislike is mutual.

"You should prepare yourself for a proposal of marriage, my lady. A proposal that your father the king expects you to welcome without argument."

My heart sinks deeper. I force a smile.

"Indeed," I say again. "Who is it this time?"

"Philip of Bavaria. He is in England to make preparation for his niece, Anne's, arrival, and will be presented to you within a few days."

Another Lutheran. How will I bear it? How can I swear duty and obedience to a heretic? How can I lie with one in nakedness? But I say nothing. I maintain my position, clutch my fingers together a little tighter and try to look mildly interested. I imagine Philip will be a foppish, insolent fellow and wonder if he will hide his horns beneath his cap.

"I will meet with him, sir, but … you must take this message to my father."

I close my eyes, picturing his rage, his disappointment, the return of his distrust of me, but I cannot deny my beliefs. I cannot be seen to go gladly into a union with a friend of the devil.

"You must remind my kind and benevolent father that, although I know it to be a matter of great importance, I can never wish or desire to enter that kind of religion. I would sooner remain a maid all my life."

Wriothesley's neck turns red, the colour creeping up to his cheeks, his eyes disappearing in a ferocious squint. He stands up, searches for his gloves and blesses me with a second sketchy bow.

"I will, of course, convey your message to the king, my lady, but … you must be aware that it will undoubtedly bring disfavour upon you again. The duke will expect to meet you in the gardens at Westminster Abbey on the twenty-second day of this month. I suggest that you be there, unless you are otherwise instructed by the king."

He quits my chamber and I am left alone. I close my eyes and a tear drips onto my cheek. *Why will they not just leave me alone?* Try as I might, it seems I can never remain in Father's favour for long, but *God must come first*. It is better to die from Father's displeasure than to burn forever in the flames of God's wrath.

I have to go, of course. I dress in my best gown, drape myself in my favourite jewels and, with only Susan and Margery in accompaniment, I take the barge to Westminster.

It is an inauspicious day for the meeting. The clouds hang low and heavy, no sun manages to find a way through and the air is cold and dank. The duke is waiting near a muddy border, the gravel path is puddled with yesterday's rain and dead, sodden plants sprawl inelegantly across the yellowing grass. It is a ruin of the summer splendour of July. The duke appears comically forlorn until, on hearing my footstep, he looks up, and his former melancholy melts away.

"My lady."

He rushes to meet me and, as he bends over my hand, I prepare myself for the burn of a heretic's kiss. I look down upon his bare head, noting the way his hair curls about the back of his ears, and then he stands and I find myself blinking into wide friendly eyes. He has a generous smile that I cannot help but replicate.

"I am pleased to meet you," I say and find, to my surprise, that it is not entirely untrue. He takes my elbow and guides me along the path.

"Oh, mind the piddle," he says and behind me, Susan and Margery titter quietly. I smother my own laughter, thank him for his gallantry, and allow him to lead me daintily through the puddles. Although he has little English, he waves the interpreter away and we move off together through the decaying garden.

"Your English weather is…" He hugs his own shoulders and pulls a frozen face, and I cannot help but laugh with him. I had not expected to like him. I had expected horns and a tail, yet he is expansive, and very funny!

"Not always," I say, fervently hoping he will understand. "Our summers are warm and sunny." I sweep my arms in an arc, playing the part of the sun, and he smiles widely, nodding his head. I notice one of his eye teeth is broken but it is attractive, and the creases bracketing his mouth suggest he laughs often and loudly.

Despite the chilly day I am suddenly warm inside, more hopeful of the future than I have been for a long while. Marriage to a man who laughs and is gentle would be a fine and unexpected thing.

"Do you hunt?" I ask, and he frowns at me.

"'Unt?"

"Hunt," I repeat, emphasising the H and aping the action of riding a horse and jumping a fence. He laughs aloud, nods frantically and pretends to blow a horn. Despite only understanding half a dozen words of each sentence, I find myself warming to him. For an hour or more we stroll about the ruined garden, oblivious to the damp, the cold, and the fine drizzle that soaks my skirts to the knee. He is telling me a story of his childhood, a tale that I only half comprehend, when a gust of wind showers him with freezing raindrops.

Covering my mouth with my hand, I try to stem my laughter, but he reaches out and pulls it away.

"Do not 'ide your face," he says. "Too pretty."

I cannot move. I stare at him entranced, my eyes roving his wet face, absorbing his thick-lashed eyes, his firm chin, his fine long nose.

Other than my father, no man has ever told me I am pretty. In fact, I know it is untrue but I don't care. This man's lies are like honey, sweetening my day, my sour difficult life. I wish I could listen to them for the rest of my life.

He retains my hand in his and without any sense of embarrassment, I place my other over them, as a priest does at a wedding.

"I am very 'appy to 'ave meet you, my lady…" he whispers.

"Mary," I say. "My name is Mary."

Somehow our eyes are locked. It is impossible to drag my gaze away; even when his face grows closer to mine, his eyes looming and merging into one, I cannot draw back. I have no wish to. As if governed by some external force, I tilt back my head, part my lips and allow him to kiss me.

I have had many suitors, many disappointments, but this is the first time I have ever been courted, the first time I've known the touch of a lover's hand on my cheek, his lips against mine. Delight surges beneath my skin, his name echoing in my head.

In the weeks that follow, I cannot stop thinking about him. His name finds a way into my conversations, he is the last thing I think of at night, my first thought in the morning.

Don't set your heart on it, I tell myself, but the other Mary, the one I keep hidden away, refuses to obey. I no longer care about his Lutheran leanings, he has unleashed something within me, something that is wild and quite ungovernable. It almost puts my passion for God in the shade.

A treaty is drawn up; I am to be given a dowry of forty thousand florins providing I waive all rights to the English throne. I do not care, my heart leaps and bounds quite frantically every time I think of his mouth and the soft kindness in his eyes. I cannot wait to see him again.

Rumours fly; it seems everyone knows of our meeting and the kiss we shared, and when I pass by, the courtiers put their heads together and I know they gossip about me. Still, I do not care.

Although we are not permitted to meet again in private, he is present at the Christmas feast. I wear my best clothes, pile as many jewels as I can upon my person so that he might be impressed at my wealth and status. Our eyes meet often across the crowd, he lifts his wine and silently drinks my health, and each time he does so, something shifts deep in my belly. Whenever his lips kiss the rim of his cup, I envy it.

But my joy is spoiled when the emperor threatens war upon the German provinces and Philip is summoned home. To my sorrow, when he takes leave of England early in January, he does not make the time to bid farewell to me. I sink into sadness again, longing for the day of his return.

Rumours of our courtship fly about the court, about Europe, and eventually reach the ear of the king. When he sends for me, I hurry to his privy chambers, sink to my knees and lower my head. He does not bid me rise and when I finally pluck the courage to look up, I find his narrowed eyes upon me.

I duck my head again and stay where I am, wracking my brains as to how I may have displeased him.

"So, Daughter," he says at last, "you welcome this match with Philip of Bavaria?"

"If it pleases you, Sire," I reply, keeping my eyes lowered, my chin dipped toward my chest as I have been taught.

"Rumour has it you frolicked together in the privy garden."

I look up, startled, and shake my head determinedly.

"Frolicked? No, Father. That is not so. We walked and talked, and he left a chaste kiss upon my cheek when we parted, that is all."

There was nothing chaste about his kiss.

"Hmm."

Father ponders the matter, drumming his jewelled fingers on the arm of his chair. "I know how the gossips like to elaborate royal matters. I will believe you but you would do well not to hold hopes in that quarter. I've changed my mind and do not mean to approve the match. You can do better than Bavaria; I allowed him to pay court to you in order to strengthen our hand against the emperor."

My mouth falls open. I stare at the king but he is gazing into space, his thoughts already on other matters.

He is unaware of my shattered hope that I might be free of him, free of England, free of spinsterhood. I try to sink lower into the floor before edging backwards from the room to the discomfort of my empty chambers.

There is a curious pain in my breast. I drop into a chair and stare down at my short stubby fingers. I will never marry, I realise that now. I will live and die a virgin, always envying the women around me who have husbands … and children. I would have dearly loved to bear Philip many, many children. I am fated, it seems, to be the unhappiest woman in Christendom.

Greenwich – January 1540

Elizabeth, dressed for Father's wedding to Anne of Cleves, has dropped something sticky on her skirt. I summon one of the women to attend it. She kneels at the child's feet.

"Keep still, my lady, please. Let me see if I can sponge it off."

Elizabeth pouts and frowns. If I was not watching, I am sure she would poke out her tongue. She abhors to be still and is full of mischief. She is always being scolded for skipping about the chamber, hiding behind curtains to leap out at the maids and make them shriek. I sigh and send her a warning look.

"Just do your best; we must not be late for the ceremony, stained skirts or not. Really, Elizabeth, what were you thinking to eat sweetmeats when we are almost ready to leave? What will your new stepmother think?"

Elizabeth ceases to dance to some music only she can hear and looks at me, her face suddenly intense.

"Her name is Anne, isn't it? Do you think Father will cut off her head too?"

My heart skips a beat and then thumps fast and loud, making my head light. What is she thinking of to speak of such a thing as if it were an everyday event? I fumble for a suitable answer.

"Of course not," I reply, far more sharply than I intended. "*Anne of Cleves* has done nothing wrong."

She narrows one eye and tilts her head to one side.

"I overheard my nurse say that Father is displeased with her already, so perhaps she has done something wrong that we don't know about yet."

"You are a silly child," I announce brightly, making a nonsense of her words but, as I straighten my hood, I frown at my reflection in the looking glass. There is something in what she says. The whole court knows of Father's reluctance to go through with the marriage. He desperately seeks an escape from it but is constrained by the treaty and dare not risk falling out with the German princes as well as the emperor.

"Come along, Elizabeth, that will have to do. If the king or – or the queen speaks to you, ensure you keep the stained parts out of their sight."

She takes my hand. "They won't even look at me, at least Father won't. I make him uncomfortable."

As we progress along the corridors and make our way to the chapel royal, I ponder her words. Do we, the daughters of his wronged wives, make the king *uncomfortable*? I doubt it. If our presence offended him he would just send us away and deny us the right to come to court. I know that better than anyone.

To my surprise, Anne of Cleves looks nothing like his previous wives. She is tall and quite plain but kindly looking, perfectly suited to the role of motherhood, if not perhaps as wife to a man like the king. In the past, he has always been drawn to women with striking looks; only Jane was different, but she made up for her lack of beauty with the kindness of her heart. I have not yet discovered whether Anne is kind or otherwise but she looks friendly. Understanding little of our speech or customs, she beams on everyone, keen to be accepted, to make a good impression.

Even from behind, it is clear that Father is furious. His shoulders are set in uncompromising lines, his head held stiffly, the feather on his hat trembling as he battles to suppress his rage. The rumours are true. The king is not happy.

Beside him, Anne smiles uncomprehendingly on the company. I watch her. How strange we must seem to her. How disconcerting it must be to find oneself in the midst of strangers, unable to speak their language or understand their customs. How must it feel to be wed to a man like Father? I try to imagine how he must seem to Anne, view him from her eyes.

He is no longer the golden prince of his youth. He is quite jaded. His face is lined, his hair greying, and his belly is becoming gross. During the marriage negotiation he had portraits painted to send to Anne. I saw them. They were not true to life at all. She will have left her homeland imagining she was to marry the man in Holbein's paintings; a glorious, godlike figure – how disappointing the reality must be. Poor Anne, forced to bed the angry, ageing Henry. Perhaps it is fortunate, after all, that I am to remain a maid.

Hampton Court – 1540

Now that Queen Anne is in residence, I return to court, taking apartments close to Edward's so I can spend as much time with him as my duties allow. My brother has just turned two and is a bonny bundle of mischief; as fat and healthy a boy as the king could wish for. I take him on my knee and kiss his damp cheeks while he tugs at my veil and refuses to sit still.

"He is like an eel!" I laugh.

"You'll make a good mother one day, my lady," Lady Bryan says as she watches us together. I look up and meet her eyes and, finding sincerity there, I relax and smile in return. She cannot know she has pierced my armour, she cannot imagine my despair of ever knowing the joy of motherhood.

"The queen came by to see him yesterday," she continues, picking up Edward's toy that he has thrown to the floor. "She was much taken with the prince. Hopefully, she will add to the nursery soon. Edward will enjoy having some brothers. My hands will be full then, my lady."

She rattles the child's toy.

"Yes," I say, kissing my brother behind the ear, making him giggle. "That would make the king happy again."

"A king can't have too many princes."

"Indeed."

I dare not speak it aloud but rumour says my father is already seeking an annulment to the marriage. Anne does not please him at all. He says she is nothing like as fair as she was painted, and her stomach and bosom are so slack he fears she is no maid. Poor Anne, I hope she hasn't heard of this. I sigh as I straighten Edward's skirts. I know only too well the fate of others who have displeased my father, but even he must see that Anne is blameless. The king leaves the whole thing at the door of his secretary, the soon to be Earl of Essex, Thomas Cromwell.

As Thomas goes about the court, he wears a very anxious frown, and who can blame him. The Cleves marriage was by his arrangement, his praise of Anne before the wedding encouraged the king to enter into the treaty. My father, now finding himself bound to a woman he abhors, is looking for someone to blame; a scapegoat.

As Cromwell's enemies prick up their ears, he desperately concocts a solution. Seizing on a pre-contract of Anne's with the son of the Duke of Lorraine, he declares there is an impediment to the marriage. This, together with Father's failure to consummate the union, serves as a way out, for the king, if not for Cromwell.

Everyone tries not to notice the relief with which Anne agrees to the annulment. From now on, she is to be known as the king's sister. She tucks a very handsome settlement and a long list of properties into her coffers, and takes up residence at Richmond; my favourite palace.

I have little to thank Thomas Cromwell for. He is not only a heretic but was instrumental in progressing my parents' estrangement. He pushed for the split with Rome and during my estrangement from the king his treatment of me was unnecessarily harsh. In recent years, he has wrought great destruction on the monasteries, inflicting suffering on monks and nuns alike. As far as I am concerned, his downfall is his just deserts. He may have orchestrated the reunion between me and my father but it falls far short of redemption … his end is of his own making. It is no concern of mine.

Rumours abound at court. His enemies take great pleasure in describing Cromwell's ignoble end. He does not face death valiantly. *What can one expect from the son of a blacksmith?* He writes from the

Tower, begging Father to spare his life and swearing unswerving allegiance, his unwavering loyalty. The king does not listen. He cannot see beyond the plain, uncultured wife Cromwell has saddled him with, and is deaf to all pleas ... whether they bear the ring of truth or not.

But after Cromwell's death, life at court does not settle down peacefully. It seems to unleash a great rage in the king and a spate of further deaths follows. Like a lion driven into a corner the king lashes out, and his claws are strong and fatal.

I weep sorry tears when I learn of the death of my mother's chaplain, my old tutor, Dr Featherston, and Father's own confessor, Dr Wilson. I cannot imagine what crimes he uses against them. These are good Catholic people who do not deserve death, and the three Protestants who follow them to the scaffold shortly afterwards do not compensate for it.

My discomfort is not eased by news of another looming royal wedding, another stepmother. When I am told her name, I wonder if the king has run a little mad for this time, he chooses a bride for himself. He cannot face a diplomatic match this time and instead he marries a child; or so she seems to me.

I am embarrassed to learn that Katherine Howard is my junior by some five years or so. She is bright, pretty and quite enchanting, but she is not the sort of woman who can successfully rule as consort beside any king, let alone a king such as my father.

She first came to his attention during her short service in the household of Anne of Cleves. I vaguely recall her exclaiming over the queen's vast array of gowns, her costly collection of jewels. She was overwhelmed by those around her, by the vast chambers, the rich fare we feasted on. No doubt most of Anne's possessions now belong to Katherine.

Anne, however, shows no malice toward the new queen, and the two have become great friends. I wince from the gossip that somehow reaches my ears but Father seems oblivious to the fact that the English court has become a laughing stock in Europe.

Foreign heads of state even go as far as to place wagers as to how long this marriage will last. The king is besotted. I blush to witness how he fawns upon her like a doting and extremely foolish old man. As for me? Well, I am eaten up with jealousy.

I can excuse her stupidity. I can overlook her impulsive childishness and her greed, but the thing I cannot forgive is that she is a Howard, and first cousin to Anne Boleyn.

At first, I am not invited to attend court. It is not until I implore Father to bring his queen to visit Edward at Waltham that I begin to accept her. She is harmless enough and while Father joggles my brother up and down on his knee, Katherine takes me to one side. She casts a look over her shoulder to ensure the king cannot overhear.

"Lady Mary," she says. "I hope we can be friends, and you will come to court soon. I will have the best rooms made ready for you."

"Thank you, Your Grace," I murmur, wondering at this show of friendship. Surely she doesn't imagine we might have anything in common. She places a hand on my sleeve and leans in close, wafting the fragrance of sandalwood and sage. I draw back a little, observing the flawlessness of her skin, the strand of light red hair that has escaped the confines of her hood. She dimples, and lowers her voice to a whisper.

"I wanted to let you know that I've sent clothes, a furred gown and slippers to Lady Pole. I hate to think of that poor old lady in that awful place. I – I know she was your friend…" She shudders, her expressive eyes rolling in her head. I raise my brows, surprised and touched.

"That was kind of you. Does … does the king know?"

Putting her hand to her mouth, she stifles a giggle. "He hasn't asked, and it isn't a lie not to mention it, is it?"

"I suppose not."

I look at her, and a quick companionable smile darts between us. Perhaps there is more to her than the latest fashions and dance steps. It is comforting to think so. I have never dared send Margaret anything other than my fervent prayers for her release, but she is condemned to die … one day it will happen. One day, when Father awakes in the wrong frame of mind, he will order it done. I dread that day.

I look at the queen afresh and wonder if she might be useful after all. Perhaps Katherine can be induced to work her persuasion on the king. Perhaps this child stepmother of mine will be the key to Margaret's freedom. Everyone knows that when Father is happy, the executioner gets to put his feet up.

I take the queen's arm and invite her to walk with me on the terrace.

"When I was growing up, Margaret Pole was like a mother to me," I say casually. "She is a God-fearing woman, a friend of the true church."

"Yes." The queen frowns at the ground. "It is sad that she is imprisoned. I remember my cousin…" She stops, belatedly remembering who I am, and her cheeks grow pinker as she continues. "That is to say, it is horrid for anyone to be shut up in there. Imagine living and waiting, in dread of the executioner's blade that has turned toward you. Every morning you'd wonder if it was your last … I wouldn't wish it on my worst enemy."

"I'd wish it on the guilty," I say as lightly as I can manage. "Those who oppose the king have committed treason and so do deserve to die, but Margaret is innocent. I am *sure* of it."

"I think we are all guilty of something." Her face falls, her eye losing its customary brightness. "The king says she wrote letters to her son, and when her house was searched, they found incriminating items that prove she is opposed to his rule."

Poor Margaret; as if she would be stupid enough to risk working against the king. She has long been accustomed to us and has never forgotten the fate of her father and brother. The queen and I continue our walk along the terrace.

"I suspect those incriminating items were placed there by Cranmer or one of his men, and where is the crime in writing to one's son?"

I dare not mention that I share Margaret's sympathies with the 40,000 men who marched on the pilgrimage of grace. It is not safe to admit to anyone that you harbour a desire for the reinstatement of the true church, least of all to the Queen of England.

"Perhaps, when you give the king a son, you can ask a boon of him and request her release. He is generous when he is happy."

She frowns, biting her lip.

"Yes," she says. "A son would be lovely but … the king…" She stops, shakes her head and gives a shaky laugh. "Oh, Lady Mary, rest assured that I shall do all I can to get with child, and then I will indeed beg for Lady Margaret's life as soon as it is meet for me to do so."

Hampton Court – May - June 1541

When the king is happy, the court is happy. For the first time in many years, merriment is the order of the day. Although I am present, I am shown little favour and I keep myself apart from the rest. While the court dances, the dying monks are forgotten, as are the churches that are falling and the heresy that continues to put out strong, evil roots. Nobody else seems to care.

I feel so alone; as if separated from them all by some invisible screen. I hear but do not share in their laughter. I watch their desperate, feigned delight and notice how like Bacchus Father has become; he has turned into an obese, overindulged god, showering merriment on his congregation. It cannot last. I wonder what will happen to spoil it all.

I do not have to wait long. In May, I wake from a restless night to the sound of weeping. I sit up in bed, fumble for my wrap and hurry into the antechamber.

"Oh, my lady. We didn't mean to wake you…"

My women stand ringed in the centre of the room; several of them have red-rimmed eyes and wet, starred lashes.

"What has happened?" I draw my shawl tighter about my chest as if it can shield me.

"It is … Lady Salisbury. My lady, she was executed … early this morning."

It is as if I've been struck. At first, I am numb with the shock, but slowly the pain spreads from the very core of me until it encompasses my whole being. It is the news I've been dreading. Lady Salisbury, my dearest friend.

"There has been no trial, she had no chance to plead her case."

Mary Baynton shakes her head, wiping her wet face on the edge of her sleeve. I turn from them to stand at the shuttered window.

Father has acted on a whim, as I feared he would. He has vented his spleen against an elderly woman who has shown the Tudors nothing but loyalty. She has done nothing wrong; he killed her because he is angry with her son.

I don't think I can bear it. My heart twists. She lived through so much. The years of civil war, a childhood disgraced by her father's attainder. Her innocent young brother incarcerated for years in the Tower, never to emerge until it was time for him to die. Yet still, she loyally served and somehow managed to love us. Out of all the people who claim to love me, she was one of the few I trusted, and loved in return. I feel so alone.

"Oh, my lady," Mary weeps as she describes the scene. "They are saying it was more akin to butchery than an execution. According to the messenger, she called down God's blessing upon you before she placed her head on the block."

I put a hand to my face, tears raining upon my fingers as Mary's voice continues to paint pictures in my mind that time will never erase. I wish she would stop but Mary goes on and on.

"She laid down her head and the executioner … oh, my lady, the executioner was young and untried, and he misjudged it. He – it took several strokes of the axe to end it; oh my lady, she died slowly and horribly … oh, I cannot speak of it!"

But she has spoken of it. Her words are branded deep into my soul. I will never forget, nor forgive this act … as God is my witness, I will not forget. I will not forgive.

Quite suddenly, Mary ceases speaking. I feel her hand on my arm. "Oh, my lady, you … I am so sorry. Come, come with me. You are ill and must lie down a while."

The sheets are smooth and cool, my pillow soft beneath my cheek. I think of Margaret's face, blooded now and pale, shoved without dignity into some roughly hewn coffin. I think of her sons … some alive, some dead ... and as I close my eyes and bury my face beneath the pillow, Margaret's whole sorry life runs through my mind. I should have spoken out in her defence. I should have begged mercy of my father. I am a coward. I sit upright, crying her name aloud until my women come running.

Sweet wine is trickled between my lips. I cough and splutter so it sprays like blood across the snowy linen. I push the hands away, roll onto my belly, clutch the pillow tight and lose my mind in the nightmare of grief.

I am sick for a long time; my face is pale and listless. When my menses come, I am wracked with pain, and the blood runs thick and dark.

I am unable to speak, unable to function. Each meal time, I turn away in disgust, leaving the platter untouched. I can find no comfort. Not even in prayer. It is the last straw. Should God choose to take me now, I would be glad of it. But He is not merciful and my heart continues to beat, my lungs continue to draw breath. I continue to live.

"You must pull yourself together," my women tell me. "It is your duty. Think what your mother would say. She lived through worse than this. She never gave up. It is a sin to deny the life the good Lord offers us."

I want to scream at them. There is nothing I can do other than hate myself, so one day I submit and allow them to bathe and dress me. After so long abed, my gown feels like a prison; the jewelled bodice a leaden weight upon my shoulders, as heavy as my heart.

At first, it is all I can do to walk about the gardens for an hour or so before retreating back to my chamber, but slowly, as I begin to eat again and take the air, I grow stronger. I bury my head in my books, refresh my studies and take up the lute again.

I am not really strong enough to agree when the king and queen request my presence on their planned progress to the north of the country. After the recent uprisings, Father means to demonstrate his power, and attempt to reignite their love for him. He is blind to the pain he has inflicted, and cannot understand their resentment. The people of the north will never forgive the closure of the great monasteries or the ill-treatment of the monks and nuns. They are not fooled by the king's accusations of corruption and immorality. As far as the northerners are concerned, the confiscation of the church treasures is theft, bred by greed. The desecration of the places where the people worshipped or turned for help in times of poverty or sickness is unforgiveable.

The king neither understands nor cares.

It will be painful to see first-hand the results of his 'dissolution' but I feel I must go, if only to test whether the northern people still bear any love for me. I put all my effort into making a full recovery while my women make preparations for the journey.

It is by far the largest progress I have been part of, and the most lavish I've ever heard of. There must be four or five thousand horse, countless carts and wagons; an endless procession of strength.

As we travel on ahead of the household, our royal party makes a marvellous splash of colour against the greenery of England. At first, I am in fine fettle. I sit high in the saddle and absorb the scenery, the love of the people, the atmosphere. Once more allowed the prominence that my status demands, I almost feel like a princess again, and everyone treats me as such. I soak in the cheers of the crowd, smiling with delight each time I hear my name upon their lips. The people of England have not forgotten me.

Ahead, the plume on Father's hat flutters; his familiar voice, and every so often the queen's merry laughter, wafts toward me on the breeze. I wonder if her incessant good humour ever grates upon him. He must miss my mother's calm intelligence, unless he has completely forgotten her, of course. Perhaps his memories of Mother and me were erased long ago by the concubine's wicked wit, or Jane's quiet humanity. But after the fiasco of his marriage to Anne of Cleves, it seems he is happy at last and for that we must be grateful. I try to be glad for him.

We stop at Enfield, St Albans and Dunstable, and when we draw close to Ampthill I recall the time I spent there with Mother and Father when I was still the Princess of Wales. I had been away from court and missed them so much and, after travelling from Ludlow to be with them, I can still feel the tightness of my mother's embrace, the approval of my father. My mind roams, tumbling down the years that followed, and I recollect that later, my mother was sent to Ampthill while the king fought for his divorce so that he might marry his strumpet. The rosy memories are pushed aside and the misery of those days intrudes, the humiliation that came afterwards clouding the present. I glance toward the king's wide shoulders and scowl. He is as far removed from the father of my childhood as the moon is from the sun.

I sigh unhappily.

"Are you well, my lady? Is the sun too hot for you?"

"A little." I try to smile but the day is spoiled, the memory of my distant past with all its brightness has blotted out any hope of joy in the present. We ride on, ever northward, but the further we get from London, the quieter the waiting crowd grows, the less welcoming the cheers. Their resentment is tangible. I feel unwelcome, but Father doesn't seem to have noticed.

By the time we reach Northampton, I am tired and disillusioned. At the end of the day, pleading illness I take to my bed, and when the royal party rides north in the morning, I remain behind, promising to follow on when I am recovered. But I don't. I can take no joy from the journey.

It is strange. I spend my life surrounded by people yet I am always lonely, displaced. I yearn for something I cannot name; I want to strike out at the bleakness of my unmarried, unlovely, virgin state. But at least the king seems happy; I should be thankful for that. If Katherine has achieved anything at all, she has managed to make him smile again. For that I owe her my thanks, for when Henry is at peace, the court is too.

Away from his presence, I forget the man Father has become and remember only the man he used to be; the man that made me laugh, the man who tickled me under the chin and called me his *little pearl*.

For the rest of the summer, the real king ceases to exist. In my mind, he is as he used to be; a figment, a dream. So when Father returns to Hampton Court in

October, I almost expect to greet the tall virile prince of my imaginings. I am surprised at the fat, cantankerous old man that stands before me.

Hampton Court – November 1541

At first, I ignore the whispers. It is just court tittle-tattle, I tell myself, people dearly love to gossip. But there is something in the air; the atmosphere is thick with intrigue. Returning from Mass one morning, I encounter Cranmer and Norfolk in anxious conversation. They stop talking when they see me, break apart, straighten their backs and greet me cheerfully, but I note their white faces, their anxious eyes.

"Is something amiss?" I ask, looking from one to the other. "Is the king in good health?"

"His Majesty is very well." Cranmer tucks a sheaf of papers beneath his elbow and bends over my hand. "The trip north seems to have benefitted him."

Silence falls. I search their faces as their eyes drift away, and Norfolk moistens his lips.

"Was Father much enraged when the king of Scots did not meet him as he requested?"

"Oh," Cranmer waves a dismissive hand. "Only for a short while. The king of Scots has nothing the king of England desires. His Majesty has better things to occupy him than troubling himself about a Scotsman."

They are hiding something and I am desperate to know what it is.

"How is the queen? Another son will please him." I cannot help pushing, I know something is amiss. Perhaps the queen is with child at last. I sense it has something to do with the succession … perhaps a match has been proposed for me.

"It would indeed, my lady. We look forward to news of it."

His words do not ring true. It is as if he is a performer in a mummer's play, reeling off rehearsed sentences.

"I hope for an audience with the queen later today," I continue blithely. "She will enjoy telling me all about the progress. I was sorry to miss it. Did Her Majesty enjoy her first trip north?"

"It seems she did, my lady. It seems she did. Now, would you excuse us, it will not do to keep the king waiting. I wish you good day."

One after the other, they bend over my hand again, and take their leave of me. I watch them walk away, note again their agitation, their sense of nervousness. I frown, pondering the cause of it before turning on my heel and hurrying off to crave an audience with the queen.

I am conducted to her privy chamber. When I am announced, she looks up from an abundance of fine fabrics. "Mary!" She rises to her feet and hurries to greet me, takes both my hands, her expression warm. "It is so good to see you. Are you recovered from the megrim that beset you on the road?"

"Oh yes, it was nothing more than my usual complaint."

"It is good to see you looking so well now." She snatches a roll of red velvet and holds it against her cheek. "Do I look well in this shade? I am choosing new gowns for the Christmas festivities. Oh, I do hope you will be joining us this year."

I nod, pleased by her thoughtfulness, but I have no need to reply for she continues to chatter as she plucks up different fabrics and holds them against her face. I take a seat near the window and mark her underlying nerves, the brittleness of her joy. She is so full of suppressed excitement it is as if she might break apart.

Katherine shuffles on her knees to another pile of fabric and holds up first the red, then the blue.

"Oh, I cannot decide," she says as if her life hangs on the choice. "What do you think, Lady Mary?"

I lean forward, test the nap.

"The king prefers blue, I think, but whatever you wear will please him. You can do no wrong in his eyes, least of all in your choice of gown."

"No."

She sobers and sits back on her heels, her wide eyes settling on mine. "I only regret I have failed to give him the thing he wants the most ... another son."

She blinks away tears, smiling blithely through her sadness, and I think how pretty she is, and how very, very young to have already despaired of a child. Perhaps Father is too old, perhaps he cannot manage ... I thrust the indelicate thought away and point to the blue.

"The blue will be the best choice, Your Majesty, mark my words."

Later, when I am brought the news that she is under house arrest, and being questioned for adultery and treason against the king, I remember her fevered conversation, her sense of failure, and understand it.

St James' Palace – October 1558

"It was an awful time. Worse, far worse than when they took Boleyn. Katherine was just a silly girl, but she was

162

free of malice … free of any common sense too, it seems."

Susan and Anne are seated at the side of my bed. When my conversation palls, they sit up and exchange sorry looks. It is Susan who speaks first.

"I recall it well, Your Majesty. It was a hard time yet … oh, you are right, she was a silly girl."

Susan shakes her head, her eyes rueful.

"… And my father was a fool for thinking a child such as Katherine could ever truly love an old man."

"Yes," Susan nods. "He married her for love when he could have made a diplomatic match. A foreign bride of noble blood would never have acted in such a way…"

I frown into the past, and find it a dark, chilling place.

"Yet Katherine was of Howard stock, her pedigree was flawless … we only discovered afterwards that her upbringing was wanting."

"It was shocking. I had known she was silly but never thought her unchaste. It shows how deceiving a pretty face can be. Her grandmother, the dowager duchess, should have lost her head for leaving such a young girl to her own devices."

They never discovered until afterwards that the household Katherine was raised in was rife with sin and Katherine exposed to it from infancy. It is no wonder she had no idea of how to behave.

"As for Culpepper, I hope the enjoyment of his queen's body was worth the price he paid for it."

I sniff, and Anne's surreptitious movements suggest she is wiping away a tear. I grope for her fingers.

163

"Let that be a lesson, my girl. Your sins will out."

She snatches her hand away.

"I doubt I will ever marry a king, let alone betray one, Your Majesty."

"A woman must be faithful to her marriage whether she be wed to king or commoner, and don't you forget that."

"But, it doesn't work the other way around." Susan has risen and is folding linen away into a clothes press. "A man can be as faithless as he wishes, and a wife has no right to even remark on it."

I laugh. "You were well rid of your husband, Susan, but for all his infidelity you did well from the match. I am sure you have no regrets."

"Well," she returns slowly to the bed. "Not now, Your Majesty, but it wasn't easy at the time." She turns to Anne. "You must pick carefully, child, when the time comes. If you can't love him, look to his wealth. There are more comforts to be found in a fat purse than in the matrimonial bed."

Anne blushes scarlet. I slap at Susan's hand.

"Don't tease her," I laugh, but the humour turns into a cough. My eyes water, my chest wheezes.

They haul me upright on the pillows and rub my back until the attack passes. When I am recovered enough to speak, I hang on to Susan's sleeve.

"Is there news yet of Jane? Has she returned from Hatfield?"

"She returned this morning. When she has refreshed herself, she will attend Your Majesty. I can send for her sooner, if you prefer…"

"No, no. I can wait. Let her rest. It is not long since she recovered from the fever and she will be fatigued from the journey."

Not as tired as I am, of course. I am sure there is no one on Earth as exhausted as I. Jane Dormer is young enough to still have hopes of finding romance, and I have stalled more than one of her relationships in the selfish need to keep her at my side. But I encouraged this latest attachment with Philip's friend, the Duke of Feria, although that marriage too has been delayed. I must remember to give her my blessing when he returns to England, before it is too late for them.

I hope all of my women will find happiness after I am gone, but it is hard to accept that life will continue after my death. I cannot imagine the world without me being part of it. The people of England will forget me, and some will even sigh with relief when I breathe my last.

I begin to speak but pain gripes in my belly again and my words become a groan. Susan's head shoots up.

"Are you ill, Your Majesty, shall I call the physician?"

"What would that serve? There is no cure for death."

"But he can ease you, help you to sleep…"

I wave her away.

"I am tired of sleeping. I have just a short time left on Earth and there are things I should do, stories I must share."

Yet, I do feel tired, and when I sleep I feel the people of the past are here with me; people who understood what it was like to live in those dangerous, dark days before I was queen.

"When Katherine was sent to the Tower, Father sent me to stay with Edward. I never saw her again."

I speak through my teeth, chasing the present hurt away with memories of a more painful time. "After that, the king was never the same. He sank into a deep woe and even after he married my final stepmother, another Katherine – Lady Latimer – he was never the man, or the king, he had been before.

"He knew that Christendom was laughing at him, do you see? No man can hold his head high while the world mocks him, my father least of all. But Katherine Parr … she changed things. She tried to pick up the pieces of our broken, tainted family and put us all back together. It worked … for a while, we thought we were whole again…"

Hampton Court – July 1543-45

The king is looking old. He can no longer walk far without the arm of his servants to aid him, and sometimes he is forced to resort to a portable chair. His face is pouched and lined, the whites of his eye jaundiced, and the stench of his festering thigh is sometimes overwhelming. Yet Katherine Parr shows no sign of distaste when she is with him. She is the perfect, willing wife and if at times she appears sad, well, she keeps the reason to herself. The role of queen suits her well and she embraces me and my siblings as if we are her own lost children. For the first time, we come close to being a family again. I look about the cosy chamber.

Katherine is feeding Father grapes, popping them one by one into his mouth and reminding him not to swallow the pips. Elizabeth is reading by the light of the fire, slowly turning the thick pages with a look of wonder in her eye. She is clever, increasingly curious and quick to learn – were she a boy, Father would be proud, but since she is a girl, he merely pats her head from time to time and looks at her askance.

166

"It is because I look like my mother," she says, with wisdom beyond her years. "He doesn't like that but I can do nothing about it."

She shrugs as if she is indifferent to his approval, but I know how much it really means. I have seen the tightening of her lips when Edward receives royal praise. He can do no wrong. Even when he rages and storms like a miniature version of the king, Father just laughs and does not reprimand him. As princesses, me and Elizabeth are expected to act like ladies at all times, and royal ladies at that, even though our titles are somewhat … intermittent.

"Lady Mary."

The queen's gentle voice draws me from my musings. I look up and smile at her open pleasant face.

"Please, you must call me simply, Mary."

"I wonder if you would help me select fabric for my new wardrobe. The king informs me my clothes are too plain for my … now I am queen."

She lowers her head, blushes as if she can scarce believe she is the queen of England, and little wonder for she was merely Lady Latimer before, the widowed wife of John Neville, the third Baron Latimer. She has risen so high so suddenly she must surely feel quite dizzy, yet rumour suggests she had not looked to be queen.

Susan told me that Katherine had set her heart on Tom Seymour, brother to the late queen, Jane. I cannot imagine they'd be suited, for Tom is a braggart who is far too full of himself. His ambition knows no bounds, and he has even gone so far in the past as to flirt with me.

"I would love to help," I say, pulling my thoughts from Tom. "My own seamstress is very gifted.

I will ask her to wait on us tomorrow. I could do with some new clothes myself."

I can ill-afford them but now I am to be at court more often, I will need new attire. People will gossip if I wear the same gown on too many occasions. As well as new gowns, I plan to have two or three of my older kirtles refurbished and perhaps new sleeves and some hoods in the latest style.

Elizabeth looks up from the pages of her book. "What about me? Am I to have new clothes too?"

Katherine laughs and holds out her arm. Elizabeth leaps to her feet and slides onto the settle at the queen's side.

"Of course, Elizabeth. You grow so quickly you will be bursting out of yours again soon."

"Kat Ashley says I am like a weed," she giggles. The queen kisses the top of her head and Elizabeth snuggles against her. I feel a pang of envy for my sister hasn't shown such affection to me since she was an infant. It is a long while since I have been cradled in anyone's arms.

Katherine is so delighted with the samples my seamstress shows her that she not only orders gowns for herself but also gifts for Elizabeth and me, and for her stepdaughter, Margaret.

The queen's apartments have become my haven from care. It is always crowded, always lively. Her ladies are known to me; Lady Suffolk, Lady Hertford and Lady Lisle are there on my recommendation. The new queen summons minstrels to fill the rooms with music, and we practise the latest dances, discuss the latest fashions. For the first time, I feel accepted and believe I can begin to enjoy life again.

For as long as I can remember I have walked in shadow, and now the sunshine that Katherine brings to

Hampton Court warms not only Father and my siblings, but me too. But the queen is not all lightness and good cheer, she has other more serious interests too. Some of which do not please me.

I am grieved by her keenness for the new learning. She is misled, and believes the Roman church to be corrupt and archaic. As much as I love her, I cannot agree, and even had I done so my own mother would turn in her grave if I was to support such heresy. But it is the only thing Katherine and I cannot agree upon, and I pray it will not come between us. When her friends begin to discuss religion, I slip away to the chapel and pray that the old ways endure.

She is always careful not to speak of such things in the presence of the king, and I wonder she does not show such sensitivity to my own views, but ... she knows that if she displeases, I would not take her head, even had I that power.

The gardens are lovely in May. Once the dew has dried, the queen and her ladies escape outside. I join them to walk in the fresh air, where the call of the birds and the droning of the bees evoke memories of the gardens at Greenwich when I was young.

Courtiers stroll among the flowers, and on the mead, minstrels are tuning their instruments. Katherine slips her arm through mine and calls to her small dog, Rig. He comes running, his curly ears flapping behind. Our women follow at a discreet distance, ready to attend us should we need them.

"Is there something troubling you?" she asks as we turn a corner and duck beneath the leafy arch. I look at the sky, screwing up my eyes against the brilliance of the sun while I think of how to phrase what is on my mind. In the end, I realise, the only way to say it is to be frank and more open than is my usual habit. I look away.

"I've been a lonely girl, Katherine. I expect you know that. I was very young when it all began; I was kept apart from my mother because we refused to acknowledge my father's whore."

She flinches at the angry word and attempts to smile.

"I know something of it, of course, but I was far away in the North at the time."

"Mother and I were kept apart for years. I was so young and it was hard. I was lonely; especially once I was forced to attend Elizabeth as if I was of no account. I was never tempted to give in but I've never once uttered a kind word about the Boleyn woman, and I never will."

My voice breaks as I swallow tears. "It wasn't until she was gone and Father married Jane that I was welcomed back at court. Jane was pleasant, quiet and timid, but she wasn't like a mother. Anne of Cleves is pleasant enough and I hope will always be my friend but … well, she's different. Foreign – and doesn't fully understand me. As for Katherine, well, she was just a silly girl … but … it hurt nonetheless to lose her, and see Father sink deeper into gloom."

The queen looks along the path, her brow furrowed as if she doesn't know what to say or where to look. I reach out, tug her arm until she turns toward me

"What I want to say is that I am glad you have married my father. At first, I wasn't sure if it was a good thing when I heard you were to marry, but you are my friend now. I have decided you are all I could wish for in a stepmother. We are a strange, fragmented family but you do us all good. I want to thank you for that."

Her cheeks are as scarlet as my own and great tears are balanced on her lashes. I blink my own away. I am not given to outward shows of sentiment and it is the longest, unguarded speech I can ever recall making.

Katherine takes my trembling hand.

"Oh, Mary. I'm so glad you think so. I've not been blessed with children of my own and have little cause to believe I will ever become a mother, but I have you and Elizabeth and little Edward now, as well as my other stepchildren. The five of you make up my own little family, and I love you all as if you were my own."

We embrace clumsily, laughter breaking through the tears. When she pulls away, she offers me her kerchief and, as I am dabbing my cheeks, she rests her hand on my arm.

"Look," she says. "Is that not Chapuys? I was hoping to speak to him before he returns to Spain."

Chapuys is being carried aloft in a chair rather like the king's own. He looks old and worn out and I guess he is on his way to take his leave of my father. The queen and I hurry along the path with our women panting in our wake. The palace dogs, thinking it a game, come barking beside us, snatching at our skirts as we run.

When he notices our approach, the ambassador signals his servants to halt. They lower his chair to the ground and he struggles to rise.

"Oh, no, please do not get up," the queen says. "Lady Mary and I merely wanted to bid you farewell. You will be missed at court."

He sinks gratefully back into his cushions and mops his brow with a large kerchief.

"I am sorry to be leaving, Your Majesty, but age prevents me from staying. I have been so long in England, it has become almost like home." His gaze switches to me, his face softening into smiles. "And I have known the Lady Mary since she was so big."

He pats the air at knee height, and I step forward.

"I will miss you, dear Chapuys. You served my mother and I loyally, and I will never forget that."

Katherine moves away a few paces to allow us the privacy to make the farewell our long relationship deserves.

"Promise me you will take care, my lady. Be vigilant and should you ever feel yourself to be in danger, get word to me. I will send someone you can trust. Spain remembers its own and will always be on your side."

Fear shivers up my spine. I hope the day will never come when I am in so much peril I need to turn to Spain. My days of danger are over, I hope. Chapuys has stood so long between me and the wrath of the king that he can imagine no other world. I hope those sorry dangerous days have passed.

"Thank you." My throat closes. "You must not keep the king waiting. Farewell, my friend."

Katherine re-joins us and assures him of England's gratitude for his lifetime of service.

He struggles to rise to make his obeisance but the queen forbids it, and reluctantly he gives an awkward sitting down bow before signalling to his men to resume their progress.

"Farewell, Your Majesty. Farewell, Your Royal Highness!" he calls, as they bear him off. I gasp at his illicit use of the royal title and turn to Katherine, ready to protest his innocence. But she is smiling, and pretends she has not heard his salutation.

"Look at Rig," she laughs, slipping her arm back through mine again and pointing to where her dog is splashing with the other dogs in the shallow water of the fountain.

It seems my brother is in possession of the keenest mind in Christendom. Father and Katherine extol his virtues at every opportunity. I could, with good reason, be envious but instead I find myself as besotted as the rest of the court.

Even Elizabeth, who is remarkably choosy about where she places her affection, treats Edward fondly. He is now under the tutorage of Dr John Cheke, and Father cannot disguise his delight when Cheke praises the prince's open mind, and his ease of learning.

Marriage to Katherine seems to have softened the king. He smiles more readily and is eager for court entertainments again. When I am summoned to the royal presence, I attend him with some trepidation, but when I get there I am overwhelmed to learn that the succession has been amended. Now, although Edward will still inherit the throne, should my brother die without issue, the crown will go to me. If I too die childless, then Elizabeth will be queen.

I don't expect it will happen, of course. Katherine may yet bear the king a son, and Edward is strong and healthy – and I would never wish ill upon my little brother merely to gain a royal crown. It is just so glorious to be fully acknowledged as the king's daughter, and a legitimate princess of the realm.

I find I cannot stop smiling. Katherine's love of learning encourages the erudite to flock to England and the court fills with the greatest thinkers of the age. I do not welcome all of them because too often they speak of heresy. I will not support those who decry the old religion. I am at a loss to understand how they can turn their backs on a thousand years of tradition and embrace these evil ways. I am disappointed in the queen's heretic leanings but if Father knows of it, he chooses to ignore the fact. The one thing I am thankful for is that, despite breaking ties with Rome, the king continues to worship in the old way, albeit without the intervention of the Pope.

And so it goes on. The slow disintegration of the church I love is masked beneath a gauze of familial well-being. Every time Katherine tries to steer me onto her heretic path, I hold her off, not tempted by the vulgar crudity of the new religion, and as much in love as ever with the gentle grace of the old.

My days and evenings are full, and I discover that, although not entirely happy, I am at least content. I eat, I pray, I dance, I attend court, I visit my siblings, I give alms to the poor, visit the sick and placate my father as best I can. It is a period of peace and in the years that follow I look back upon that time with deep longing.

But such halcyon days never last and our tranquillity is shattered when Father, seemingly recovered from his recent megrim, declares war on France. All talk at court now turns to war. Father thinks it will be an easy victory and no one dares to disagree.

He spreads the map across the table in the chamber where the family have gathered after supper and invites us to examine it.

"While Spain keeps France occupied on the opposite border, we will regain all our lost territories. Remember Agincourt?"

"I wasn't born, Your Grace," the queen replies with a laugh.

"Well, I remember it, and France remembers it too. How could they ever forget such a sound beating? I tell you, we will have Montreuil and Boulogne under our control within the blink of an eye."

He pokes the map and Katherine leans over his shoulder while we all follow his stubby finger around the rugged south coast of England.

"The south is well-fortified now. The new defensive outposts I've raised in the last few years will stand us in good stead. I'm not prepared to wait for France to come to us, so we will invade just here. While Spain keeps them occupied over there, we will split the French forces in two. Norfolk will take Montreuil, and Suffolk and I will besiege Boulogne. The plans are already underway."

"Is Norfolk not a little too old?"

"What, Norfolk? The man is still in his prime."

The Duke of Norfolk must be close to seventy but nobody argues. Our duty is to amuse and support the king, not to give him cause for concern, but I cannot help being worried.

"What about the Scots?" I ask. "What will they do? Won't they join with France against us?"

"Hertford will keep them busy. Don't you worry about that; and while I'm gone I will be trusting all else to the Queen. Kate will be regent in my absence."

This is clearly news to the queen. She sits down suddenly, her face paling.

"Regent, Henry? Of all England? Me?"

"Why not? You're the queen, aren't you?"

The king stands feet akimbo, hands on hips in his old manner. I avert my eye from the stained bandage spoiling the line of his hose and hope he is still as invincible as he imagines.

"In charge of the whole country? To sit at council and make decisions?"

She looks at me. I raise my brows and pull a face at the enormity of the expected task. The king takes her wrist and pulls her close, his arms sliding about her waist. She doesn't pull away.

"You can do it, Kate. Long ago, when I rode to war, I left another Queen Catherine in charge. I trust you to do just as well."

My mother. My mouth falls open in surprise. He is praising my mother who not only stood as regent over England but fought and defeated the Scottish king at Flodden too! My heart swells at the thought. I step forward.

"I will help you, Katherine," I say, without thinking what it might entail. "I will be glad to."

I am more often in the queen's company now. We have a shared love of fine clothes, jewels and music. It is only in matters of religion that we differ but I am so starved of affection that I push that to one side. When I see her in animated conversation with followers of the new learning, I try not to mind. With gentle persuasion I try instead to turn her from the path of reform and she, in turn, tries to turn me. It is like a half-hearted tug of war in which there is never a victor.

I come upon the queen one evening as she is writing, her nose bent close to the parchment in the ill light.

"Oh," I say, ready to withdraw. "I am sorry, I didn't mean to disturb you."

She puts down her pen and swivels in her seat.

"No, please, Mary. Come; I have worked too long. I will develop a squint if I do not stop soon."

She summons a servant to pour the wine.

"What are you working on?" I ask as I watch the liquid swirl into the cup.

"Oh, just a few thoughts of my own."

"Oh. Is it a translation? I recently read my great grandmother, Margaret Beaufort's *Mirror of Gold for the Sinful Soul*. I should really undertake something similar myself, I began to once but … well, I didn't finish it."

"You should indeed, Mary. I find it so difficult to be idle when I have so much to say."

I smile, wondering if she will tell me what she is working on but the conversation moves on, as conversations do, and in no time at all we are talking about Prince Edward's latest achievements in the schoolroom.

I should accomplish something too, I think, something that will please Father and make him reconsider his opinion of me. I am so much more than a royal ornament – in fact, I am not even that. The older I become, the harsher my monthly courses affect me, and more often than not I am too pale, my complexion sour.

That night, I take up Great-Grandmother's book again. Like me, Margaret Beaufort was small of stature and plain of face, but she was equipped with such intellect that she battled her way through civil war until she and her son won the crown of England. Through her, the Tudor dynasty was born. If only I was more like my great-grandmother; perhaps I should write something in her honour and prove to myself, and everyone else, that I am as capable as she.

Calling for paper and ink, I pick up my pen and work steadily for a few weeks, hoping to please the queen with the result of my labours.

In the king's absence, poor Katherine is beset with the trials of running the country.

"The council resents me," she says. "Hertford continually tries to oust me from the proceedings, keeping back matters of import, undermining my decisions. He delights in making me look foolish."

"You must not let them," I tell her. "They think, because you are a woman, you are weak and feeble. You must prove to them you are not."

"Oh, I wish you could accompany me to the council meetings," she says. "They are so rude. They speak across me, interrupt me. It is as if I am not the queen at all. Gardiner is the worst."

He would be. Gardiner resents Katherine because she supports reform. He is a conservative and aggrieved at her influence over the king. I think back, remembering how powerless I felt when Cromwell and Norfolk sought to bring me down. I recall the cold, hard armour I hid behind.

"You must act the part of a man," I say. "Wear your most masculine gown, the most sombre colours. Do not smile or show any sign of frivolity or weakness. Adjust your posture … stand … like this, like Father does."

I put my hands on my hips and splay my feet. Katherine's merry laughter fills the room.

"You look just like the king! I am not sure I can stand quite like that, but I can certainly do my best. Your advice is very welcome…"

"And when you speak, lower your tone. Fix them with your eye and make your words clipped, as if you are instructing in the school room. The council members are nothing more than naughty schoolboys, so treat them as such."

The queen evidently takes heed of my counsel, for when she emerges from the next meeting she is far less flustered. Her face is flushed with triumph. I wait for her outside the council chamber and when she sees me she clutches my sleeves and puts her hand to her mouth, disguising her laughter.

"I did just as you suggested. I barely let them speak more than was necessary and to my relief, Cranmer has proved an ally and supports me in all I say."

Cranmer will always take the opposite stance to Gardiner, that can be relied on, just as much as Gardiner is sure to speak against Katherine.

Whispers against the queen begin to float around the court; she is a heretic, they say, a traitor to the realm and, more to the point, she is barren too. It is clear to me that these rumours can be traced back to Stephen Gardiner, who will do all he can to bring her down as he has brought down others before.

One evening we are invited to see a play, and before it is half done it becomes clear it has been written as a slight against the queen. I glance at Katherine, who is sitting beside me, and notice that her face in the flickering torchlight has turned quite pale. I grope for her hand but as the scene comes to an end and the actors take their bows, she snatches it away and claps and laughs blithely as if she is unaware of the cruel intention behind it.

At first, I think the meaning has passed her by but, as I watch her, I realise that she is perfectly aware. I shouldn't be, but I am astonished to discover that despite her gentle manner, she is brave; as brave as a royal lioness. So I clap loudly too, as if I do not despise them at all.

Father promised the war with France would be dealt with swiftly, but it drags on. Katherine eagerly scans each letter that arrives but lets it fall to her lap when she realises the king will not be returning home soon. *Does she miss him?* I wonder, or is she just looking forward to relinquishing the reins of government?

She does look tired, as if all the cares of the world are upon her shoulders. I had truly meant to be of more help to her but I have been ailing, my monthly megrim and blinding headaches stretching far beyond the usual week of suffering. The physicians offer no lasting remedy or explanation, and so I suffer on, barely recovering from one month before the next begins.

It is not until summer's end that news comes of the fall of Boulogne. The court sighs with relief. The king will be glad now and proud of his second 'Agincourt', but before we can celebrate we learn that Charles of Spain has betrayed our agreement and made peace with France.

The French king now sends reinforcements against us, isolating our forces. In great panic, the queen summons more men to Father's aid. But, before they can embark, we receive news that the king is returning home.

To my surprise, the time he has spent away at war seems to have done him good. He looks much better, his step is a little quicker and he speaks with vigour. Instead of the thwarted warrior I had expected to return, he speaks eagerly of taking up hunting again.

The threat from France is not over. In fact, the danger of war is greater than before. Not only are the forces of France and Scotland united but Spain, the country I always think of as my own, is ranged against us too.

It is not my place to worry, and I dare not even ask Father for his opinion. I am forced to wait until he offers it. In the end, it is the queen who informs me that the king is looking to Saxony and Antwerp for an alliance with the Duke of Holstein and the German princes.

But war doesn't go away. For months it looms over us, a shadow on our gayest feasts, our brightest days and then, while Father is in Portsmouth surveying the fleet, the French navy sails almost into our harbour and, almost under the king's very nose, sinks his favourite ship, the Mary Rose.

Father rages and storms, weeping one moment over the loss of life and his beautiful ship, and the next he is ferociously cursing his enemies, demanding to know who is to blame. When he cannot lay hands on the French, he turns on his own.

Lord Lyle bravely defends our shores and prevents the French from invading, but Father takes no comfort from that. He wants vengeance.

"I will crush the French! I will see every one of their ships on the bottom of the ocean!"

He clenches his fists, red-faced with fury, and then, like the turning tide, his rage recedes and he descends once more into self-pity.

"My ship," he moans. "My lovely ship!"

He subsides into sentimental reminiscence while the queen and I sit in silence, unable to think of a single word to offer by way of comfort.

He recovers, of course, but his confidence has taken a heavy blow. As the months pass, he becomes ever more suspicious, ever more vindictive towards those who attempt to thwart him. Everyone at the Palace, be they high or low, treads with caution.

"When my father was angry, people crept about the palace fearful for their lives and liberty, and I was no different."

I slump into my pillow, the discomforting memory of Father's last few months of life painful to recollect. I blink away the fear of it.

"They were hard times. I'd no idea then that harder times were to come, of course. Much harder times."

"We never know what the future holds." Susan snips her embroidery thread and folds her linen away. "It is time you had something to eat, Your Majesty, before you fall asleep again."

I glance toward the window and sense the light of the day is beginning to fade. The days pass so quickly. Who knows how many more I have left. I pleat the edge of the sheet between my bony fingers.

"The king grew rapidly ill after that. He was always irascible of course but now there was no one who could predict his moods. He swung left, and then right, and if you weren't careful and drew his attention, you'd like as not find yourself in the Tower for the least offence."

Anne's eyes are wide, glistening and full of youthful vigour. I would give all I have to be as young as she with all my life ahead of me. Not the life I've lived but a new, untroubled one.

"And in his sickness, the queen was vulnerable. The encroaching death encouraged the queen's enemies to work against her. The old war between Gardiner and Cranmer raged on."

"I thought Queen Katherine was a good woman, why did she have enemies?"

I throw back my head and make some semblance of laughter. "We all have enemies – even you, if you thought about it. Royal enemies are just more dangerous. As for Katherine, she had too much influence and she was a reformer – as far as Gardiner was concerned, she should have gone to the scaffold ... as other queens had before her."

"But she hadn't done anything wrong."

"Oh, that didn't matter; she'd have been found guilty of something."

Behind the shock in Anne's eyes, I sense sadness ... disappointment. She is still young enough to believe there is such a thing as justice, and I feel a twinge of regret at disillusioning her. I reach for her hand; my rough old fingers rasp against the smoothness of her skin. "There is little fairness in this world, child. It is more about power than goodness. Yet, sometimes, no matter how good we are or how much we pray, we are punished. God's ways are mysterious and harsh, child. Remember that."

"Queen Katherine's enemies ... she wasn't sent to the Tower, was she? So if she won, it proves that sometimes the good do win."

I think back, through the days of my own triumph, the days of treason, the dark days of my brother's reign, to the last months of my father's.

"Gardiner worked hard against reform and I applaud him for it but ... Katherine was different. She was a wise woman but a misguided one. Imprisonment wasn't for the likes of her. She needed a talking to, an education, do you see? All heretics should be shown the error of their ways and then, if they refuse to see sense..."

Anne nods, her eyes fixed on my face. I dab some spittle from my lips.

"At that time, reformers were being taken left and right. Everyone was treading on glass. The queen, fearful of arrest, cleared her apartments of anything that might condemn her. She was afraid. *I* was afraid. People were being arrested and thrown in the Tower. When the heretic Anne Askew was taken and tortured, that was one thing, but then Father's friend Sir George Blagg was arrested and the king stepped in and stopped it. He was reprieved in time. Gardiner was getting above himself but, although Blagg was freed, the rest were burned."

"Burned?"

"At the stake, for heresy, as is the law of the land."

There is horror in her eye. A memory stirs of a time when my own stomach turned at the thought of roasting men alive. Those have passed.

"When they came to take the queen, she must have been terrified. The warrant was signed but at the last minute the king changed his mind. Katherine must have already felt the lick of flame against her skin when Father clouted Gardiner about the head and sent him away. He couldn't go through it all again; do you see? Even had Katherine been the worst heretic in England he'd not admit it, because he couldn't bear to lose another wife. He was too old. Too fragile."

"So, her enemies were thwarted by the king, even though she was guilty of ... heresy and deserved to be punished? She didn't die?"

"Well, she is dead now, of course, but no, she didn't die then. Father died instead."

January - May 1547

The world is very different without Father. Although I was never in the habit of seeing him every day, the fact of his existence was what held us all together. I am shaken by his death – we all are. It is as if we are a pack of dogs whose tether has been severed; we are no longer sure where to run, or who to bite. The court is edgy, and the queen is now so vulnerable to her enemies that her hands tremble. Everyone speaks in whispers, there is nobody living who can clearly recall life in England before Father took the helm. He may have been erratic, he may have been terrifying, but he was there, like an immoveable mountain beneath which we all sheltered. Now, with just my small brother to take his place, we are faltering, and the future is uncertain.

"It won't be Edward leading us at all, will it?" the queen whispers. "It will be the council, led by *Hertford,* at least until the king reaches his majority."

She plucks at her skirt, her face drawn and pinched with concern.

My brother is just nine years old. I remember my school lessons where I was taught of other boy-kings, other protectors. It never turned out well but Hertford's wife is my friend … or she was. I can't imagine her or Hertford resorting to infanticide.

But the old ways are swiftly overturned and there are new men at the helm. Norfolk, after falling victim to Father's displeasure, languishes still in the Tower, and Gardiner no longer holds a position of power. In fact, most men who support the old church have been ousted from prominence by those who support the new. The reformers are in control and I sense division such as the country has never yet seen under Tudor rule.

For all his bilge and bluster, my brother is a small worm, ready to be gobbled up by the flock of reformers who surround him. They will take his infantile mind and mould it to their will.

"We must pray they take as much care over the health of his body as that of his soul."

I am with Katherine and her sister, Anne, in her private chamber, her women are seated a short distance away. Like us, despite their leaning, they are uncertain of what will happen next and full of horrified speculation. Katherine has never been a friend of Hertford.

"My Lord Hertford has bought himself the support he needs, offering titles and property in return for the backing of the council. John Dudley has been made the Earl of Warwick, and Wriothesley is Earl of Southampton. In all but name, Hertford is now king. He has made himself Duke of Somerset while only allowing his brother Thomas a barony."

Her voice softens, and she caresses the name of *Thomas,* who was her sweetheart long before she caught the eye of the late king.

"He has been given Sudeley Castle," I remind her. "That is not something to be sniffed at."

"No." She smiles vaguely, and doesn't meet my eye.

"Somerset should be careful. He raises himself too high, too fast, as other Lord Protectors did before him … they who climb too high, often fall…"

"Hush, Mary…" The queen, whom I must now learn to call 'dowager', leans forward, glancing toward her women. "You must promise me not to speak so. We lack the protection of the late king now … we are more vulnerable than ever before. Remember that."

I frown at her serious face.

"But … my brother…"

"… is nine years old. He is powerless. A figurehead and nothing more. It is Hertford – Somerset – and his ilk whom we must answer to now."

Belatedly, I recall that Lady Hertford is one of Katherine's women, but I do not see her gathered with the others. No doubt she has abandoned her post and is enjoying her husband's new-found status, swanning about court and waving her title of Duchess as if it is a swansdown fan. I have often wondered if her friendship with me has more to do with status than liking. I frown at my own thoughts.

Katherine sits back and fumbles with her embroidery before tossing it aside again with a gusty sigh.

"It is best that we trust no one other than our closest kin. Mary, despite our differences in matters of religion, you and Elizabeth *are* my family. I would never wish harm to come to either of you. Therefore, heed me, keep a close tongue, and your own counsel and your opinions to yourself – especially when it comes to religion. You can sometimes be quite outspoken."

We clasp hands. I am thirty-one years old and although I have never enjoyed the full extent of a father's affection, without him, I am like the most wretched orphan. Katherine is the closest thing I have to a mother.

"It has been agreed that Elizabeth will join my household," she continues. "What do you propose to do, Mary? You are now in possession of a vast fortune, with many houses in which you could make a home."

I frown, a little piqued at not being invited to remain with her but … I would have refused anyway. I want the freedom to follow my own heart when it comes to religion and pray in the manner I see fit. I'd never be free if I shared a house with Katherine.

"I will retire to my estates, Hunsdon perhaps or Kenninghall," I say. "I must confess, it is very satisfying to have inherited so many of the great Howard properties. It is little in the way of compensation but … well, perhaps I am petty."

Katherine smiles. I smile in return. She knows well my abhorrence for the Howards, the kin of Anne Boleyn. Then her smile fades and she bites her lip. "Mary," she says, and pulls a face.

"What is it, Katherine? Is there something…"

"I do have something I must tell you. I am loath to take such a step behind your back but … I am more afraid of losing him again."

I sit tall, my back straight.

"Him? You mean Thomas Seymour?"

She nods, dabs at a tear and looks down at her kerchief.

"I have loved Thomas for … oh, for so long I cannot quite remember. While I was wed to your father, I did my duty as queen and as his wife, but now … Mary, I have been wed *three* times and never once where my heart dictated. This time, I want to make my own choice. It is my last chance at happiness."

"And you think the admiral will make you happy?"

I had not meant to sound so doubtful but my reservations are loud in my voice. She looks down and begins to pull at her kerchief, shredding the fine lace edging.

"I can only hope he will."

"Do you expect the council will permit it?"

She is silent for so long that I speak again. "Oh Katherine, surely you don't intend to wed without the permission of the king?"

She lets out a sound, halfway between a sob and a sigh.

"Thomas says we must. He says they won't allow it because I am the dowager. They will insist we wait to be sure I am not carrying the late king's child … but I know I am not. It is not possible. If we wait, I will lose him again … I know it! Do – do we have your blessing?"

Silence falls like a portcullis. She sits like a lamb awaiting slaughter while I mull over what she has told me. If I give my support, it will go ill with the council when they discover it; if I refuse it, I will lose a valued friend, my substitute mother. I shift uneasily in my seat.

"Katherine. Privately you have my blessing but I cannot openly support such a match. And need I remind you, you've just been warning me to tread

189

carefully yet … here you are about to commit social suicide."

Her tears are flowing freely now; they trickle down her cheek and drip from her chin. She puts her hands over her face and I notice that her women have fallen silent and are watching us, their sewing abandoned in their laps. I shift in my seat so my back is turned toward them, blocking the dowager from their view.

"Oh Mary, I have no choice!" Her hands drop, she covers her stomach and my mouth falls open as shock drenches me.

"You are with child?" I hiss, leaning forward so her women cannot overhear. She puts up a hand.

"Oh no, no, I am not. I swear it, but … perhaps … soon."

I have never been so disappointed in anyone in my life. She is the dowager queen of England, a woman of integrity and grace, a woman of intelligence, yet she cannot govern her own conduct. She has allowed lust to obliterate her common sense. She should have known better. She should have waited. Why does love drive out all sensible thought? I suspect I will never discover the answer to that.

I stand up, smoothing my skirts. She grabs my hand.

"Mary, please, do not deny me your friendship."

I look upon her lowered head and speak quietly.

"I will never do that, Katherine, but you must see that I need to distance myself from this. If the council were to suspect that I knew of or condoned your actions, I would risk my own security. Believe me, I wish you well, you and your admiral. I hope all goes well with you."

I fear it won't. The admiral is a rogue, a flirt and a villain who once even approached me with the idea of marriage, but Katherine shall not learn of that from my lips. Shortly afterwards, with a sense of impending doom, I leave her company, obliterate all thoughts of court intrigue from my mind, and travel to East Anglia to inspect my new properties.

Kenninghall – Summer 1548

"Oh, my lady, you shall enjoy being in residence here!" Susan leans from the window and looks out across the gardens.

"Yes, it is most pleasing." I look around at the refurbished apartment, the new tapestries and cushions. My women are busily delving into chests, arranging the chairs to make the most of the light from the tall windows.

I think of Norfolk living here. While he worked against me and dreamed of smashing my head against a wall, these were the ramparts that sheltered him. The man is a monster. I am glad he is in the Tower – I hope he rots there. As I live and laugh in his house, I shall think of his present suffering often.

I have no plans to attend court. Already they are making changes in the realm that I can never agree with. I know I would be unable to govern my rage were I to witness at first hand the heresies that they are allowing to creep into England. No, I shall remain here, away from it all and, as long as they leave me to my own devices, all will be well.

After a walk in the grounds, I sit down to write to Katherine. I extol the virtues of my new house, exchange some light gossip about women of mutual acquaintance, but I do not acknowledge her marriage, or her husband's ambition to get closer to the throne. Somerset will keep his brother as far from the king as possible, I have no doubt of that. From her last letter, Katherine is happy in her new state. Elizabeth has been joined at Chelsea by our cousin Jane; the cleverest pair of girls ever to enter the schoolroom.

My sister has always been bright – precocious some might say, and Jane is similarly gifted but unfortunately she is a strong advocate for the new religion. Elizabeth will be targeted both by Jane and the dowager queen. Katherine will encourage them both. It is a pity. It would be far better to concentrate such minds upon truth and tradition.

The pair of them dress as plainly as paupers and keep their noses so deep into their books that they become like moles; short of both sight and insight. But it is no matter to me what they think or how they worship, so I do not chide them.

From time to time, I get a long erudite letter from my sister with a gift she has sewn or a passage she has translated. Her letters are dutiful rather than affectionate and it is impossible to detect in the words any semblance of the child I once doted on.

At first, all seems well. But even though I am far from court in the depths of the Norfolk countryside, rumours reach me of events taking place there. The protector is allowing changes that violate the six articles laid down by my father. They do not merely meddle with Mass but order that images be destroyed; processions are to be abolished and the ringing of bells and the lighting of candles is to be forbidden. Cranmer, in his Book of Homilies, attacks the Mass. His beliefs are heretical but when Gardiner rightly points this out he is swiftly imprisoned and the abuse against the Mass increases.

They order an English Bible to be placed in every parish church and, horror upon horror, the clergy are now to be allowed to marry! In the end, when I can contain myself no longer, I sit down to write a letter outlining my objections. England is no longer the peaceful and stable kingdom my father left behind, but our realm must not become so divided.

Somerset's reply, when it finally arrives, is disappointing. He states, to my great chagrin, that my father did not leave a *peaceful* kingdom but an incomplete reformation. He believes it to be a situation that can only be remedied by completely abolishing Popish doctrine as well as the authority of Rome. In other words, he infers that my father had not yet completed the changes he intended to the church. But he is very much mistaken. My God-fearing father would *never* champion Lutheran teaching; to break with Rome is one thing but to work against God? That is something he would never do!

I screw Somerset's letter into a ball and toss it across the room with a futile scream of rage. He has no right to make such changes to the constitution; he is a protector, a servant of the king! Only my brother, the reigning monarch, can contradict the six articles … when he is of age to do so. Until then, the matter should be left alone.

Shortly afterwards, I begin to receive bullying letters from court informing me that my religious practices are in opposition to those accepted by the crown. My response is to increase the number of Masses I attend daily; sometimes hearing as many as four in a single day. I ensure that in all my households the traditional rites are followed to the letter. Somerset and his ilk can go hang themselves. They can hardly have me thrown into the Tower. I am, after all, the heir to Edward's throne.

So, my hopes of a peaceful life in the country are spoiled by intimidating messages from the protector. I write to Spain, who warns Somerset to leave me in peace, claiming there is no harm in me following the faith I was born into. But the orders continue to arrive from court. I deal with Somerset as politely and as coldly as I am able but, when fresh news comes from Queen Katherine, it takes the strength from my knees.

It breaks my heart to write of this, dear Mary, but I have discovered Elizabeth indulging in lewd behaviour with Thomas. At first, I though it only play but then ... then I came upon them together and I saw quite plainly that I was wrong...

My mouth drops open. Poor Katherine! She must be distraught. Not only betrayed by her husband but by her beloved stepdaughter too! Two of the people she loves most in the world have committed sin beneath her very roof. *What was Elizabeth thinking? What was Seymour thinking?* It is not as if he can divorce Katherine and wed Elizabeth. Katherine is expecting his child!

Katherine, of course, is reluctant to speak ill of Seymour and her tight lips make me suspicious. Perhaps it wasn't his fault at all. Perhaps he wasn't the one to initiate the ill behaviour. Perhaps Elizabeth is her mother's daughter after all.

Anne Boleyn somehow induced my father to act like a man possessed, to throw away all he valued for the promise of her bed. Elizabeth might be young, but she is sharp. Is she likewise able to bewitch men with those Boleyn eyes?

I peer into my looking glass. I have my father's small and unprepossessing eyes. I will never bewitch anyone with them. No man will ever dance to my tune. I sigh and turn away, my head beginning to ache with the worry of it all.

I learn that Elizabeth is to be sent away from the queen's Chelsea household in disgrace, while Katherine takes up residence at Sudeley to await the birth of her child.

The poor infant will be born into a world of turbulence, the child of a rogue. It is well her mother is possessed of such sweetness. Hopefully she will make up for Thomas' lack. Despite her love for the new religion, Katherine has always been good to me … and Elizabeth. She nurtured all of us. She was born to be a mother. She does not deserve to be so ill-used.

During the weeks that follow, I fashion some small garments and send them to Katherine with my next letter, bidding her luck in her coming confinement. I make no mention of either Elizabeth or Katherine's husband. After the messenger has ridden away, my thoughts turn to Elizabeth. Perhaps I should invite her to live with me. She is young, in dire need of a mother figure to look up to, to emulate. If anyone could set her on the correct religious path, it is me. But for now, she remains in Katherine's guardianship. I will discuss the matter with her when the child has been born.

Almost by return, a letter arrives informing me she has given birth to a daughter, and my ladies and I drink to her long life and happiness. But, just six days later, I receive further word. Turning my back on my women, my temples begin to throb as I break the seal and see the words, scored so heavily on the page.

Katherine has died, taken suddenly by childbed fever, leaving her daughter, whom she named Mary in my honour, to the devices of her wayward father.

It is cool and dark in the chapel and I relish the silence. I send my women away that I might pray for Katherine alone. When I am at prayer, I seem to leave the world behind and exist in a high and lonely place where sin can never intrude. There is only me and God and the love I bear Him. As the cares of this world melt away, I stand before Him and beg that Katherine's soul be allowed to pass quickly from purgatory.

She was the best of women, the kindest of souls who may have been misguided in life but surely is deserving of the sweetness of Heaven. Before I leave, I remember to pray for the child too, for only God knows what her future will be – daughter of a queen and a reprobate.

My heart is heavy. I grieve for Katherine, for the loss of my father, and for the end of the world I loved, the religion I refuse to divert from.

I pray for little Mary Seymour, and for all the children of the true church in these perilous days. The summer passes, wet and warm, the crops rot in the fields, the cattle take sick and die. And, months later, when Thomas Seymour is taken up for treason and condemned to death by his own brother and nephew … it seems somehow fitting. I never expect to hear good tidings in these sorry days. As the world slowly implodes, the only thing in my power to do is pray.

"Were those times truly perilous, Your Majesty?"

I squint at the child, flexing my toes beneath the covers.

"Of course they were; it was terrifying. I could trust no one. I had never had faith in Thomas Seymour but I cannot truly believe he meant to hurt the king. He was always fond of children, especially us royals, and he never once called without a gift of some kind; a box of sweetmeats for Elizabeth, a toy for Edward. I recall he once gave my brother a pet monkey. It may have all been … to the purpose of securing favour and a place in the future royal household but … I will not believe that. He was a fool but he did not deserve to die.

"In those uncertain times, peril was around every corner especially if, like me, you refused the jurisdiction of the protector. I, and people like me, found ourselves caught in a cleft stick. I could not forswear Christ, and I could not in conscience obey the law of the land. I stood in direct conflict to Somerset's wishes and yes, my life was in great danger just like anyone else who stood in opposition to him."

Anne shuffles closer, her face shining like a moon in the darkness of the chamber.

"What happened? Why did they not arrest you?"

I sniff, wipe the tip of my nose on the edge of my sleeve and try to blink away the darkness that encroaches on my vision.

"Ah, well I had the backing of Spain, you see. I've relied on Spain, some might say unwisely, throughout every crisis of my life. Had Somerset come down too hard on me, he'd have been ever after looking over his shoulder to see if my cousin was coming for him. The Spanish ambassador ... what was the fellow's name ... Van de Delft ... he suggested I flee the country and take up residence at Charles' court but ... I could never leave England. It is the only home I've ever known. I always looked upon it as *my* country ... even then, when I appeared to have no part in its future."

"So what happened next?"

I peer into the past, that seems to have come to life among the bed hangings.

"Well, in the end, after months, years of bullying, even the council had enough of Somerset. The citizens whom I lived amongst in Norfolk rioted – I swear I had nothing to do with it. Somerset sent Dudley to deal with the trouble and the fighting was fierce, and the punishment of the rebels fiercer still. The people of East Anglia hated Dudley ever after ... and Somerset too. I was powerless while England balanced on the edge of civil war and could do nothing but pray, but ... it seems that God was listening after all."

"What did He do?"

Anne's eyes are shining as if she expects me to reply that Heaven sent a fearsome angel

198

to smite down His enemies. I smile at the image, laughter bubbling in my belly.

"He just made Warwick, Southampton and other members of the privy council come to their senses and toss Somerset from his pedestal.

"He didn't go easily, of course. As soon as he got wind of what was happening, he took possession of Edward and bundled him away to Windsor Castle. To speak plain, he kidnapped the king."

Her mouth falls open, her eyes swivelling as she tries to absorb the enormity of the events I describe.

"Kidnapped the king?"

She plucks a grape from my bowl, forgetting whose company she is in, but I don't mind. I rather enjoy her lack of fear, the absence of false deference. I have the feeling that when God finally frees me from this earthly penance, she will be one of the few to regret it.

"Yes. He wrote to me of it afterwards; the king, I mean. He complained of rough treatment and of catching a fever. He said he greatly missed his chamber and servants, and having books or toys to play with. As I recall, Somerset had forgotten to take the king's spaniel along. I laughed when I read that. The country in turmoil, an anointed king in danger of his life, and my precocious little brother is angry that he has mislaid his pet dog."

Our conjoined laughter makes the candles dip but I sober quickly and frown at the top of her head. "The truth of the matter is, the coup turned my brother, who was the hope of Tudor dynasty, from a revered king into a frightened little boy. I never forgot that and neither, I suspect, did Edward."

"So, everything was all right after that?"

"I thought so, for a while. I imagined the coup was a triumph for the old church and that the ancient ways would soon be restored but I was wrong. Northumberland was just as ambitious as Somerset, you see; another scoundrel who was just as wed to heresy as the rest of them."

A door opens, the past and the people who inhabited it with me trickle away and I remember I am trapped in the present.

"The doctor is here, Your Majesty."

I tug the covers to my chin.

"I have no wish to see him."

"But you instructed me to send for him, Your Majesty."

"No, I didn't. I've been talking to Anne here."

I glance at my companion, but her seat is empty, the skeletal remains of the grapes she has eaten the only testament to her having ever been with me. I frown at her absence. I don't remember her leaving me.

The doctor steps forward from the shadows, clutching his robes. He clears his throat.

"Your Majesty, your woman tells me you are having trouble passing…"

"I have no wish to discuss that."

"Your Majesty, if I might just..." He rubs his hands together to warm them and Susan, like a traitor, snatches back the sheet. My bedgown is bunched about my knees and my lower legs are swollen and pale like those of an invalid. I remember when they were shapely, and muscled from dancing and long days in the saddle. Not that anyone ever saw them.

"Come, Your Majesty, let me remove the pillow that you might lie flat."

There is no use complaining so I do as I am bid and submit to the indignity of examination. My bedgown is tugged higher and I raise my knees. As cool air wafts around my quaint, an aroma of piss and sickness rises, but nobody dares remark upon it.

The doctor's hands are warm and dry. He presses my flaccid belly, making me wince.

"You feel pain, Your Majesty?"

"Of course I do, man. You'd feel pain too were you so ill-treated."

"There has been no return of..."

Susan shakes her head and covers my nethers, her face pink with embarrassment on my behalf.

"Her Majesty eats very little and says she isn't hungry, but she drinks copious amounts. Yet ... well, she doesn't pass much water."

"That will account for the swelling in her ankles and the pain in her stomach."

He scratches his chin, frowning at me, and I wonder if he thinks my body is like a bucket and my ankles are full of piss.

It is not so long since this fool of a doctor concluded that I was pregnant, and set all England rejoicing. The fool.

For a short time, I was so happy. Preparation was made for the birth of a prince – the hope of the realm. The royal cradle was brought out and dusted down again, my women made garments, and swaddling bands were prepared.

The lying-in chamber, when I entered it, was dark and warm, the shutters sealed, the bed hangings showing only images of peace and fertility. For months I waited, Philip waited, my women waited, the realm waited and, as their hopes receded, my mortification grew. Of the myriad humiliations I have suffered in my life, that was surely the greatest.

"I will have a powder prepared," the doctor says. After a perfunctory bow, Susan follows him from the chamber, murmuring secrets as to my diet, and my bowel movements.

I hate sickness. It is weak. A monarch should never be weak. I am not a child as my brother was. I should not be at the mercy of fools such as these. I should be strong as I was in the beginning.

Kenninghall – 1548-49

When I refuse to attend the Christmas court, I am not as sick as I pretend. The truth of the matter is that I am loath to rub shoulders with reformers or be refused the right to hear Mass. Sometimes, it seems as though all the demons of Hell have been unleashed in England and now gather to cavort in a lewd heretical dance at my brother's court. It is wiser not to visit him if I cannot obey his laws.

When the Mass is forbidden in June of 1549, I continue as before; the aroma of incense is thick in my chapel, the bells ring loudly and the forbidden candles burn just as brightly as they ever have. Some faithless jade, and I know not who, carries word of this to the privy council who send word, demanding that I stop my practices immediately or find myself in defiance of Edward's authority. In other words, guilty of treason.

How does one make a heretic understand?

They are blind and deaf to my defence. They are ignorant of the sin they themselves are committing against God and I cannot make them see it. There is no question of the path I must take. I can choose to defy my king or my God, and if death is the punishment for making the right choice then, so be it.

My Lord, I perceive by the letters with which I like received from you, and all of the King's Majesty's council, that you be all sorry to find so little conformity in me touching the observation of His Majesty's laws; who are well assured that I have offended no law, unless it be a late law of your own making, for the altering of matters in religion in which my conscience is not worthy to have the name of a law, both for the King's honour's sake, the wealth of the realm ... and (as my conscience is very well persuaded) the offending of God, which passes all the rest.

Before I can change my mind, I dispatch a servant with the letter and await the consequences. I do not have long to wait.

I am up and breakfasted, my women just completing the last of my toilette, when I hear a party of horse arriving. One of my women, Margery, I think, cranes her neck at the window to see who calls so early. She turns, white-faced.

"I believe by his badge it is Lord Rich, my lady, and some other gentleman. Oh, my lady, do you think they will arrest us all? I only ever did as you instructed!"

She screws her skirt into a crumpled ball, her features turning upside down with fear.

"Don't be foolish. They cannot arrest my entire household. I doubt very much if they can even take me; not unless they want my cousin to send his armada. Pull yourselves together. These men are bullies; rogues and bullies. We have God on our side."

My brave words do not prevent my knees from quivering. I clasp my hands tightly together, stiffen my spine and await their coming with my head high.

They enter in a flurry of cloaks, with a gust of fresh air at their heels, and I suddenly have the urge to be outside, on the chase, in pursuit of a hind. Here, inside, I am the quarry instead of the huntsman.

"Lady Mary."

Lord Rich bows over my hand but he does not allow his lips to touch my skin. His fellow, whom I recognise as Sir William Petre, does likewise. They are warm from the ride and I note a sheen of sweat on Rich's brow, and the way Petre's hair is plastered to his scalp. Perhaps, I think with a stirring of confidence, they are as ill at ease as I.

Lord Rich pulls out a chair from beneath the table and bids me sit on it. I obey as slowly and as regally as I can, perching perilously on the extreme edge and clasping my fingers tightly together. My whole body is tense, my muscles clenched as I wait for the blade of their displeasure to strike.

Rich clears his throat.

"My lady, I will not mince my words. You are in breach of the king's law. Despite our several attempts to dissuade you from it, you and your household…" he looks pointedly at my hovering women, "… continue in your heresy."

"*My* heresy, sir? It is your reforms that have invited the anti-Christ into our church."

I stare coldly into his face. His lips compress, turn white, and the lower lid of his left eye twitches.

"You must – we all must – comply with the changes in the law. You and your household imperil your lives by ignoring the reforms."

"You are mistaken, sir. My cousin, the emperor, believes I should be allowed to worship as I see fit in the privacy of my home. He would be sore displeased were I to be arrested for it. He has made that quite plain. Perhaps you would like him to come and tell you so in person."

It is like Hatfield all over again. I am a defenceless child, pretending to be strong when inside I am secretly quaking. My words are bluster and I fear he knows it.

"Lady Mary, you are the king's beloved sister, the favourite of noblemen and commoner alike. We would be loath to fall out with you in this…"

"Loath to take my head, you mean." Rage stirs in my belly. I have never been able to carry out a measured debate, as always my ire rises and obliterates my reason.

He laughs humourlessly. "It will not come to that … unless, of course, you should persist."

I stand up, take three steps away from the table and turn abruptly.

"Persist in what, my lord? Praying in the manner I have been taught? In the manner of my father and his father before him? Where is the sin in that? If there is sin in it now, why was there none before? I have not changed, God has not altered. It is you, it is the king. I am constant. I am Mary of England and before God I swear my loyalty to the king, my brother, but … I am a good Catholic first and that will ever be the case. Whether you use threats or violence against me, you will *never* sway me from the true church."

While Petre fumbles with a sheaf of papers, Rich regards me narrowly. I can almost hear the words he stifles behind his beard.

"Very well. I shall convey your message to my Lord Somerset and to the king. No doubt you will soon be hearing from us again."

He nods curtly but does not take my hand this time. As their footsteps clatter down the corridor, the company in the chamber sighs with combined relief. Someone giggles nervously. We exchange tense glances, my stomach lurching at their white faces, wide dilated eyes. I have put them all in danger.

"Oh, my lady!" Susan hurries forward and takes both my hands. "You were magnificent!"

"Was I, Susan? Magnificent? I didn't feel it."

I manage a dilute smile but my counterfeit courage is rapidly dwindling with my rage, for Rich is right about one thing. They will be back.

It is as well that I am far from court, for events are happening swiftly, the seat of power shifting and changing. My spies bring me tales of dissention at Edward's court; resentment of the Duke of Somerset is high and it is not long before he is ousted. The Earl of Warwick, John Dudley, having become too big for his boots after his success in the war with Scotland and putting down the recent rebellion in Norfolk picks up the reins of government.

I've never had any love for Somerset but John Dudley makes my hackles rise all the more. He is an upstart, an ambitious, remorseless bully, and I hate to think of my brother in his hands. While Edward is kept fast within the palace, a ring of protection about him prevents even his closest kin from seeing him. I would wager my favourite horse he has no idea of the peril his councillors have placed me in.

My life is in the deepest peril. I am in more danger now than I have ever been. My man, Rochester, having met secretly with Dubois, visits me in my chamber; his presence more a worry than a comfort. He tells me the plans laid down by my cousin in Spain are underway, his ships lie off the coast ready to take me to safety.

"I am loath to escape England," I tell him. But, what else can I do? It is all in hand. The emperor has sent ships to escort me to Spain. It is what my mother would wish.

Spain. All I know of that land are stories my mother told; tales of a bright sun, exotic fruits and mosaic halls, blackamoors and olive trees. I picture it now as I did when I was a child, at my mother's knee – a one dimensional world, painted in primary colours. The thought of leaving England fills me with fear but my enemies are real, and my brother lacks the authority to control them. Perhaps it is better that I leave.

Rochester screws his cap between his hands and comes closer to speak urgently in my ear.

"My honest opinion is that you should stay, my lady. It isn't safe. Watches have been posted on every road. If you decide to flee, then you must be prepared for a fight, but I think you should stay. If you leave England's shores, you do so for good. I think it would be wiser to remove to your house at St Osyth – that way you will be close enough to escape to the sea should the need arise later."

My bags are already packed, my women primed and ready to leave, but my love of England has me tied fast to the bedpost. I grasp the lifeline Rochester offers.

I stand up and move toward the hearth, staring into the leaping orange flames. I can feel their heat on my face and hold my hand closer, wondering how it feels to die by the flame, a martyr to the one true church.

Rochester coughs, drawing my attention back to the matter in hand. He tugs the edges of his furred collar together.

"There is danger in flight, my lady, but there is danger in staying too. I don't know what else I can say on the subject."

For a long moment I stare into his eyes; they are tired, ringed about with lines and care. He has an honest face and I trust he will not lead me with false lights.

"My brother is young, Rochester, and it is a cruel world. Should, and God forbid it does, should anything befall him, I need to be here in England, to stake my claim on the crown."

It is treason even to hint at the death of the king.

"I agree. If you are overseas, you will have lost the throne before you even have a chance to bid for it."

"It is mine by right; I am the heir."

His eyes slide away, his optimism diminishes.

"What? What have you heard?"

208

I step forward, tugging his sleeve, drawing him close again.

"It may be a rumour," he whispers, his beard tickling my cheek. "But I heard that Northumberland is trying to persuade the king to allow a match between his son, Guildford, and your cousin, Jane Grey…"

I raise my eyes and see my own suspicions mirrored in his. My brow lowers.

"Dudley would not dare…"

"I fear he would, madam. I fear he keeps you occupied with matters of liturgy to distract you from his real plan."

My cousin Jane is clever. Too clever surely to fall victim to Dudley's plots. But … she is also keen for reform and hates the old church as much as I loathe the new. For those who embrace the new religion, Jane will be more favourable an heir to Edward's throne than I. But they wouldn't dare … would they?

I turn suddenly, my skirts sweeping the floor, fanning the flames in the hearth.

"I will stay, Rochester. I will stay and fight."

All thoughts of escape abandoned, I make ready to leave for Beaulieu, sending my chaplain, Mallet, on ahead to prepare for my arrival and the hearing of the Mass.

The admonishments from court continue, almost daily, and I have messengers night and day, bringing orders that I desist in my method of worship. I take no notice, ignoring their authority and endangering my life.

In the end, the king writes demanding my presence at court, warning me that I should be more like our beloved sister, Elizabeth, his 'sweet sister

Temperance,' who has obeyed every edict laid down by king and council.

Of course she has, I think. *Elizabeth will always appear to do what is expected of her. Nobody can ever guess what she is really thinking.*

London – December 1550

Unable to think of an excuse to refuse another summons to the Christmas court, this time I agree to go. It has been a long while since Edward, Elizabeth and I were together in the same room. On the day of my audience with the king, I dress with care, defiantly adorning myself with as much finery as I can stand up in. Susan arranges my hood and ensures my skirts hang straight at the back.

"You look very gracious, my lady," she says, as she hands me my prayer book and forbidden beads.

The king will take immediate issue with the elaborate style of the gown I have chosen, but it is not for others to rule how I live my life.

When my name is called, the company falls silent. I sweep into the great hall with my head high and kneel before the boy who is seated in my father's chair.

"Mary," Edward's piping voice cries. "We are right glad to see you."

I rise from the floor and kiss the knuckles he presents to me.

"Edward, my dear brother," I smile, my maternal longing rising to obliterate my detestation for his method of worship. "I am pleased to see you looking so well."

In fact, he looks rather pale, as if he should spend more time in the sun, or ride to the chase as often as our father did. He has the face and hands of a scholar

210

and, so his tutors say, the mind of one too. His face is thin, veins visible at his temple, a crease of worry between his brows, and more than a hint of my father's determination about his mouth. He looks anxious rather than happy.

"I haven't been too well, actually," he says with a pathetic droop to his shoulders. "I am troubled with a persistent cough." He thumps his chest and gives a few short barks like a dog, to demonstrate.

"Oh, Your Majesty, I am grieved to hear it. I will send your man a receipt that I have found most beneficial. As you know, I am often ailing myself..."

I trail off as the doors are thrown open again and the king's attention drifts away from me. The courtiers turn their eyes from me to a newcomer waiting at the door.

"The Lady Elizabeth," the herald announces, and the slight figure of my sister sweeps forward. She pauses to allow the company to acknowledge her unmistakeable presence. Then, keeping her eye on the king, she makes her way to the throne. My spirits plummet and the former confidence I had in my appearance ebbs away.

I chose my jewel-encrusted velvet gown and headdress to show off my status, make everyone take notice and remember that I am next in line to the throne. Elizabeth, however, has chosen a different way.

Her gown is plain, almost severely cut, and her only necklace is a single cross hanging on a golden chain. Her fingers are bare of rings, her hair tucked tightly beneath a demure cap. It seems as if she is lit from within. She is young. She needs no jewels, not with eyes that shine brighter than any candle.

Before she reaches the dais, she sinks low and remains there while the court drinks in the scene.

"My good sister, Bess! It is too long since we saw you last!"

Edward leaves his seat, descends the steps and holds out his hand to assist her to rise. They are of similar height. They smile into each other's eyes and I notice how alike they are. Similar chins, similar smiles – only the eyes are different. They have the eyes of their mothers while I have my father's. I feel separate. Isolated and irrelevant.

Elizabeth is economical with her words. Unlike her mother, she says little, but what she does say has immediate impact. She turns belatedly to greet me, sweeps a disparaging eye over my elaborate gown, my pale and unprepossessing face. The fingers that lie in my palm are cool and slender, her smile bewitching.

"It is good to see you again, Sister," she says with no hint of irony. She kisses each cheek, her hands firm on my shoulders, swamping me with the scent of citrus and cinnamon. Her fragrance is as exotic as her appearance.

From looking, one would never know the extent of the scandal that taints her name; there is certainly no hint that she cares. *Did she really dally with Thomas Seymour?* I wonder. Has she already tasted the mysteries of a man's body?

As we take our seats, one either side of the king, I take note of the gracious slope of her shoulder, her long graceful neck and the youthful glow of her cheek. Perhaps it wasn't just ambition that tempted Seymour to sample her; he certainly never came back for a second try at me.

"I have a gift for you, Your Majesty," she says, signalling to her woman to pass her a small package. "I translated it myself, and embroidered the cover too, for your delectation."

Edward takes and unwraps a small book, and even from my seat I can see the skill of the needleworked cover. I wish I'd chosen something more personal than the jewelled candlesticks I'd bought for him. Elizabeth has always managed to get everything right, seemingly without effort. I, on the other hand, misjudge everybody and get everything wrong.

For a few days, all is well. We eat too much, drink too much, and I even take to the floor and dance a few times. Elizabeth dances too and is never short of partners, but the king, declaring it makes him cough, is content to watch from his throne.

For all the show I make of festivity, I do not enjoy my time at court. I am too aware of the heresy that surrounds me. My cheeks burn when I notice the sideways glances at my clothes, and the raised eyebrows of the courtiers when I take my seat beside the king. Everyone stares, everyone whispers, barely disguising their disapproval. I feel like a foreigner; an interloper, a stranger with stranger habits who is forced to pray in the privacy of her chambers instead of joining the rest of the court at chapel.

Most of my friends are in disgrace, either in the Tower or uninvited or unwilling to attend Edward's Protestant court. The Catholics of England keep to their own houses, risking life and liberty to pray in the secrecy of their own chapels.

But I have managed to avoid offending the king and so I must conclude that the visit has gone well. Soon I will be able to return home, and breathe a little more freely, away from the spies of the king's council. It is the day before I am due to leave when Edward summons me and tries to gently persuade me as to the error of my ways.

"I am concerned, sweet sister," he says gently, "that you risk everlasting punishment for praying as you do. It is against God's wishes. You should pray with the rest of us in the chapel, not in your own closet like some leper."

I sigh inwardly and force my angry features into a smile. He is little more than a child and cannot really understand.

"My dear brother, my sweet king, you are not yet old enough to make your own decision as to religion. Pray allow me to make up my own."

"And you, sister, are not yet too old to learn that you are mistaken."

Not too old? I clamp my lips together as the words echo in my head, the response I long to make is frozen upon my tongue. *It is not Edward's fault.* I will not blame him. He is merely repeating lessons he has learned by rote. I know he loves me and has no inkling of the hurt he inflicts.

I bite my tongue, bow my head and execute a deep curtsey. When I rise, I cannot hide the sorrow or the moistness of my eyes, and on seeing my tears, he leaps to his feet.

"Mary, sister!" He holds out his hands and hurries toward me, places his palms upon my cheeks, his face close to mine.

"I would not injure you for all the world," he says. "You were a mother to me when my own was taken but … I fear you will *burn*, Mary! There is nothing I can do to…"

I snatch his hands away from my cheeks.

"You are the *king*, Edward," I hiss. "Of course there is something you can do to stop them. You can stop all of this!"

I sweep my arm at the gathering and, turning on my heel, I quit his presence without waiting for his permission.

As I hurry along the corridor, expecting any moment to hear the tramp of the royal guard behind me, I tear the veil from my hair, scattering pearls as I go. On entering my chamber, I cast it aside.

"Get out!" I shout and my attendants scurry away with white, shocked faces.

I sit on a low stool at the fireside, my head in my hands until Susan enters, breathless from her hasty pursuit of me from the hall. I look up and let out a scream of frustration.

"I cannot bear it, Susan! They are like devils. How can they be so blind to their own sin? They have turned my noble brother into a bigot and a bully!"

I break into sobs, my head heavy in my hands.

"Oh, my lady, he didn't mean it…"

"Start making ready for a journey," I snarl as I dash my face dry on my sleeve. "We are leaving."

Copped Hall, Essex – August 1551

So I retire to Copped Hall and shroud myself in misery. I know the world cannot be exactly as I would have it. I understand that Edward is the king and I love him dearly, it is the men who rule him that I abhor. They are tainting all England with their evil beliefs and spoiling my brother who, without such influence, could bring England back to Rome.

If I allow myself to dwell on the absurdities taking place in the realm, I may run mad. I pick up my lute again and fix my mind on more pleasant matters. From now on, I shall try to see only flowers in this beautiful world, and if there is muck in the garden, I will navigate a path carefully around it.

But they will not leave me in peace. In August, three members of my household, Robert Rochester, Francis Englefield and Edward Waldegrave, are summoned to Hampton Court to appear before the council. They are accused of 'keeping the princess in the old religion.' This is nonsense, of course. They are my servants and do as I command them. I need no man to tell me how to think.

They return from London full of 'advice' as to how I should open my mind to the new learning, read heretical works and submit myself to the devil. They have clearly been coached in what to say. I cannot in all conscience allow them anywhere near my household chaplains. Instead, I send them straight back to Hampton Court with a verbal message for the king's council, and a letter addressed privately to the king. As they ride away, I bite my lip at the things I have said in it and wonder if I might have gone too far.

Having for my part utterly refused heretofore to talk with them in such matters, trusted that Your Majesty would have suffered me, your poor humble sister ... to have used the accustomed Mass, which the King, your father and mine, with all his predecessors did evermore use: wherein also I have been brought up from my youth, and thereunto my conscience doth not only bind me, which by no means will suffer me to think one thing and do another, but also the promise made to the Emperor, by Your Majesty's Council, was an assurance to me that in so doing I should not offend the laws, although they seem now to qualify and deny the thing... Bear with me as you have done, and not to think that by my doings or example any inconvenience might grow to Your Majesty or your realm

I fear that in the writing of it, my brain seemed to overtake my fingers and I added: *...rather than offend God and my conscience, I offer my body at your will, and death shall be more welcome than life with a troubled conscience.*

Now that the letter has been dispatched, I begin to fear the council might bear upon the king to act upon my offer. The thought of the Tower fills me with dread. It is a drear place, a palace of lost hope, peopled with ghosts and scented with treason.

To my great chagrin, my messengers are immediately incarcerated in the fleet. No amount of complaining or ranting can persuade the council to free them. Consumed with a mix of fury and remorse, I turn to Susan, who is my only friend.

"Oh Susan, I should not have instructed them to say such things. My hasty words have stolen their liberty and Rochester is not well…"

"You were not to know, my lady, and the council should not have taunted you. They've no right to treat you so. It is they who sin."

"It is me they want to lock up really but they daren't – not with Spain waiting for an excuse for war. Rochester and the others are being used as my whipping boys; they suffer in my place and the council know that I am impotent against them."

The door opens and a servant offers a letter on a tray. I take it, recognising the royal seal. I glance up at Susan and she smiles encouragingly … so I break the wax and unfold it.

"They are coming to see me, on Tuesday next."

"Who is, my lady?"

I hand her the letter so she can see for herself.

"The lords Rich, Wingfield and Petre; bringing further instruction from the king."

The next few days pass in an agony of the unknown. They might come with chains to take me into custody; they might come with an assassin to put an end to my impertinence. Briefly, I consider the possibility that they come to offer a solution that is suitable to us all ... but no, I am certain that they will come with threats and admonishments. I can sense it.

I keep them waiting while I slowly attend to the final details of my toilette. Then, dressed in deep black velvet and as many pearls as I own, I descend to the hall. The servants throw open the door and I march in, my head high, ready for the fight.

Three bearded faces turn toward me. Their expressions are hostile, their eyes cold as they regard me. The troublesome princess whom, I'd lay money, they wish had died in the womb like her siblings.

They do not beat about the bush. Rich draws out a piece of paper and starts to read from it.

"We have orders from the king; His Majesty does resolutely determine it just, necessary and expedient that you should not any ways use or maintain the private Mass or any other manner of service than such as by the law of the realm is authorised or allowed."

I narrow my eyes.

"I am and ever will be His Majesty's most humble servant but in matters of conscience I must let God be my guide. I cannot hear any service other than that left by my father until such time as King Edward reaches his majority..."

And is no longer led by fools, I add silently. Rich's face grows purple, his eyes bulging with suppressed fury. It must be difficult to stand before a princess of the realm, bastard or not, and not take measure of one's words. It must have occurred to them that I may one day be their queen. They know I will never forget this. Lord Rich takes a deep impatient breath.

"These are decrees laid down by the king…"

"Decrees put into his mouth by the likes of you, my lord, and you, Petre. My brother can order the kingdom as he likes but I will not be so ordered. I will lay my head on the block if I have to."

My belly flips at my own words and I send up a silent prayer that they take as little notice of this as they have my other offers of martyrdom.

They bilge and bluster for a while longer; angry one moment, cajoling the next. I remain on my feet, forcing them to stand too, preventing the meeting from becoming too comfortable. We are eye to eye, chin to chin, their stubbornness matching mine, but their dislike cannot compete and neither can their resolve.

"The king does not wish to take your life!" Rich shouts. "He merely seeks your obedience, your loyalty. You must see it is your duty to submit."

How I despise these men.

"You give me fair words, sir, but your deeds are ill toward me. I will never consent to your wishes."

It might be easier to give in, as I gave in once before. Once, when my father's men bullied me to admit my parents' marriage was no marriage, I thought it would be easier to be a bastard than an unloved princess, spurned by the father I adored. I gave in once before. I will never do so again, even if death is my reward.

Petre throws down his hat and storms from the room, quickly followed by Rich. Wingfield hesitates, then gives a sketchy bow and a look of helplessness before scurrying after them. As their footsteps dwindle, I remember something I have forgotten to say.

I hurry to the window, clamber on to the seat and wrestle with the casement catch. It opens so suddenly that I lurch forward, the ground below rushing up to meet me, seemingly close. My head swims and I pull back, catching my breath before looking down again.

From my vantage point the enemy is foreshortened, like midgets that amuse us at court festivities. I notice the beginnings of a tonsure on Rich's scalp – and note that a man less like a monk has never walked this earth. As they storm across the bailey, he harangues his companions, furiously wagging a finger and no doubt cursing my very name.

"Master Rich!" I call and they stop, turning a circle before locating my voice and looking up at my window.

"I forgot to say." My veil, caught by a sudden breeze, blows across my face. I push it aside and shout into the wind. "I require the return of my comptroller, Robert Rochester. I am having to take account of how many loaves of bread be made of a bushel of wheat. My father and mother never brought me up with baking and brewing, and to be plain with you, I am weary of the office. Therefore, my lords, send my officer home with all good speed, and my other men too."

I slam the window with satisfaction and plump suddenly onto the seat.

"Good lord, Susan," I say. "After that, they will either leave me alone or hang me. Only time will tell."

February 1553

The council allows me no respite until its attention is taken up by renewed hostilities between France and Spain. Worried that England will join with France against them, the Hapsburgs consider invading us and placing me on the throne. I know of this only through the small gossip that filters through the ever increasing security measures imposed by the council. I know of it when it would be safer not to. It will not take Edward's council long to see the benefits of implicating me in the plot.

I am enjoying a rare day of sunshine when a messenger arrives from court. I break the seal and scan the contents.

"Blast."

"What is it now, my lady?" Jane and Susan stroll toward me and join me on the arbour seat, one to either side.

"The king requests my presence at court, to help entertain Mary of Guise. No doubt they wish to prove that I am no threat and all is well between me and the king."

"Shall you go, my lady? You could wear the new velvet gown with the high collar. It becomes you so well…"

"No. I won't be attending. You must tell my secretary to inform the king that I am unwell. I shall retire to my bed now in case anyone is sent to test the truth of it."

I remain in bed for the duration of Mary of Guise's residence in the capital. The weather turns nasty so I am missing little. In fact, it is quite comforting to prop myself on pillows and leaf through books, write letters or strum my lute. It is like a holiday that requires none of the discomforts of travel.

When at last Edward and his council cease to bombard me with demands for compliance, I sigh with relief. It is many weeks later when the reason for their silence becomes clear.

Edward, after a bout of measles in April, has taken sick again and this time his physicians fear it may be the consumption. With the king's health deteriorating, the council dares not risk offending me. I am, after all, the heir to the throne. They are well aware that my vengeance would be harsh should I suddenly become sovereign.

Their efforts for church reform do not cease during the king's malady; instead they grow apace, and the royal council does all it can to push through the changes in law. They work desperately. As the king's health continues to deteriorate, they know that, should Edward die, my accession to the throne will mean the reversal of their heresy, and the end to their reformation.

A return to Rome.

But, although the idea of the crown is thrilling, the thought of losing my brother is not. I order my household to make ready for a journey and leave for London, determined to gain admittance to the king.

With two hundred lords and ladies in attendance, I ride along Fleet Street toward the city, where I am met by John Dudley and a cavalcade of knights and gentlemen. He makes a great show of friendship but I am not deceived. I know he conceals some nefarious scheme. I take comfort from the crowd that gathers to greet me, their roars a delight to my lonely heart. I lean from my saddle and make a great show of calling down a blessing on those nearest to me.

Dudley pushes back his cap and scratches his head, clearly disconcerted by their devotion.

'*Mary! Mary!*' I hear them call and I twist and turn in my saddle, my hand raised in acknowledgement. How I have missed this feeling; I relish the honour done to me and, as the city gate grows near, I sit taller, more confident of my future than ever before. These are Edward's people, but they love me. They will allow nothing to injure their princess. *They love me!*

I repeat those words silently, the truth of their affection soft and warm about my chilly heart. But the next morning, when I request an audience with the king, I am told he is too sickly. Not one of the council members can look me in the eye; instead, they exchange glances, stare at the floor, anywhere rather than at me. *What are they hiding?*

"I will not tire him. I will just stay a moment, just to wish him well."

The greybeards shake their heads, looking to all corners of the room instead of into my eyes. Once more, I force my irritation down and try to accept defeat cheerfully.

"Then I shall write to him instead," I say. "You can convey my letter to him, my lord. It will cheer my brother as he recovers."

There is little they can do other than reluctantly agree. I write Edward a loving letter, hand it to Dudley and return to Copped Hall, promising to visit the king again when he has recovered his health. But, although I cannot pinpoint the reason, in the weeks that follow, I am unsettled and wake every morning to a sense of doom; as if someone has unleashed the hounds of Hell.

"Hounds of Hell? What do you mean?"

"I mean that if I thought Dudley was evil before, in the months that followed he turned into the devil himself."

The aroma of citrus fills the chamber and I realise Anne is peeling an orange. She presses a segment into my hand and I pop it in my mouth, the sharp flavour bursting on my tongue and making me cough. I wipe my watering eye on my sleeve and when I am calm again she urges me to continue with my tale.

"Dudley was pure evil; that I know for sure. It was a sharp lesson to me when I heard how they'd been working against me for months, seeking to put me down before I'd even risen. I should have been more wary when I learned he'd secretly wed his spindly-legged son to my cousin, Jane – the clever one, the reformer that I spoke of before. His intention all along was to put her on the throne in my place. I never found out what he intended to do with me. He probably would have taken my head if he could have got close enough."

She gasps, puts a hand across her mouth and turns at Susan's approach.

"Did you know of this, Lady Susan?"

"Know it? I was there. I've always been there, at Her Majesty's side."

She places a hand on my arm and I pat it.

"So you have, Susan. Through thick and thin…"

We smile at the memory of it all. The tears, the laughter, the terror, the joy – life is like a pudding; a mix of all those things; without dark times there would be no light – and vice versa. But, sometimes I think the cook neglected to give my pudding a good enough stir, for the mixture was ever uneven – the odd taste of sugar but mostly bitter, bitter rue.

"Did they send you to the Tower?"

"Nay, child, but they would have, had fortune not smiled upon me."

"Dudley persuaded the king to change the succession," says Susan, taking a seat at the girl's side and picking up her needlework. "Weeks before his death, the king disinherited both our queen and the Princess Elizabeth, declaring them illegitimate again. He named the Greys instead; they were the heirs of Henry VIII's sister, Mary. Jane was Mary's granddaughter."

The child turns from Susan to me. I see her face change as she notices the tears on my cheek. I seek to explain further.

"I was injured by the treachery of my Grey cousins, more than any others that worked against me. Edward's last actions were to my detriment. I was still grieving for him when I discovered it. I still remembered the weight of his infant body in my arms. My mind was full of memories. I recalled how I used to kiss his fingers, count his toes, smell the scent of his hair – to think he had been warped so much, and taught to hate me…" My voice breaks. The women make soothing sounds.

Swallowing my grief, I shake my head, dispelling the grimness of my thoughts, but Susan, noticing my struggle, fills the brief silence.

"It was politics, Your Majesty. The king loved you well. You know that."

"He loved the devil more; his desire to deny Rome outweighed any love he once had for me. He went so far as to reconfirm that my parents' marriage was invalid, and I was declared a bastard all over again."

"He disparaged the Princess Elizabeth too…"

"Yes. I wonder what she thought about that? He declared that, since Anne Boleyn had been inclined to couple with courtiers and paid the penalty with her head, her daughter was unlikely to be the king's. Even I could see that was nonsense – Elizabeth is made in our father's image; a Tudor through and through."

"Had it not been for my spies, I'd have known nothing of this. Had those true to me not brought me news, I'd have been thrown into the Tower before Edward could draw his last breath. Imagine that. If I'd been replaced by Jane Grey! Oh, when I realised the truth, and the fight I had on my hands, I could do nothing but step up to the mark. The days that followed were fraught with danger but they were indeed my most glorious days…"

Norfolk – July 1553

I am at Hunsdon when Northumberland finally summons me to court. I order the servants to make ready for a journey before retiring to pray for Edward's gentle passing in my private chapel. It is dark and quiet, the beads of the rosary cool and solid beneath my fingers. *I will soon be queen.*

The knowledge intrudes upon my prayers, softening the sharp stab of sorrow I feel for the loss of my brother. I shake my head to dispel the thought. There will be time enough to think of the future when Edward is gone. And I know now that he will not survive.

As I whisper the familiar words, his face swims in my mind's eye. I persist in remembering him as a laughing infant, his baby chin damp with dribble. I see his first steps, his first time on a pony. I see him, older now, on my father's throne; a child too young to resist the pressure put upon him by our enemies. For his council were enemies to both of us. They *corrupted* him. He could have been so much better than he was. My throat closes and a small groan escapes me. I pray harder, my voice rising…

"My lady?"

I raise my head sharply. They know better than to disturb me at prayer. Something must be very wrong. I cling to the altar rail and clamber to my feet.

"What is the matter?"

Susan hovers in the half light, the unshaded side of her face taut and white.

"Rochester is here and wishes to see you, my lady. He says the matter is most urgent."

He is waiting in my privy chamber, examining a portrait of my father that hangs above the fireplace. When I enter, he turns and takes two steps toward me before bowing low.

"What is it, Robert? No problem with the travel arrangements, I hope."

His expression is grave.

"No, my lady. It is more than that. I have received intelligence from court that you should not travel to London at all."

The words are ordinary enough but I sense danger lurking behind them.

"Not travel? But I must. There will be arrangements to be made once he has g … for the king's funeral and my coronation."

"That is the crux of the matter, Your Majesty. My source, one close to Northumberland and a member of the privy council, informs me of a plot to entrap you, and to … to crown Jane Grey in your place."

"*Jane Grey* … I do not understand. Even Northumberland cannot ignore the will of my late father … and *Jane Grey*? It is absurd. It is *treason*!"

"Yes, my lady. My advice is that instead of travelling to London, you make haste to Norfolk. On the way, we can muster support for your cause. I will send word ahead to John Huddlestone. I am confident he will offer us shelter on our way to Kenninghall."

"My cause?"

"Yes, my lady. Your cause. Good Catholics will flock to your banner. Nobody wants a Protestant, and nobody wants Dudley and his puppet queen."

I had suspected skulduggery when Dudley married Jane to his son. Now I understand the full duplicity of his intentions. This is no spontaneous act. He has been working toward this for months. He means to rule England himself through his son's wife. Jane will be nothing but a figurehead.

I clench my fists as blood surges beneath my skin, fury gathering in my heart. One day I will have the pleasure of taking Northumberland's head, but for now that must wait. I spin on my heel, walk the length of the floor and back again.

"Give the order," I say. "We must hope our unexpected arrival does not scare our host out of his wits."

Rochester clears his throat. "We will not be entirely unexpected, my lady. A few days ago, I took the liberty of laying down some contingency plans."

I narrow my eyes.

"You knew this was coming? Why did you not warn me?"

"It might not have happened, my lady. I did not want you to worry over something that might never come to pass."

I nod slowly, my eyes pricking.

"Tell me the arrangements you have put in place."

He draws a paper from inside his doublet and moves closer to the fire, where we lean over the itinerary together. He flicks it with his forefinger.

"As I said, first we should stop at Sawston Hall. Sir John Huddlestone is expecting us."

"He is on my side?"

I am unused to people championing my cause; all my life I have been shunned. Even those who love me have ever lacked the courage to speak out against the king. A warm feeling is unfurling in my belly, an unfamiliar sensation, as if I have just supped strong spirits.

"He assures me so, my lady. Then it is but a short journey to Bury St Edmunds and Hengrove Hall, where the Earl of Bath…"

"But he is on the king's council…"

"He was, my lady. I am informed he has declined to support Northumberland and retired to his estates on the grounds of ill health."

"I am surprised Dudley didn't have him thrown in the Tower."

"Lady Burgh is ready to receive you at Euston Hall…"

"And from there to Kenninghall, I presume?"

"Yes, my lady."

I look toward the unshuttered window where night presses like velvet against the glass. Until today, I had felt safe here, sheltered by thick stone walls, cared for by my vast loyal household, but now, suddenly, I feel vulnerable and cold. I wrap my arms about my torso and shudder.

"Put the arrangements in place, Robert. I shall be ready to leave when you send word."

He bows, flashing a brief encouraging smile before leaving me alone with my rampaging imagination.

I watch the horizon turn from a faint pink into a bright sun-drenched morning. It is full light before we leave although the hour is just after five. Rochester assures me Sawston is merely thirty miles or so and I have easily travelled that far in a day before.

Today however, we seem to cover the miles very slowly. Leaving the bulk of our household behind, I ride ahead, keeping only Rochester, Susan and Jane, and a small guard with me. We travel hard, my mount tossing her head as if it is a lark but soon, the relentless pace begins to tire her and green froth flies from the bridle to spatter my clothes. I am fearful, afraid of a future I cannot see, yet I am alive, my heart is pounding, and my mind more alert than it has ever been.

"We should stop so the horses can rest," I shout over my shoulder, but Rochester shakes his head.

"We can slacken our pace to let them get their breath but we cannot afford to stop."

If my horse dies beneath me I will be in worse peril than if we take a short break, but … I do not argue. This kind of adventure is foreign to me. The pounding of my heart, the terror in my belly is something new and terrifying, yet somehow I am eager for what is to come.

Susan smiles encouragingly from her saddle but Jane crouches low over her horse's head, her face grim, her brow scored with a deep frown. Jane's determination to reach safety is as keen as mine.

Rochester allows us only a brief stop at midday and another a few hours later. It is late afternoon when he points out the top of Sawston church above the trees.

"Nearly there, my lady."

I am so tired I could fall from the saddle. My thighs are raw, my lower back at breaking point and my fingers seem to be fused to the reins.

"Oh Robert," I say, my voice husky with thirst. "I hope there is a chamber ready for me ... and a bath. I'd give anything for a warm bath."

The horses clatter into the yard and John Huddlestone hurries out to greet us.

"My lady." He offers me assistance from the saddle and when my feet touch the floor I find the strength has gone from my knees. I clutch at his arm, almost falling, but his strong hands keep me upright until Rochester pushes forward.

"Forgive me, my lady," he says and, sweeping me into his arms, proceeds to carry me up the steps to the hall.

"I can walk, Robert," I protest, embarrassed by my hitched skirts that are revealing my knees.

"No need to walk if you don't have to, I always say."

Robert carries me up the steps and into the welcome darkness of Sawston Hall. I see almost nothing of the interior on our way through the house, but I am grateful for the welcome fire in my chamber, and the large wooden bath that stands before it.

Susan, dusty and tired as she is from the road, steps forward to help me disrobe, but I hold up a hand.

"No, Susan, you and Jane must be as tired as I. You look to your own needs. Sir John will find a maid who can assist me."

Sir John's servants are, of course, not as sensible of my particular preferences as my own women, but I make no complaint when they help me into a robe before my skin is quite dry. When one of them snags my hair as she combs it, I do not remonstrate with her. My mind is focussed on the large bed, the promise of a soft mattress and pillows.

"Pass me my rosary," I say, and one of the girls takes it up and carries it gingerly toward me. I remember that my brother ordered rosaries to be banned. She is probably fearful that the king's men will suddenly appear and place us all under arrest.

My bones shriek as I rise from the chair at the fireside to kneel at the *prie-dieu* in the corner. Although I am thankful to have survived the journey so far, I do not pray for long. My knees are full of knots and my back aches keenly. The thought of climbing into the saddle again in the morning is not a welcome one.

The next day, and the day after, I am faced with a similar ride. It is as if I am caught in some recurring nightmare. On the seventh day of July, we set out in drear drizzling rain, the clouds low in the sky.

"It will be brighter by mid-morning," Susan assures me but I cannot find it in me to make reply. I am so tired, I put my head down and focus on the ground, watching the miles pass and wishing my horse could move faster.

Euston Hall lies close to Thetford, and when I spot it through the trees, I have never known a more welcome sight. Although it is only a little past noon, after greeting and thanking Lady Burgh, I am conducted straight to a chamber where I manage to snatch a few hours sleep. When I awake, I call for my women to help me rise. I am just slipping from the bed when someone knocks upon the chamber door.

"Who is it? Go and see," I say.

Susan opens the door, and I hear her whispering.

"Lady Mary is not yet risen from her bed," she hisses, and I hear the rumbling tones of Rochester. I'd have thought he'd be resting too, given the ride we've shared, but perhaps he is made of sterner stuff.

"Rochester?" I call. "What is it? Have you news?"

With an appalled expression, Susan opens the door wider and allows Robert into the sanctum of my chamber. His face flushes at the sight of my bed gown, the braided hair across my shoulder. I draw a shawl across my chest.

"Forgive me, my lady, but … Robert Reyns has arrived and he brings grave news from court."

He doesn't need to tell me, I can read the news in his face.

"My brother is dead, isn't he?"

His face is calm, deeply cut with lines, worry lines engraved by his years of service to me.

"He is, my la … Your Majesty."

He drops to his knees, and somehow my hand is in his and he is kissing my fingers. From somewhere deep within me a bubble of laughter emerges at the ridiculous picture we must make. Here I am, barefoot and exhausted, stripped of every vestige of royalty, and a man kneels at my feet, swearing fealty.

I push my amusement aside and concentrate on the severity of the moment.

"And Dudley, what is he doing?"

"By all accounts, he has installed Jane in the Tower."

"So they control London, the armoury, the munitions and gunpowder … and the great seal of England."

He inclines his head in agreement.

"They do, Your Majesty, but I swear before God they shall not hold it for long. I offer you my lifelong allegiance and pledge to assist you to your throne."

"Get up, Robert," I say, aware of my women's scandalised faces. "Our journey is not yet done."

"No, Your Majesty, but we have begun. Already, men are flocking to your cause. In the morning we will continue our journey to Kenninghall."

My face falls at the thought of more hours in the saddle.

"Don't worry, Your Majesty. It is a mere ten miles or so. We will be there in a matter of hours."

I am bone weary. Lady Burgh will be hoping for us to stay and enjoy a light supper at least.

"I feel we should not wait. We should leave right away."

"My – Your Majesty, we cannot. At least … not until you have eaten…"

"I will hear Mass, partake of supper, and then we will ride through the night. Order preparations to be made for a further journey."

"As you will, Your Majesty." He bows low again and leaves me.

"Susan," I say, "you must dress my hair, it feels like a bird's nest at the back…" but when I turn, I find she is on her knees, her head lowered, her hands raised so I might bless them.

"I pledge my allegiance, Your Majesty, the great honour that you do me…"

"Oh, for Heaven's sake, Susan! Get up, you fool, and see to my hair."

The rhythmic motion of the comb lulls and soothes me, and my thoughts float like white feathers in a breeze. My little brother is dead but I am still one step away from the throne. All I need do now is deprive Dudley of his power and snatch back my crown from my cousin.

The feather, suddenly tarnished, drops like a stone and doubt intrudes, begins to dominate. *I am accustomed to failure, why should this be any different?*

"Dudley will capture me, I know he will," I whisper, suddenly glad of Susan's comforting arm that creeps about my shoulder.

"It will soon be time to leave, Your Majesty. You will be safer at Kenninghall."

"Framlingham will be safer still," I reply, allowing her to push me onto a stool and pin on my hood. "Northumberland's men will not be far behind us."

We pass through unfamiliar corridors, descend the stairs to the hall where a hasty supper has been laid out. When I enter, the babble of conversation ceases, servants dissolve from sight, and Lady Burgh steps forward.

"Your Majesty," she says and, to my astonishment, the entire company drops to their knees. I had forgotten for a moment that I am queen. It feels so strange.

"Up, up," I say and, pushing my shoulders back, I hold my head high like my father used to, and move forward. I hold out my hand.

"Lady Burgh, what a lovely welcome. You have conjured an appetising supper for us, I see."

"It is my pleasure, Your Majesty. I am honoured to be of service."

She ushers me toward the top table and I take my seat, picking up a napkin.

"We must eat and leave, I am afraid, Lady Burgh. Important matters await our attention."

"Yes, Your Majesty, so I have been informed. I – I will join the party, if you will allow. I have no wish to confront Northumberland's men when they arrive. You have heard he is in pursuit … and of what happened at Sawston after your departure?"

"No. What happened?" Suddenly alert, I seek out my comptroller. "Rochester? What happened?"

Robert rises to his feet, places his cup on the table.

"I would have informed you of it later, Your Majesty. It seems Dudley took offence at the support they offered you and … he ordered Sawston Hall be put to the torch, Your Majesty."

"They burned it?"

"Yes, Your Majesty."

I do not answer at once. In my mind's eye I see the noble building, the elegant interior, the mullions twinkling in the sunshine. Now it has been engulfed by flames. Hate grumbles in my heart.

"We will rebuild it, in gratitude for Huddlestone's assistance."

A murmur of appreciation eddies around the room but, looking down at the plate before me, I find I have lost my appetite. Dudley's men are not far behind me, and they are burning and murdering in my wake. *How dare he? How dare he injure and punish my subjects for assisting me?* He will suffer for this. If I am ever in the position to wreak justice upon him, he will suffer greatly.

My growing company takes to the road again just after supper. It is a warm night, the gathering dark hampering the speed at which we travel. Rochester has set men at the head and the rear of the party, and my women and I are ringed by a small guard. Despite the precautions, I still feel vulnerable, exposed to the elements, sure there are assassins hidden in the trees. Susan waves her hand to gain my attention.

"We will soon be there, Your Majesty. Safe in your own bed chamber."

But there is little hope of sleep, and somehow I no longer crave it. Although I am weary to the bone, my mind is sharp and my blood surging, ready for the fight of my life.

As soon as we reach the security of Kenninghall, while the men loyal to me hone their swords and prepare for battle if needs be, I will take up my pen. I will write to the loyal Catholics of England, the former friends of my mother, and beg their allegiance.

It is almost morning when we ride into the bailey. As I hurry through the hall, tearing off my gloves and casting my cloak to the floor, my women scurry behind, picking up after me.

"Gather the household, I want to address them," I order as I march into my privy chamber. The servants scurry round, a girl throws logs on the fire while another closes the shutters and brings a tray of wine.

It is comforting to be back in my own house where things are governed to my own will. Without stopping to refresh myself, I sit down and draw up a list of men in whose loyalty I trust. Then I descend to the hall. At the turn of the staircase, I pause and look down at the upturned faces of my household. As one they fall to their knees.

Most of them have been with me through the darkest days of my brother's reign. They are good honest Catholics and I must do my best to defend their liberty, their church. I descend further and make my way to the dais where I clasp my hands, lift my chin and begin to speak.

"You will have heard that my brother, King Edward, has departed this life. The right to the crown of England has, by divine and human law, descended to me."

A great cheer arises, caps are tossed high in the air. Their joy is so great that in spite of everything, I find myself smiling. I wipe away a tear and hold up my hands.

"Good people!" I cry over their jubilation. "Our job is not yet done. Our country is in the hands of the Duke of Northumberland. He has named Jane Grey queen; Jane, who is a Protestant and his son's wife too! This is *treason* and as yet we lack the numbers to stand against him, but every day our number is growing. I am not yet defeated, not so long as I have your stout Catholic hearts behind me!"

Their cries are deafening. I smile, my cheeks stretching, my jaw aching. "I implore those of you who can to ride out and muster men and ammunition, while I send word to those loyal to me who live farther afield. We will build a great army and muster at Framlingham."

Men mill about the hall, kissing their wives and sweethearts, and calling for horses that they might galvanise this thing … this war … into action. For war it shall be.

"Come to bed, Your Majesty," Susan yawns. "You can write in the morning."

The candle at my side is smoking. I light a fresh one and extinguish the old, picking up my quill again.

"Not yet. This needs to be done now. The letters must be ready for dispatch by dawn. There will be time to rest once this battle is won."

She goes to the window and opens the shutters a crack, I glance up and notice a bright stripe on the horizon. Morning is not long away. She turns and, picking up a jug, carries it toward me.

"At least pause for sustenance," she says. I watch the wine slowly fill the cup, and she hands me a wafer filled with honey. "You need your strength."

Reluctantly, I take a bite and honey runs down my chin, dripping onto my bodice. I blot it with my finger.

"Now look, Susan," I say. "I will be a target for the wasps now."

***

"When they proclaimed Jane Grey queen, nobody cheered, Your Majesty. The crowds in London were silent."

"Silent?"

"Yes, although they say a few called out her name; those wise enough to pay lip service to Northumberland's game. For the most part, the announcement achieved a chilly reception. One poor soul who called out your name in defiance was taken and his ears nailed to the pillory."

"For calling my name?" I ponder on this nameless fellow for a while, his futile bravado in the face of treason is … comforting. "Remind me, Robert, to see the fellow is well rewarded."

I am strangely calm.

239

"What does Spain have to say of all of this?" I ask. Rochester glances at Waldegrave, who clears his throat.

"I believe they think the deed is done and your cause is lost, Your Majesty. Their advice is to wait and see what happens but … they do not understand the mood of the people." He clenches his fist, a rock of victory. "The people don't *want* Jane or Northumberland. They want you!"

I stand up, my throat tight with emotion.

"Then, we must give the people what they want, Rochester."

I sit down again and write to the council – the traitorous supporters of Jane's coup.

We are not ignorant of your consultations, to undo the provisions made for our preferment, nor of the great bands, and provisions forcible, wherewith ye be assembled and prepared – by whom, and to what end, God and you know, and nature cannot but fear some evil.

I demand that they put aside their treason and pledge loyalty to me. I even promise them each a pardon if they obey me but … I have no intention of pardoning the ringleaders. I will watch and laugh as Northumberland dies.

If I had expected them to lay down their weapons and fall to their knees, then I am sore disappointed. Instead, Northumberland has my messenger thrown into a dungeon and writes back in his own hand.

My claim is spurious, he says, and reminds me of the act of parliament that illegitimised and disinherited me in my father's day.

My anger inflates into fury. I send word via the ambassadors to my cousin Charles in Spain, but there is little time for him to take action. As Northumberland, with the contents of the Tower munitions at his disposal, masses an army against me, I look at my band of trusty Catholics with debilitating despair.

I must not be thwarted by my own lack of confidence.

As my resolve begins to crumble, new arrivals ride in through the gate of Kenninghall: Sir Henry Bedingfield, John Shelton, Richard Southwell, Henry Radcliffe and with them they bring money, armed men and provisions, and above all, a determination that we *will* have victory. It is the fillip I need.

I hurry down to greet them, look fondly on their lowered heads as they take knee before me. My former despair lightens, and I spy a glimmer of hope on the horizon.

"In the morning," I say, "we will ride on to Framlingham."

Framlingham – 12th July 1553

Framlingham is the ancient seat of the Howard family. It is a vast structure, built for defence, and provides the perfect protection against Northumberland should he bring his forces against me. This time, when Rochester helps me into the saddle, I spare no thought for the fatigue of the journey. I now have men and arms at my back. Our army might be inferior to that of Northumberland but I have *right* on my side. The crown is my birthright and I have already suffered enough for it. Now, I shall make England mine, and punish those who dare attempt to wrest it from my grasp.

As we ride out from Kenninghall, the locals gather to wave us off and their blessings fall like warm rain upon my face. I raise my gloved hand; a clenched fist to mark our imminent victory. I no longer even feel like Princess Mary, the suppressed and besmirched bastard of England.

I am Queen of England now.

I beckon Rochester to ride beside me.

"Will they come, Robert? Do you really believe enough men will ride out in support of me?"

"I believe they will, Your Majesty."

He waves his arm at the company that surrounds me. "Are these men already mustered not proof enough of the legitimacy of your claim."

I flush at the word *legitimacy*, so long used to hearing it directed against me. I glance at the riders ahead and behind. Strong, steel-clad men, well armed for battle. They will fight and die for me if needs be. The bright day darkens as the road dips into a wood, and I shiver in the sudden chill.

"Don't be troubled," Robert says. "There is light ahead, look."

And, in the distance, I see the tunnel of darkness open again into the brilliant warmth of the sun. It gives me heart. I turn the full strength of my approval upon Rochester.

"I am not afraid, Robert, I was merely chilled for a moment. How can I be afraid when men such as you are ready to lay down their lives for me?"

It is coming on to dusk by the time we see the towers of Framlingham Castle in the distance. As we draw closer, the roadside begins to fill with people, ragged people; farmers, blacksmiths and women with children at foot.

"God bless, Your Majesty!" they cry. "God keep you!" and I feel again that surge of love that has been missing from my life. While the allegiance of the upper classes shifts and turns, these people, these common simple folk, do not change.

A slight incline rises ahead and the party breaks into a trot, increasing to a slow canter as we reach the summit and then…

I draw in breath, pull my mount to a halt and look down on the meadows that surround Framlingham Castle. Wide acres of undulating pennants; fields spiked with spears; the setting sun glinting on a sea of shining steel. I raise a hand to my mouth in disbelief at the great concourse of men who have come to offer up their swords.

Let battle commence in the morning, for tonight I will go to my bed happy, and confident that God will send us victory.

I sleep like one blessed.

St James' Palace – November 1558

"And did God send you victory, Your Majesty? Was there a great battle?"

Anne's voice drags me back from the past. The chamber has turned quite, quite dark. I am surprised to find myself in my bed, startled by the sudden ache in my joints, the gripe in my belly. For a while, I'd been young and victorious again; a rightful queen taking back her throne.

As my consciousness returns to the miserable present, I wish I could have my life to live again. There are things I'd do differently, of course. I doubt there is a

243

body on earth who would not make some small changes to the past. At the start of my reign I'd had such a sense of righteousness. I felt my trials were over and a new life beginning. If only I could have hung on to that feeling.

On the day when Northumberland's army conceded, my future stretched out like an endless golden sea. I would restore the old ways; make England merry again. I would marry, bear a string of heirs, and lead the Tudor dynasty into a new era of unblemished Catholicism. But I was blinded by it; by the crown, by the power, by false hope, by my own unshakeable faith.

I believed all England longed as I did for a return to the true church but I was wrong. I had not yet learned that most men yearn for power and wealth; they have little care for the method of prayer. Even God in his Heaven cannot compete with the human lust for power on Earth.

"No, Anne: there was no real battle. The people resisted Northumberland's plan. Jane Grey was a stranger to the commoners but they had known me from my infancy, seen the indignities I had suffered. The people were the first to show their support for me and then, one by one, the knights and nobles followed. In the end, with few supporters left and knowing his cause was lost, Northumberland had no option but to surrender."

"What did you do?"

Her face comes into clearer focus as she sits forward. I cannot make out the contours of her face but her hands are lit by the candle, and I notice they are clasped so tightly the tips of her fingers are turning white. I don't remember ever having enjoyed such a captive audience.

"What did I do? I sent the Earl of Arundel to arrest him, of course."

"And what about Lady Jane?"

I sigh. Poor Jane. I'd rather not think of that.

"Well, she was kept in the Tower. My hands were tied. I couldn't let her go free. She had allowed herself to be declared queen, she had endorsed an army to be sent out against me. My advisors urged me to take her head but ... I couldn't, in all conscience, do that. Honourable confinement was the best I could offer."

"It must have been hard for you, she was your cousin."

"Yes, it *was* hard, and painful too. I'm glad you can see that. She might have been an annoying little Protestant who constantly tried to convert me but, first and foremost, she was my kin. We had been friends for a time. We had walked together in the garden at Chelsea with Elizabeth and Katherine Parr. Jane was family, and her betrayal was the worst of all ... well, almost the worst."

A door opens. I cough feebly and turn my face toward the sound of swishing skirts, unsure who it is.

"Susan?"

"Yes, Your Majesty, it is me. I came to tell you that Sir Thomas Cornwallis has returned from Hatfield."

"Does he wish to see me?"

"I believe so, Your Majesty. I will tidy you up a little first before I summon him."

I grimace at the child as she rises from the bedside to allow Susan access. A thrill of cold tingles on my scalp as my cap is removed and a comb is gently run through my thinning hair. I wonder what I look like these days. It is a year or more since I was able to clearly see my face. Of course, my women assure me I am still beautiful to behold, but they'd hardly dare say otherwise.

Even in my youth I was merely *pleasant looking*, never beautiful like my mother. I have my father's snub nose, his clenched stubborn chin, his direct gaze. A firm eye is never appreciated in a woman. It gained me the reputation of being difficult even before I'd had cause to be defiant about anything.

Susan bids me sit forward. I groan while she fastens a clean shawl about my shoulders and eases me back on the pillows.

"There," she says. "You look lovely now."

"Do I, indeed?" I grumble. My head feels heavy, my neck aches. I slump on the pillows like an aged monkey. "Bring him in then," I say.

After a while, brisk footsteps enter the chamber, I hear a nervous cough and a flurry of movement. I imagine Cornwallis has swept off his hat and is making a gallant bow. A ridiculous gesture since I cannot see it.

"Your Majesty, I hope I find you in good health."

"No, sir, you don't. As must be quite plain."

"The physicians will have you well in no time…"

"No. No, they won't. Now, enough of your flannel. What did my sister say? Did she manage to hide her glee long enough to wish me well?"

"She did, Your Majesty, and is most distressed by your present malady."

"Codswallop. She can't wait to see me in my tomb. Did she swear to uphold my laws, protect the true religion?"

I squint, longing to be able to see the lie in his face as he makes reply.

"She did, Your Majesty. She also regrets that she cannot be with you in your time of…"

"I have no wish to see her."

The only sound is the crackling of flames in the hearth, the sudden slump of a charred log. I cough at the smoke that wafts uninvited into the room.

"They've already begun to leave me, you know. Flocking to her at Hatfield, no doubt. I imagine her court there is now larger than this one … just as her mother stole courtiers from my mother, now she is stealing mine."

He stumbles and stutters, unwilling to comment.

"Oh, be quiet, Cornwallis. You can go. Tell them to send that child back … she is the only company worth having these days. She doesn't argue, she doesn't flatter…"

"I am here, Your Majesty. I didn't leave."

I grope for her and the comfort of a small smooth hand creeps into mine. Ignoring Cornwallis as he takes leave of me, I urge the child to sit again.

"Your eyes are bad again today, Your Majesty?"

"The sight comes and goes, child. One day I can see shapes and colours, the next I see nothing at all. Today is a dark day but tomorrow I might look upon your face again."

"And the pain in your belly?"

"Not so bad this morning. Don't worry, I shall live to finish my tale."

"What was it like to be queen, after so long of being ill used? Did you wreak vengeance on your enemies straight away?"

I laugh, and my chest crackles with the effort.

"Some of them, but with others … leniency was best. Those I allowed to live were spared for the sake of England. The men who had supported me were good

247

men, stout Catholics and loyal to the realm but ... they were not politicians and state craft is a specialised matter. I had to pardon some whose heads I would rather have taken, but a monarch's life is always one of compromise ... or it should be."

<u>Richmond – September 1553</u>

As I had expected, there are many complaints from the Protestants in and around court. I am advised to treat them with forbearance, and hope that Rochester is right when he advises me that persuasion rather than force is a better method of ensuring the return of the true faith.

Simon Renard, an ambassador from the court of my cousin, Charles, quickly becomes my loyal adviser. Trying to ignore their failure to come to my aid when I needed it, I place my trust in him. I invite him to attend me without the knowledge of my council and he comes under cover of darkness.

He is small, dark and bearded with large sad eyes like a spaniel. He bends over my hand, his lips rather too moist on my wrist.

"I agree with the advice you've been given," he says when I put it to him. "Leniency and patience is the best path ... although your cousin, the Cardinal, will be difficult to convince."

Cardinal Pole, the son of my dearest friend, Margaret, is renowned for his intolerance. He fiercely desires England's return to Rome no matter the cost.

"I know little yet of such things, Renard, but even I can see that it is a matter that should not be hurried."

"Let them come back to grace of their own volition, Your Majesty. I am sure that once they see the error of their ways, the preferment good Catholics receive, they will realise it to be for the best."

It is not until it is over that the full extent of the damage caused by my brother's regime becomes evident. They destroyed centuries of devotion; stripped the cathedrals and the parish churches bare. They silenced our religious music, our Latin prayers, and smashed our glorious architecture; our statues, our beautiful stained glass. So much has gone and so much of it is irreplaceable.

I am determined to return as fully as I can to the old ways. I will replace the great roods burned in the heretic fires. I will restore the gilded lofts, the high gleaming altars of the true church, but I must do it slowly, by degrees.

When the abbeys fell in my father's time, the church properties were given to some of the most powerful lords in the kingdom. To demand the return of what they now see as their homes will only offend and alienate them against me. It is not enemies but friends I need.

Within a few days of taking back my crown, I realised the loyal men who helped me were not politicians. I was forced to maintain the council that served my brother. They pushed a usurper onto my throne yet I now have to trust them; I can only hope that the realm of England means more to them than their aversion to me. It is while I am pondering on their dislike of me that I remember Norfolk is still in the Tower, as he has been since the last days of my father's reign.

There were many in England who cheered my father's death, but I have no doubt Norfolk topped the list. Had the king not died when he did, the duke would surely have followed his son to the scaffold.

Lazily, I recall my terror in the face of his mistreatment. I can punish him now. I have his houses, I have his wealth. Now, I can take his life.

The only thing that stays my hand is his support for the old church. He can help me erase heresy from this land as no other can. I push aside the memory of his ill-treatment and sign his release from the Tower.

A few days later, he comes into my presence, and I discover his arrogance is untainted by years in a Tower cell. He has shrunk in body, his skin is jaundiced from lack of air, but all else remains the same. Even his nerve.

He removes his cap and stiffly lowers himself to his knees. "Your Majesty," he says and I wait unsmiling and watch his discomfiture increase.

Clutching the arms of the throne tightly, my knuckles white, I suppress the teenage girl that still lingers within me and longs to batter him about the head … *until it resembles a baked apple*. I wonder if he too remembers that day or if it is lost amid a thousand other insults... Our eyes meet and I see that he does. He both remembers and rues it.

"My lord." My lips curl into a sneer of their own accord. "You seem to be in good health considering the years you have languished at the king's pleasure."

"Oh, my bones do ache a bit, Your Majesty."

I expect they do. He must be eighty if he is a day but I feel no pity. Where was his compassion when he was in his prime and I a young defenceless girl?

"You must be surprised to see me here, on the throne of England, my lord … after you fought so hard to keep me from it? I imagine you thought it a day that would never come."

"Indeed, it makes me very glad, Your Majesty. Had I been free I would, of course, have ridden in your support. I can only be thankful that my _ my former home at Framlingham offered you such lavish hospitality."

His smile is cold, his rhetoric like stones against a frozen window.

"I suppose you'd like it back? And your former office too?"

"I am undeserving, Your Majesty, but nothing would give me greater pleasure."

My upper lip snarls.

"And you swear to serve me, as loyally as you did my father?"

"I will serve you loyally whether I am returned to royal favour or not. You are my queen, and I am yours to govern."

He bows low again. I am sickened by his smooth insincerity and long to unleash the fury I've suppressed for so long. But I must not. I need his experience and the support that only he can provide.

I hold out my hand and try not to gag as he kisses my knuckles and pledges his lifelong fealty. When he has gone, I wipe the back of my hand on my skirt and call for wine.

My heart is heavy. I doubt any service he does me can recompense for the despairing time I spent at Hatfield, but at least I have him where I need him. At my side.

Within days of my entrance into the capital, Elizabeth arrives to congratulate me on my accession and swear allegiance. She rides into my capital and the crowds flock to greet her, all suspicion of her involvement in Northumberland's plot forgotten by the public. They call out her name, throw greenery in her path as if she is some pagan goddess.

As always, I am surprised when we come face to face. When we are apart, it is easy to forget she is a grown woman. Expecting a young girl, I am stunned by her composure, her flawless appearance, and her infuriating charm.

As soon as she enters the room, I feel old and stout, and wish I'd chosen a different gown. She is neat and plainly dressed, presenting herself as a demure and obedient subject. When she falls prostrate before me, I look down at the top of her bowed head and bid her rise. She raises her face and I look at her clear brow, her wide innocent eyes and flawless skin, and push back the resentment of my own wasted youth. Trying not to see her mother reflected in her eyes, I open my arms.

"Elizabeth."

As she comes into my embrace, her skin sweet on my lips, her fragrant hair tickles my face. I kiss her on either cheek. "My dear sister, you look so well. I heard you have been ailing."

"It was just a passing thing, Your Majesty. I hope you are in good health and haven't found the last few weeks too taxing."

She will have heard of my desperate flight into Norfolk, the near loss of my throne. Were it not for the men who flocked to support me … she will have heard of that too. My confidence increases.

Although she tries to conceal it, I can see that she is not really pleased at my victory. As far as she is concerned, I have stolen her future. I am the queen now, and soon I will marry and bear a son to rule after me; she knows she will never wear the crown. I expect she would prefer our Protestant cousin, Jane, to be sitting here in my place.

But she keeps her resentment concealed behind a ready smile, and as we discuss the downturn in the weather, and the arrangements for the coronation, Renard's warning rings like an alarm bell in the back of my mind. Elizabeth will always be a thorn in my flesh. She is, and always will be, a Protestant alternative to my rule. Those who are keen for reform will flock to her at the slightest provocation.

I must find a way to be rid of her; she must marry overseas. I will arrange a marriage with some elderly prince who can give her no children; a Catholic who will demand her conversion to the true faith.

As she speaks, my eyes fasten on her long fingers that she uses to embellish her words. She is quiet, self-assured, and righteous. She will not be easily persuaded. I would not put it past her to pretend to embrace the faith, but I will *not* tolerate anything less than a whole-hearted conversion.

It must not be a sham.

But, first things first. Once my coronation is out of the way, I will turn to the matter of finding a suitable husband for myself. My future consort must be of royal blood and he must be a Catholic; I need a man in his prime who can give me children. Above all things, I need a son, and I need one quickly, for I am past the first flush of youth.

Elizabeth promises faithfully to study, and contemplate whether or not her conscience will allow her to return to the true church. When I invite her to join me for Mass at the chapel royal, she tries to wriggle out of it, claiming a headache and a sickness of the stomach. But I insist and, reluctantly, she accompanies me. Throughout the service she makes loud complaint of griping pains and swears she is in imminent danger of vomiting.

Although I am fuming at her tricks, I ignore her, shut out her irreligious voice and give my full attention to God. She might complain, she might protest, but she is here, praying in the true manner whether she wants to or not.

Of course, I am not without empathy for her situation. It is akin to mine when Edward tried to force me to his will, but mine is the *true* faith. Elizabeth is not as devoted to heresy as I am to my God. She is not prepared to suffer for her beliefs as I was. Outwardly, as the weeks pass, she plays the part of a good Catholic, but I am not convinced by her compliance. I know her of old for a hypocrite.

Fabrics and trimming for my coronation gown start to arrive. By the middle of September, the cities are being decorated to mark the day. Scaffolding has been erected, scenery for the pageants is built and painted, and a great walkway installed along the coronation route. At Westminster Abbey, a stage has been constructed so everyone can see the glorious moment of my crowning. A moment I have only ever dared to dream of.

Of course, England has never had a female monarch before and there are arguments as to how the ceremony should be conducted. Some call for a rite similar to the crowning of a queen consort, but I veto that idea. I am queen in just the same way my father was king. I see no reason why the two should not be treated equal. The wrangling of my ministers floats over my head as the sense of unreality increases.

In the end, I will get my way.

Fearing an outbreak of violence, both against my gender and the reestablishment of my faith, some of my council suggest the ceremony should be postponed until parliament has restated my legitimacy. I grow restless as their droning voices go on and on. We have sat here for hours while the same problems circle the table, resulting in the same dead ends, the same barriers.

"Enough!" I spring to my feet and thump the board as my father would have done. All heads turn to me, eyes wide, faces paling as they are reminded whose daughter I am.

I am Mary, and I am the queen.

"The date, gentlemen, has been set for the first day of October, and the first day of October it shall be. If there are problems then they must be overcome so I suggest, if you value your heads, you will stop your quibbling and get on with the job!"

Leaving them to wrangle on without me, I join my women in the privy chamber and turn my attention to the cut of my gowns, the selection of my jewels. Then, just as I am beginning to relax, someone mentions the arrangements for the procession through London on the day before the ceremony.

Who is to accompany me in the litter, and who shall follow on behind? I bury my head in my hands. The minutiae of policy and the etiquette of my women is as tedious and tiring as the statesmanship of my council, but when the day comes and the arguing is over, I conclude that it has all been worthwhile.

In the end, Elizabeth, as second person of the realm, accompanies me on the royal barge to the Tower. The river is full of boats, pennants wave and people cry my good health from the banks and bridges. It is a bright day of cheer, the river is green and deep and slow, the sky a brittle blue canopy. I sit upright on cushions with the curtains drawn back so that everyone can see and glory in my presence. The next morning, on my way from the Tower to Temple Bar, I ride in an open litter drawn by six white horses apparelled in mantles of cloth of gold.

It is another bright day; the gold tinsel cloth that covers my hair casts a myriad of tiny lights all around the litter. My heart is light, but the coronet is so heavy and ponderous I can scarce hold up my head. My neck is aching before we've travelled a mile.

Ahead, I see the Duke of Norfolk, all reservation of my legitimacy forgotten as he leads the way, carrying the royal sword. Behind Norfolk comes the mayor of London who bears the golden sceptre. Beside my litter, clad head to toe in scarlet, rides Norfolk's wife, Elizabeth Stafford, and beside her, the marchionesses of Winchester and Exeter. Elizabeth Stafford, long estranged from her husband, takes delight in flaunting her prominent place in the royal party. Every so often, their eyes clash, the air between them seeming to hiss with hatred. I wonder what happened between them. They are certainly no great advocate for marriage. I will make sure that when I select my own spouse, I will choose with greater care.

Following behind me, Elizabeth and Anne of Cleves share a carriage. Once or twice, the crowd catch sight of my sister and call out her name, but they shout mine the loudest for I am their queen.

Lines of peeresses, and ladies and gentlewomen complete the parade, the younger girls laughing and waving to the crowd. The royal henchmen all clad in Tudor green and white follow in their wake.

The skies of London resound with joy as the procession, which is more than a mile long, winds its way through the streets. We pass through a massed crowd, the city aldermen to the fore, the multitude behind, and I wave and smile upon them all. These people have put aside their everyday lives and travelled from far and wide to welcome me to my throne. Such an array of civic pageantry has not been seen in many a year. The dark days are done, forgotten, and England's capital sparkles like a new minted shilling.

I spy a boy dressed as a girl carried on a throne by men and giants. At Cornhill, Florentines pay tribute to my triumphant ascent to the throne with an image of Judith saving her people from Holofernes. I am touched by their recognition of the struggles I have suffered. I twist in my seat, turning back and forth so often that my neck grows tired, but I don't want to miss a single display laid on for my delectation.

"Oh look, an angel!" I cry, and Elizabeth Stafford turns and smiles, snatching at her veil as it is blown across her face by a playful gust of wind. She laughs as she struggles to free herself, and points to a city conduit that is issuing wine in honour of the day.

The celebrations will last long into the night and into the next day. England well deserves this happy time. We pass a group of children, singing sweetly. I smile and blink away tears as their voices fill my heart with sentiment. The people love me; the citizens of my capital and far, far beyond, love and welcome me as their queen.

This day, the day the crown of England is lowered on to my head, is the greatest of my life. It has *all* been worthwhile; the loneliness, the shame, the suffering. Misery has only made me stronger, and that strength has brought me to this moment.

My first action following my coronation is to declare that the marriage between my father and mother *was* valid. I am legitimate again, in the eyes of the law and of the people, and there is no one living who dares deny it.

At last, I have achieved the thing I have fought for since I was a young girl. I have redeemed my mother who, from now on, will be referred to as *the late queen*, not the late *Princess of Wales*. If I could erase the whole affair of the king's great matter from history I would do so, but the product of my father's liaison with the Boleyn woman is living testament to it. She resides at my court; a slim, elegant reminder of my past unhappiness.

I have not yet determined what I shall do with Elizabeth. It is as well to keep her under my watchful eye but her presence irks me and serves as a constant reminder that I am growing old. As the queen in waiting, Elizabeth is in her prime and a constant reminder of my mortality.

Her existence taunts me.

Of course, my council has already begun to discuss the idea of marriage, but now that the time has come to choose a husband I find myself reluctant. I do crave a child of my own, someone who will love me for who I am, and whom I can love in return. I need an heir, but a husband is a different matter.

I have seen too clearly the discomforts of the marriage bed. My father's multiple wives brought him little peace, and my stepmother Katherine Parr, when finally able to wed the man she loved, soon came to regret it. If I am to marry, the man I choose must be devoted, but loyalty is a fluid thing and apt to change as quickly as the tide.

I would never tolerate infidelity and it seems to me that marital faith does not really exist. I would always be watching, waiting for his eye to fall on someone younger, someone fairer. My jealousy would be untenable and I think I would rather be childless and live in peace than bear the shame of a faithless husband. But when I broach this idea with the council, they throw up their hands in horror. It seems chastity is not a permitted state for a queen because a queen must bear an heir.

I wonder if it is usual for the royal council to be unable to agree on anything. It seems each step of the way I am faced with opposition – not an open fight, of course, none of them would dare to blatantly disagree with me. They are too wary of my temper. But I am constantly tripped by subtle argument.

I push for a return to Rome but, although they agree to be rid of Edward's prayer book and priests are once more forbidden to take wives, I cannot persuade them to accept the authority of the Pope. It has nothing to do with their faith, of course. They are not afraid of God's wrath but of losing their lands, the fine houses they've built on church property. There is no way around it. I am forced to concede and let them keep their land but, although I agree to remain Head of the Church in England as my father was, at least I can make sure that England now prays in the old way – whether they like it or not.

Although I feel the restoration is incomplete and I like the situation little better than my cousin, Reginald Pole, I accept that we must move slowly. *Slow but sure* as my old nurse used to say. England has changed since my father's day, and will not easily be persuaded to revert. As soon as can be managed, the gentle old ways are reinstated. The work is done by degrees, the crosses are restored to the rood lofts, the gilded wall paintings repaired, and Latin prayers are murmured once more in the dead of night.

"Your Majesty, you must choose a husband. If the old religion is to continue after … ahem … Your Majesty cannot be here forever. You must have a son to rule after…"

"Yes, yes, I know."

Rochester is like a dog with a rat, he will not let the matter drop. I wonder which member of the council has prompted him to accost me.

"I am not a young woman, Rochester … you are aware that there are certain dangers attached to marriage and the childbed?"

"But … Your Majesty will concede it to be her royal duty."

I sigh, and stare unsmiling into his dark eyes. He does not flinch away. I cannot argue. He is right. My father moved heaven and earth to get England an heir. I should put my personal fear aside and do the same. I sigh heavily and throw my book onto the table.

"I will wed nobody until I have met and spoken with them at length. I refuse to take a stranger into my bed. Have the council make up a list of suitors, and I will scratch through any I am not prepared to consider."

I recall my father suggesting a similar thing and someone quipped that selecting a bride was not dissimilar to choosing a new horse. I glare at Rochester, daring him to remember that also.

"Very well, Your Majesty." He bows low, backs from the room and, as the door closes, Susan comes forward.

"Is there anything you require, Your Majesty?"

I lean back in my chair and scowl into the fire.

"My father was right. I should have been a boy. If I were a king, marriage would be a simpler thing. Wives are dispensable but a queen is not. If I die in childbirth, all England will be affected. There will be chaos. But supposing when – if – I marry, my husband seeks to rule in my stead or tries to use my power to his own ends? He might argue that as the male he is my superior. Even if I wed one of my subjects, a man far beneath me in status, he might still seek to raise himself or fill his coffers at my expense. Oh, Susan, how can I trust any of them? Men greatly dislike being ruled by a woman and I long for peace. I fear marriage will bring me little of that."

"I fear it brings few of us comfort, Your Majesty."

"What would you do if you were me, Susan?"

"Me? Well … if I might speak frankly, Your Majesty, I think it unlikely you will find personal satisfaction with any man. Perhaps it would be best to choose a husband who will be beneficial to the church. Select a Catholic gentleman, someone with authority who has the strength to stand against Protestantism not just in our realm but overseas too."

There are Catholics aplenty to choose from in England, but an English gentleman would have little influence abroad.

"What you mean is that I should take Philip of Spain, isn't it?"

She crosses her hands on her bosom.

"Yes, Your Majesty. You are half Spanish yourself so it would not be like marrying a foreigner, and he is kin too. A perfect match, I'd say. Think how it would have pleased your mother."

My mother always favoured a match with Spain. She was furious when my betrothal to Charles came to nothing.

"Philip is younger than I, yet not too young. Some of the names put forward by the Imperial Ambassador have been young enough to be my sons."

261

"They say he is handsome."

"I was betrothed to his father once, when I was an infant. There may be an impediment."

"Surely not, Your Majesty. Who else has been suggested? Dom Louis? Are you considering him?"

"I'm considering them all, as the council suggests. Many of them are suitors of old. It seems I am more desirable now I am queen than when I was a princess of nebulous status."

"You can hardly blame them, Your Majesty. Your position was always so uncertain before."

"How gallant of them…"

"Perhaps you'd prefer an Englishman?"

"Hmm, the list is most unprepossessing. They've even suggested Reginald Pole."

"The Cardinal?" Her brows shoot upward. "Is that … permissible?"

"In theory. He has never been ordained into the priesthood but he is far too … forthright, a little too earnest for me. I fear we would clash most horribly."

"Edward Courtenay then?" She gets up and brings a tray of victuals closer, and then taking her seat again, she picks up her sewing.

"He is the favourite of those who prefer an English match."

"But not those who mistrust his Plantagenet blood."

"Well, there is that but … he *is* peculiar. The years in the Tower have taught him no manners."

Courtenay, another cousin of mine, has spent most of his life in the Tower, since his family were attainted after the Exeter conspiracy in my father's day. When I ascended the throne, I was glad to offer him liberty and restore his title and honours at court. But, while I deeply pity the life he has led thus far, I cannot reconcile myself to the idea of marrying him. His royal blood makes him a good match, as does his faith and age, but his sudden liberty has gone to his head and I've heard he favours a dissolute life. I pull a face.

"If he behaves so badly at court, imagine what he might descend to in his private life. Imagine what he might subject a wife to…"

I catch Susan's eye, our imaginations romp along a similar path and we both dissolve into laughter. Ruefully, I shake my head and let the list fall to the floor.

"Oh, Susan, I am bored to death with talk of marriage. Summon the other women and let us have a game of cards or something. There is an hour or more before bed."

After much heart searching, I decide to marry Philip of Spain and all hell breaks out in the council chamber. Gardiner, Rochester, Englefield and Waldegrave insist I should make an English match.

"The English hate foreigners!" Gardiner exclaims. "There could be war with France over this! Your Majesty will be happier and more secure with Courtenay…"

"Don't be so dramatic." Paget stands up, waving a sheaf of paper. I close my eyes and let their wrath wash over me. They are all fools. When I stand up and face them, I do not speak at once but wait as their argument slowly disintegrates. One by one they turn toward me.

"Thank you," I say when silence has resumed. "I have given this matter much thought, considered all things, pondered upon every one of your opinions. The matter of marriage is a personal one, or it should be. Although matrimony was contrary to my own inclination, my sources tell me that Philip is a kindly man who will ever show me consideration, and observe the conditions that shall be put in place to safeguard the welfare of this country. God has performed many miracles for me of late and now, he offers me a husband; a husband who will love me perfectly and never give me cause for jealousy. Therefore, gentlemen, can you not just be glad?"

I watch them wag their heads and scratch their beards. Their arguments die unheard for they have the good sense to heed my wishes. When we turn our attention to other matters, I find it difficult to concentrate. I am to be married and while most women welcome a union and the promise of children, I only fear it.

St James' Palace – November 1558

"Why did you fear it, Your Majesty?"

I turn toward the sound of her voice, her guileless question reminding me of her youth. She knows nothing of life, or marriage, or what is expected of us. Nothing at all.

The shutters are drawn, I am unsure if it is evening or early morning. These last weeks the hours seem to merge one into the other until time is both endless and static.

"On my wedding day, I was approaching thirty-eight years old and knew nothing of men. Philip was nigh on ten years younger than I, and had been married before. She, Maria Manuela, died in childbed. I imagined he'd adored her and I hated being second best. I needed him to love me. Our marriage was one of arrangement. We'd never set eyes on one another, yet I was expected to share his bed, and allow him to look upon my nakedness."

The child makes a small embarrassed sound and I reach out for her hand before I continue.

"What I couldn't work out was how to maintain my *queenship*, shall we call it, while suffering the indignity of consummating our marriage."

"Oh, I see," she says in a small, tight voice. She doesn't see at all, of course. No woman can imagine the realities of the marital bed until they've experienced it. It was terrifying to me at the time, and I never found joy in it. Evidently, passion was not in my nature. I found more excitement in my dogs and horses than I ever did with Philip. Perhaps it was him. I'd no gauge with which to judge him by, whereas he ... not only had he been wed before, but half the whores of Europe had been at his disposal.

There is more I'd like to say on this subject but, taking pity on Anne, I sway the conversation and spare her blushes.

"Anyway, child, I am getting ahead of myself. Before we could marry I had to deal with something every monarch dreads."

"What is that, Your Majesty?"

"Rebellion. I love my people and when Wyatt rose up against me, the hurt I felt was overwhelming but then, when it passed, I found I was furious."

265

"Why did they rebel? Was it because of the church?"

"That; and their distrust of Philip. They were afraid, so they said, that the country would be overrun by the Spanish. The English don't like foreigners, Gardiner was right about that. Their fear of our blood being diluted rules their silly little hearts. They had no love for Philip because of his nationality yet they love me, or most of them do, and I am half Spanish. Any child I bore Philip would be more Spanish than English and they didn't like the idea of that. Of course, they didn't like the changes taking place in the church either. Every one of the men who rose with Wyatt against me were secret heretics."

"What, why – was Your Majesty in danger?"

"I would have been, had they laid hands on me. I have no doubt that had my army not been the stronger, I'd have been taken down and thrown in the Tower while Elizabeth or Jane were raised in my place."

"Lady Jane Grey? I thought she was imprisoned."

"So she was, but once they'd murdered me, they'd have soon had her out again. Her father was involved in the intrigue, fool that he was. I had pardoned him once but I wasn't about to do so again. That was why Jane had to die, do you see? I tried hard not to do it. She was my kin and I loved her, but she had to die, for the sake of England, for the sake of the church."

"It's time for your physic, Your Majesty."

266

I turn toward the sound of Susan's voice, and wave her away.

"Leave me alone, that stuff tastes vile and does little good. What is the use?"

She sighs gustily, and when she speaks her tone is patient and caring.

"It can't do any harm though, can it? Take it for me. To make me feel better."

She places cool fingers beneath my chin and guides me to the spoon. Small gestures like this prove that she knows my sight has gone, although I've admitted to no one that I am now almost completely blind.

The concoction she feeds me is foul, I almost spit it back at her but she keeps a hand on each cheek, as if to help me swallow. Just how old must one be before free of the obligation to the bidding of others? First my father, then his bullying henchmen, then my council and now in my final days, I must obey my servants.

"Take this now, Your Majesty." I open my mouth and she places a segment of orange on my tongue. Flavour floods my mouth. I grunt my appreciation as the taste brings memories of my infancy when my world was full of sunshine and flavoured with citrus.

"So, you cut off her head, Your Majesty?"

"In the end, I had to."

"Why?"

"Because of the uprising; because of her father; because while Jane lived she provided a rallying point for every heretic in England, and every exile overseas."

"It doesn't sound very fair to her. She didn't do anything."

"No; you're right, it wasn't. Life is seldom fair for noblewomen; especially Tudors." I snatch my hand from hers. "Are you criticising me?"

"Oh no, Your Majesty. I am merely curious. I know you acted for the sake of England and the church."

"Yes, I did. Mostly the church. Heresy is a plague, blown on the evil wind from Europe. It began in my father's day and where it will end ... I can't imagine. It is every Catholic's duty to stamp out heresy whenever they see it."

Silence falls. I can almost hear her thinking. I play with my rosary beads, the worn familiar surface bringing a small glimmer of light into my darkness. I begin to mutter a prayer.

"I beg pardon?"

"Nothing, child, I was speaking with God but no matter, there will be time for that later. He is always there. Was there something you were going to say?"

"Your Majesty, if the new religion is wrong, why does God not strike the heretics down?"

Good question. I often wish He would.

"It is a test. He likes to test us. I am His instrument and He is striking out and showing His displeasure through me. I am His tool."

"So, the fires ... the fires at Smithfield, they are God's will too?"

"They are."

"I see. Tell me more about the rebellion. Why did it begin and who started it?"

I motion for the cup and she holds it to my lips while I moisten my tongue. Dabbing my chin with a kerchief, I think back to the early days of my reign. I had wanted to focus on my marriage and the promise of children, but instead I had to defend my throne against another rebellion.

Susan said it wasn't a personal attack; the rebels had little argument against me. It was the true church they hated. As soon as I realised that, I knew they were fiends, instruments of the devil, sent to test me. I knew I would beat them for God was on my side.

Richmond Palace – February 1554

My women and I are sorting through a pile of fabric samples and trims for the fashioning of my wedding clothes. Someone is singing, the high melody accompanied by a lute. Bobbing her head in time with the music, Susan holds a piece of lilac velvet against my cheek.

"Hmm," she says, "too pale." She rummages through the jumble of velvet, and draws a deeper hue from the bottom. "This is better..."

The nap is thick and warm. I am rubbing my face against it when the door opens and Stephen Gardiner is announced. I sigh and do not rise to greet him but wait for him to approach me.

"I hope you are well today, Your Majesty?" He bows over my hand, looking about the chamber as if wary that my women may be concealing an assassin. I regard him quizzically, growing suspicious of his errand.

"I am in good health, sir, but please, dispense with formality. I can see you have news, so impart it quickly."

"I have been informed by the Imperial ambassador…"

"Renard?"

"Yes, Your Majesty. He informs me that he believes there is a conspiracy brewing … a possible rebellion in the making."

"Rebellion?" I am alert now. I stand up, straighten my shoulders and narrow my eyes, all thoughts of my forthcoming wedding forgotten. "Tell me."

I beckon him to the privacy of an alcove.

"It seems that a small group of disaffected men —"

"Such as? You have names?"

"Erm…" He clears his throat, swiveling his gaze toward the upper corner of the room as he reels off a list. "Wyatt, Carew … Croft … and Suffolk is also involved, or so we believe."

"Suffolk? Jane Grey's father? Is he an utter fool?"

"I believe he must be, Your Majesty."

I spin sharply, stride the length of the chamber and pause at the window. He follows, his footsteps soft on the floor behind me. Reluctantly, and sick at heart, I turn and face him again.

"Heretics all."

"So it would seem, Your Majesty."

"What must I do to please these people, Gardiner? My only wish is to set them on the truthful path. Why will they not see the error of their ways?"

"I know not," he says, raising his hands and letting them drop again. "I must inform Your Majesty that Courtenay is also believed to be in the thick of it."

Courtenay; my erstwhile suitor. This would not have happened had I settled for him. These men that have taken up arms are not just against my church but against my union with Spain. The dogs think to rule me and tell me where I must wed. I swear to God they never dared to instruct my father. Like a cork from a casket, my temper suddenly explodes.

"By God, the man must be missing his Tower cell! Bring him here to me! I would speak with Courtenay myself and hear first-hand what he has to say."

Gardiner cringes, bowing several times as he backs toward the door. I yell after him, "And ensure he is found quickly!"

I turn from the door to find my women grouped at the table, slack-faced with surprise. I laugh without humour.

"You look like a gaggle of drooling fools," I frown. Susan is the only one courageous enough to brave my wrath.

"What did Gardiner want, Your Majesty? I thought I heard him mention the word *rebellion*."

"You heard right."

I slump into a chair and strike the table with my fist. Pain shoots up my arm. I cradle it to my bosom, rocking back and forth. "A party has risen against my rule and plans to put Elizabeth in my place … or Jane. I should have had her head, as my council advised."

A shudder runs through Susan as she makes a soothing sound that riles me further.

"It is my marriage they dislike! They seek to force me to their will. Should it not be the other way

271

round? Are they not the ones who should do my bidding?"

"Men will always seek to rule us, no matter what our station."

Our eyes meet. Hers are sad; mine are no doubt furious. I clench my lips and run my tongue around my dry teeth.

"Perhaps I should not marry at all. I'd sooner have my council fuming about my virginity than be at the beck and call of a man ... any man. There is not one male on this earth who can be trusted."

"But, Your Majesty, you have given your consent. Surely it is too late now to change your mind."

I stand up again.

"Yes, because I am a woman. It was not too late for my father to annul his union with Anne of Cleves even after they'd shared a bed. He found a way to be rid of her, or his henchmen did. I cannot envisage my council ever being as careful of my wishes as they were of my father's. God's teeth! It makes me mad."

"Do not fret, Your Majesty. Come, sit by the hearth and I will ask Margery to fetch her lute and play for us."

Reluctantly, I allow myself to be guided to a favourite chair, while the women gather round me, their faces tense and unhappy.

"What will happen now, Your Majesty?" Jane Dormer asks, and Susan scowls at her to be quiet. I turn to look at her and something about their quiet presence calms me ... just a little.

"I have sent for Norfolk. He and the council will send out an army to quell the rebels."

Poor Norfolk must be tired of rebellion. His service to my family has been peppered with revolt and unrest yet ... I know the people love me and desire peace as much as I. It is the nobles who are full of disquiet.

"Will there be a battle?"

I sigh and accept a drink that Susan offers.

"I hope not but it is possible."

I think back over the last few weeks. While I've been enjoying the Christmas festivities and planning my wedding, members of my court have been plotting against me, arranging my downfall. There is no one I can trust. I narrow my eyes.

Elizabeth *must* surely be involved in this. Why else would she choose to spend the Christmas season at Ashridge rather than with me at court? All those promises to study her Bible and learn to be a good Catholic were a deception. How was I ever taken in? She is a traitor of the highest degree. *How could she do this to me?*

I can find no joy in the sweet music that Margery plays. I am restless, unable to settle. Gulping my wine, I bang the cup on the table, get up and begin to pace the floor. When will I ever know peace? How can I ever feel secure with half my realm up in arms against me?

Courtney is brought before Stephen Gardiner. I conceal myself behind a screen and listen with growing rage to his cringing remorse. There is no need to resort to the thumbscrew to get his full confession, for his former arrogance has been entirely quashed by terror. Gardiner does not speak at first, but waits and watches while Courtenay squirms in his chair like a worm on a hook. Through a gap in the curtain, I see him lace his fingers together as if in prayer.

"Edward," Gardiner says, his voice neutral. "Do you understand why I have summoned you here today?"

Courtenay shakes his head.

"No, no, my lord. I had thought perhaps t-to arrange a pageant to _ to entertain the queen on her forthcoming…"

"No. There is no pageant, but there is another matter … isn't there?"

He sweats, wipes a hand over his face. Shaking his head, he swallows.

"I am at a loss then, sir."

Gardiner settles deeper in his chair.

"I am informed that you and certain of your friends have spent the dark days of Yule concocting a revolt; a revolt in which you mean to depose our anointed queen, marry the Princess Elizabeth and together make a bid for Queen Mary's throne."

He jumps up, his chair crashing to the floor.

"Nay, sir, that is not so! It is a foul lie!"

He runs a hand through his hair so it stands like a rooster's comb – *coxcomb that he is*. Gardiner sits back and regards him with cold, unblinking eyes.

"I have sworn statements that state otherwise."

"Then they are false, my lord. I swear, on my life, I am a true subject of the queen."

His face is pale, his tongue emerges in a vain attempt to wet his lips.

"You deny that you have sought the hand of Princess Elizabeth?"

Courtenay coughs, splutters. I can almost see the cold sweat breaking on his brow.

"I – I admire the princess greatly, but I would never do anything to place her in danger. I have no wish

274

to put her on the throne. I don't want to marry her and have no plan to."

"Since Her Majesty has been magnanimous enough to restore your lands and title of the Earl of Devon, there are a hundred noblewomen who would welcome a match with you. Is that enough for you?"

"More than enough, sir, truly. I greatly value my liberty. Her Majesty has been my very good friend, and I am hers."

He takes out a kerchief, mopping his forehead while Gardiner's lip rises in one corner and answers with a snarl.

"So say Wyatt and Carew, so say James Croft and Henry Grey. The secret is out; you might as well assist us further in our investigation, unless you'd prefer to face the consequences."

Courtenay slumps, his head lolling with the whisper of a sob. Gardiner strikes while his foe is weak.

"Come, sir, sit down and tell me all about it. It is the only way to save yourself. I swear, if you co-operate, the queen will hear no ill of you from me."

I bite my lip at Gardiner's lie, and hold my breath while I listen, sickened to the core as Courtenay vomits up every detail of the treachery against me.

"Summon my sister to court. I will brook no delays." I march along the corridor toward my privy chambers, scattering orders while a scribe follows, his pen sputtering beneath the speed at which I travel.

My instinct is to strike hard and fast, but Gardiner urges a soft approach.

"We need not hurry, Your Majesty; I think it wise to let them all implicate themselves so we have something to use against them. Let them make the first move. We know everything and will be ready to strike as soon as they act."

"I will not be governed by my subjects."

"No, madam."

I peer at him, scrutinising his face. He has no love for Spain and has championed an English marriage often enough. Perhaps even he is against me. Can I truly place my trust in him?

"I will give notice of my forthcoming nuptial, let there be no mistake. Perhaps an announcement will prompt them to act sooner – force them into action."

He closes his eyes, inclining his head in agreement.

While my women gather muttering in the opposite corner, I sit and compose a statement to be sent out across the realm.

'Certain ill-disposed persons, under the pretence of misliking this marriage, mean to rebel against the Catholic religion and divine service within this our realm, and to take from us that liberty which is not denied to the meanest woman in the choice of husband, spread false reports of our cousin stirring up our subjects by those and other devilish ways to rebel.'

Within days, we learn that Carew has fled to France, and Suffolk, for the intention of raising a rebellion in Leicestershire, is arrested and thrown into the Tower. Wyatt, however, continues to elude us and remains at large with the men of Kent behind him.

"I need Elizabeth under lock and key," I rage at the council, "she is a loose cannon, a rallying call for my enemies."

I sit down and write her a letter, demanding her attendance at court, leaving her in no doubt that I expect to be obeyed.

'Tendering the surety of your person, which might be in some peril if any sudden tumult should arise, either where you be now or at Donnington, whither, as we understand, you are bound shortly to remove, do therefore think it expedient you should put yourself in good readiness with all convenient speed to make your repair hither to us, which we pray you, fail not to do.'

As soon as the message is on its way, I begin to bite my nails, worrying she will disobey me and ride out to lead the rebel army herself. I can imagine her, pale and valiant upon a white palfrey, winning the hearts of the people as she rides against me. I shake my head, dispelling the image.

She will, of course, have been expecting my summons and has already ignored one polite request to come to court. It is clear to me that someone, some spy, is keeping her abreast of events. I have no doubt she is as deeply involved in this treachery as it is possible to be.

A few days later, she sends word that she is ailing and cannot face the difficulties of travel when the roads are so heavy with winter mud.

I remember how as a child she used imagined headaches and belly upsets to get her own way. I remember how she'd wilt on her bed, feigning sickness while her women rushed to fetch warming possets and extra blankets, and then she'd catch my eye and wink at me.

Elizabeth has not changed at all. She is lying. I know she is.

Westminster Palace – February 1554

As my courtiers dissolve into hysteria and the Imperial commissioners flee in fear of their lives to the Netherlands, Wyatt's army draws closer to the capital. The news on every hand is not good. To his fury, a section of Norfolk's men have deserted and joined the rebels. While my army depletes, Wyatt's force increases. With thunderous brows, my ministers stalk the palace corridors, arguing and shouting while clusters of women snivel and gossip in the corners of my privy apartments.

They are driving me mad!

I leave them to their tears and go in search of my advisors and, while the citizens of London go in peril of their lives, I discover my council chambers a riot of conflicting advice, and portents of doom.

"You must leave the capital, Your Majesty, take refuge at Windsor; preserve yourself that you might fight another day."

"No, Your Majesty!" cries Paget, leaping to his feet. "That is the worst thing you can do!"

I watch the anxious faces ringed about my table and don't know who I should heed. Paget was part of Northumberland's coup attempt; he preferred Jane to me then. *Can I trust him?* Even Gardiner is wary of my proposed marriage to Spain. *Can I trust any of them?*

I look upon their grey faces. Most of them haven't washed this morning, they've been up all night, their beards bedraggled, their eyes ringed with shadows. I rub my chin, as my father used to, and squeeze my bottom lip as I struggle to reach a decision.

Affecting a calm I do not really feel, I place both hands palm down on the table and speak quietly.

"We will remain where we are. It is my city. The inhabitants deserve our protection."

A wave of voices assaults me. I close my eyes, seek a grip on my patience and hold up my hand until their protests dwindle.

"The people are afraid for their lives. This morning I shall ride out and offer them comfort, reassure them of our unstinting protection." I rise to my feet and, with much muttering and shaking of heads, the council does the same.

I order my women to dress me in sombre hues, and wear a coat cut in the masculine fashion. My palfrey is caparisoned like a warhorse. As we near Guildhall, the crowd increases, the cries of the people making my blood throb. These people are loyal but they are full of fear. Their terror is infectious. My head is pounding, but I cannot relax. I keep my back straight, and my shoulders as tight as a vice.

Ahead, the guildhall gleams white against a blue sky, black carrion birds circling high above it. I manoeuvre my horse so that all assembled can see me, and I hold my right hand high to silence the crowd. Slowly, the shouting lessens, and the clamouring bodies grow still. Their faces turn up to look at me. I lower my arm.

"Good people," I cry and a cheer goes up at the sound of my voice. If only all men could love me as these humble folk do. I smile lovingly on them, my eyes misting, but I blink the tears away. There will be time for weeping later. My horse's hooves shift and slip on the wet black cobbles, but I hold him firm.

279

'I am your Queen, and at my coronation, when I was wedded to the realm and laws of the same, you promised your allegiance and obedience to me…. And I say to you, on the word of a Prince, I cannot tell how naturally the mother love the child, for I was never the mother of any; but certainly, if a Prince and Governor may earnestly love her subjects as the mother does love the child, then assure yourselves that I, being your lady and mistress, do as earnestly and tenderly love and favour you. And I, thus loving you, cannot but think that you as heartily and faithfully love me; and then I doubt not but we shall give these rebels a short and speedy overthrow'.

Cheers shatter the quiet of the street as a sea of hands waves and eddies. Gardiner and Paget, whose horses flank mine, exchange grim nods of satisfaction. Rochester goes as far as to wink at me. Ignoring his impertinence, we push our way back through the crowd, and as we do so, the people surge forward to touch my horse, grasp my heel.

I reach out to bless those closest, to reassure them with my presence and the touch of a royal hand. But in truth I am the one more comforted; their willingness to fight for a queen who refuses to flee revitalises my resolve.

When Wyatt attacks our city gate, we will be ready for him and the citizens of London will show him exactly what they think of his intrigue and treason. It will not be long before London Bridge boasts the head of another traitor.

The bridge is secured, and every city gate is guarded night and day by men in harness. At first light, when Wyatt leads his army toward Southwark, he finds his way forward is barred. My informants tell me he lingers there for three days before riding off.

"That was easy," I remark to Rochester, but he shakes his head.

"Your Majesty, I fear Wyatt has not given up but has merely gone to seek another passage into the city."

I wait at the palace, asking every few minutes if there has been any word. I am still standing at the window when Rochester at last brings news that Wyatt has now marched his army west, along the south bank, and managed to cross the river there. He is now trekking back north toward the city again, where Lord Clinton's army, positioned at St James' Field, lies in wait for them.

I pray to God he manages to hold them back, for the news from elsewhere is discouraging. Some of my forces are proving craven in the face of action. When Wyatt fires his first shots, Sir John Gage, whose army is almost a thousand strong, turns tail and flees. When this news reaches us, the palace falls into confused panic and I am filled with a greater fury than I have ever felt before.

At three in the morning, I am roused by the sounds of hurrying footsteps. Men are shouting close by my chamber. A thundering of fists sounds on the door.

"Your Majesty! The city is under attack!"

I leap from bed, pull on a loose gown and hurry to the council chamber with my feet bare, my braided hair flying out behind. When I crash into the room, not one member of my council bats an eye at my dishabille.

"What news, gentlemen?" I demand, bending over the table and drawing a candle close so I can read the messages. For my protection, the room is ringed with men at arms; my women, who have followed me, cling together. One of the youngest girls is sobbing hysterically, her high-pitched whimpers like nails in my head. Such behaviour will diminish us all.

"Shut her up before I slap her myself!" I cry before turning my attention back to the matter in hand. The men of my council flock around me and bleat like sheep.

"Your Majesty, I really think you should try to get to safety. Shall I order the royal barge? Wyatt is close to breaking through…"

"Hold your breath, sir, I am not going anywhere. Where is my Lord of Pembroke? I would have a word with him."

They stammer and stutter, raise their hands at a loss for words, until Paget steps forward.

"Your Majesty, Pembroke is on the field, where he should be."

I look into Paget's eyes, noting his underlying fear, his flagging confidence that we can win this day. He is a heretic and a weak one at that. Dismissing his concern, I nod and smile in the face of it. Confidence is required. I have learned that if you believe hard enough that a thing will happen, it usually comes to pass. Good or bad.

"Then, if that is the case, we are well served. I suggest we calm ourselves and pray, gentlemen. I warrant we shall have better news come morning. Pembroke will not desert us and neither will God, in whom my chief trust lies. Go you to your beds, safe in the knowledge that the palace is secure, as is our city."

I speak with a confidence I do not really feel. When we return to my apartments, I turn on my women.

"Keep her quiet!" I run a disdainful eye over Dorothy, whose face is red and drenched from weeping.

"For Heaven's sake, child, have peace! Turn your attention to God; have some faith in Him."

But my anger exacerbates the maid's fear and, as others give in to their terror, the sound of weeping intensifies.

I utter a foul word.

"They are afraid, Your Majesty, but I will do my best to quiet them."

My heart softens, just a little.

"Let them sleep close by, if it will help…" I wave my hand and watch as the mother of maids settles them to sleep on cushions about my chamber. Running my hand across my face, I turn from them towards the window and open the shutter. A ghostly moon is sinking in the west, the sky to the east is striped with pink and grey, proving dawn is not far off. I wonder what the new day will bring.

I close my eyes and, swaying slightly on my feet, I offer up a silent prayer.

Do not forsake me, Lord. Send me strength.

I remain at the window for a long time and when at last I allow my women to persuade me to lie upon my bed, I do not sleep. As the light of day imperceptibly increases, I lie wide-eyed, listening to the night mumblings and snores of my companions. If Wyatt succeeds it will not just be me who falls; my council will be scattered, my women will be forced to flee. If the reformers prevail, all the good Catholics of England will be driven from the land. It must not come to pass.

I am just leaving Mass the following morning when Paget brings me the news that Wyatt, having come as alarmingly close as Ludgate Bar in the midst of an disintegrating army, has surrendered and is pleading for a pardon.

Relief steals the strength from my knees. Almost falling, I cling to the rood screen.

"Then we must thank God for it. I knew we would prevail for our cause is righteous."

But as I give my thanks I cannot help but consider my fate had the outcome been different. I must rid this land of my enemies for if I don't, I myself will be destroyed.

I am exhausted, I am anxious and I am relieved. This must *never* happen again. I am *queen*. How dare men try to deny me? Summoning the council, I spend less than an hour deciding how to deal with the perpetrators. I have been lenient in the past but I will never be so again.

Carew and his brother have somehow managed to escape to France, but others remain and they shall be given the full force of punishment. Carew, in his exile, will have to learn to live with that.

"Throw Courtenay back in the Tower. We shall deal with him appropriately later."

"Once we have evidence of his…"

I stab Paget with a glare and he backs down, fumbling with his pile of papers. Crossing my hands over my belly, I lean back in my chair.

"And evict his mother from my court. I can no longer bear her near me."

Gertrude Courtenay, my one time friend, has been a thorn in my side for months, ever urging me to select her son as my husband. I see now that my refusal forced them to seek other avenues to power. Let them suffer the consequence.

"Guildford Dudley and his father, to whom you will remember, gentlemen, I showed leniency before,will this time die. I will not be made a fool of and can tolerate no more of their disloyalty."

I try not to think what death means. I am not committing them to an easy passing but a prolonged and painful punishment, followed by an eternity in Hell.

"As for Wyatt, question him and do not go lightly. We must know every single traitor involved in this. We must clear England of traitors. They will all be punished."

Paget stands up, hesitantly clears his throat.

"And Jane Grey, Your Majesty?"

I look up sharply, my narrowed eyes clashing with his. I turn away first, unable to withstand the suggestion I see mirrored there.

"She has done nothing," I shrug. "As a prisoner in the Tower, what involvement could she have?"

"She didn't need to do anything, Your Majesty. That is exactly my point. The simple fact of her presence is, and always will be, a trigger for Protestant uprising. Her father and husband plotted together with Wyatt to place her on your throne."

"That, sir, is not *her* fault."

He puffs his cheeks, rolls his eyes and turns to Gardiner for support. Gardiner clears his throat.

"Your Majesty, I think we all believe that, for the safety of your good self, Jane Grey cannot be allowed to live. For the security of the true church and of all England."

At this moment I hate Paget and all he stands for yet … deep down, I know he is right. I stand up so suddenly my chair topples backward. I kick it aside, yell for the guard to open the doors, and stride from the room.

I am in the garden at Chelsea. Katherine Parr sits beside me, sewing a long seam. The sun is warm on my cheek and her voice buzzes like a lazy bee in my ear. One of her small dogs is cradled in my lap, its coat silken and soft beneath my fingers. Far off, I can hear Elizabeth and Edward at play; their laughter grows loud as they appear through an arch in the yew hedge, and I look up and wave.

They wave back at me.

Their clothing makes a colourful splash against the solid green of the yew. As they come closer, throwing a ball back and forth between them, Elizabeth's voice is high and happy. Edward opens his mouth, his infant merriment floating on the breeze toward me. He launches his ball toward our sister but misthrows it, so it lands with a heavy thump in my lap.

The dog yelps and leaps off. I look down at the ball and time slows. Sounds are distorted, and my scream unfolds slow and loud. When I raise my hands it is as if I am swimming through treacle.

I strain away, struggling to free myself as blood soaks through the skirts of my gown, hot on my thighs, filling my nostrils with heavy sweet scent. Katherine's mouth opens wide, her screams piercing, merging with mine, rising upward, as the blood bubbles to our chests, our throats. The whole world is screaming. The ball in my lap grins up at me. I see it is not a ball at all. It is a head, a head I know well. It is the severed head of my cousin ... Lady Jane Grey.

"Your Majesty, Your Majesty, wake up! You are dreaming!"

"Susan!" I cling to her, still trapped in the grip of the nightmare.

"You are safe. You are in your bed at Westminster. You are queen. You are queen…"

"I am queen," I repeat as I look wildly about the room, ensuring the horror of my sleeping mind has not followed me into the morning.

There is no severed head here. I am safe.

The room is shadowed, a warm fire glowing in the hearth, my startled women grouped at the foot of the bed. Nightgowns. Braids and bedcaps. I gasp for breath and try to smile, and make light of my dream. But my mouth will not obey.

This morning I cannot pray, I cannot eat, I cannot even *think*, for today is the day my cousin Jane must die.

St James' Palace – November 1558

In the darkness, a hand tightens in mine. I turn my face toward the murmuring voices and tuck my chin down, close my eyes. Let them think I am sleeping.

"How did the queen bear it?" I hear the child whisper.

"Not very well," comes Susan's muted reply. "She was never the same afterward. All the time the Princess Elizabeth was in the Tower, the queen wavered between the conviction that she'd been involved in the plot against her, and the belief that shared blood holds precedence over politics."

"What did you think, Lady Susan? Do you believe the princess was part of it?"

A rustle of silk breaks the short silence.

"We will never know. Elizabeth has always kept her own council. Nobody ever knows what she is thinking. Some say she has no feelings."

"I've heard she is clever."

"Oh yes. Very clever … and agile too. A quick thinker, with a mind more akin to a man's than a woman's."

"Will she make a good queen?"

Another silence, this time broken by a sigh.

"No. It is a shame she is not a true Catholic. None of us, not even the queen, have really been fooled by her pretence. When she rules, England will become Protestant again and I, and others like me, will be unable to stay. I could never live a lie and so I must see out the last of my days in exile."

The rattle of a rosary informs me that Susan is kissing her beads.

"Where will you go? I can't imagine ever leaving English shores."

"Spain perhaps. I have always wanted to go and there I can worship as my heart dictates, not my monarch."

I open my eyes but the darkness remains.

"Your Majesty, you are awake."

I make a sound that falls somewhere between a word and a grunt, and attempt to pull myself up the pillows. I am too weak. I give up and slump down again.

"Let me help you."

Susan leans over me, and my nostrils fill with the fragrance of lavender. She places a hand beneath each armpit and hauls me higher up the bed.

"Thank you," I say and hang on to her hand when she would remove it. "Can you light the candles, please?"

"It is full day, Your Majesty, but I will if..."

"No matter." I sink my head into my shoulders, hunching beneath the blanket like a wizened crone. It is frightening to be in the dark with my eyes wide open. "I am quite blind now," I say and when they do not answer, I realise it is because they are weeping.

Someone holds a cup to my lips and I freshen my mouth. I will die soon. I have only a short time left. They know it and so do I. But I am too young, despite the lines upon my face. Groping on the coverlet for the girl's hand, I give it a squeeze.

"I must finish my story, child, while there is time. I regret it is not a pretty tale from here on; not the fairy tale I hoped it would be."

She gulps audibly. "Yes, Your Majesty. Do not worry. I am brave enough to listen."

"Where was I?"

"Your sister was in the Tower and you were just about to marry Philip of Spain."

"Oh yes ... Philip."

Winchester – February 1554

Months of wrangling pass, and I am exhausted from quarrelling with my ministers over tedious details before my future husband agrees to set foot in my realm. Why must they constantly raise political irrelevances designed to postpone the day of our wedding?

Perhaps, had they not tried to thwart my wish to marry into Spain, I would not have fought so hard to make it happen. I have always resented instruction and grudge it even more now I am queen. Nobody tells a king how to act; why should a queen be at the beck and call of her advisors?

Elizabeth has become the thorn in my side I was warned she would be. No matter how hard the council tries to implicate her in the rebellion, she fends them off with ready answers and makes no effort to disguise her contempt for them.

"She shows no hint of fear, Your Majesty. Not even a touch of guilt or weakness, but I know she was involved...."

I look up at Gardiner and do not miss the reluctant admiration in his voice as he relates the details of the interviews. Somehow, she has managed to dip and dive around the most agile minds in the kingdom and emerge unscathed. Short of putting her to the rack, I can only surmise her innocent, but I am not yet ready to free her.

I read through the reports once again, the words on the page evoking her so clearly the scene runs like a mummers' play through my mind. I imagine her entry into London dressed all in white, the curtains of her litter open so that all might look upon her. She woos the people with her pretty face and youthful innocence, and her sudden descent into fever increases their pity further. *I don't believe a word of it.* She claims to be ailing, covered in bumps and pustules, sick unto death, and the physicians I send to determine the truth of it also swear it to be true. But Elizabeth will not die. She is too clever.

But then a rumour starts up that she is not sick at all but pregnant – although whose child she is supposed to be carrying is not certain. Again, I know it is a lie and she is quick to prove it. She parades herself before the people, standing tall and enviably slim to prove to the people she is not and never has been with child.

Later, when the moment is described to me, Renard is clearly impressed.

"She was lofty, somewhat scornful but rather magnificent, Your Majesty," he says and I lose my temper, swipe a tray of cups to the floor and leave the council to it. They must find a way of removing her, she is a barb in my finger and must not be allowed to turn bad.

Later, the Earl of Sussex brings me a letter, written in haste by my sister.

If any ever did try this old saying that a king's word was more than another man's oath, I most humbly beseech Your Majesty to verify it in me and to remember your last promise and my last demand that I be not condemned without answer and due proof which it seems that now I am for that without cause proved. I am by your counsel from you commanded to go unto the Tower, a place more wanted for a false traitor, than a true subject which though I know I deserve it not, yet in the face of all this realm appears that it is proved. Which I pray God I may die the most shameful death that ever any died afore. If I may mean any such thing; and to this present however I protest before God (Who shall judge my truth, whatsoever malice shall devise) that I neither practiced, concealed nor consented to anything that might be prejudicial to your person any way or dangerous to the state by any means. And therefore I humbly beseech Your Majesty to let me answer before yourself and not suffer me to trust your counsellors yea, and that before I go to the Tower (if it be possible) if not before I be further condemned, howbeit I trust assuredly Your Highness will give me leave to do it before I go, for that thus shamefully I may not be cried out on as now I shall be, yea and without cause. Let conscience move Your Highness to take some better way with me than to make me be condemned in all men's sight before my desert known. Also, I most humbly beseech Your Highness to pardon this my boldness which innocence procures me to do together with hope of your natural kindness which I trust will not see me cast away without desert, which what it is I would desire no more of God but that you truly knew. Which things I think and believe you shall never by report know unless by yourself you hear. I have heard in my time of many cast away for want of coming to the presence of their prince and in late days I heard my lord of Somerset say that if his brother had him suffered to speak with him he had never suffered, but the persuasions were made to him so great that he was brought in belief that he could not live safely if the admiral lived and that made him give his consent to his death. Though these persons are not to be compared to Your Majesty yet I pray God that evil persuasions persuade not one sister against the other and all for that they have heard false report and not harkened to the truth.

Therefore once again kneeling with humbleness of my hart, because I am not suffered to bow the knees of my body, I humbly crave to speak with Your Highness which I would not be so bold to desire if I knew not myself most clearly as I know myself most true, and as for the traitor Wyatt he might peradventure writ me a letter but on my faith, I never received any from him and as for the copy of my letter sent to the French king, I pray God confound me eternally if ever I sent him word, message, token or letter by any means, and to this my truth I will stand in to my death.

I humbly crave but only one word of answer from yourself.

Your Highness's most faithful subject that hath been from the beginning, and will be to my end.

Elizabeth.

It is a long and somewhat repetitive letter and Elizabeth has filled the blank areas of the page with thick black lines to prevent her enemies from adding a damning codicil. I squint at the page in the poor light.

It is untidy and mis-spelled, the script is cramped and blotted, yet my sister's voice is clear in every line. *How can I not remember writing similar letters to my father, to my brother?*

Elizabeth lives in dread of the Tower and who can blame her? The memory of her mother, if indeed she remembers Anne Boleyn at all, must be at the forefront of her mind. She knows too well that those who enter the dark recesses of the Tower of London as prisoners rarely come out alive.

Yet, my hands are tied. I shake my head.

"She must go to the Tower, Sussex. I must be seen to be doing what is right. It is what Spain expects."

I find it difficult to speak, for grief is strangling me. The thought of my pretty, lively sister incarcerated in the terrible darkness of the Tower is unbearable.

"Give her apartments that befit her status and ... and, don't take her in through Traitor's Gate," I add as they leave the room. One by one, they bow and take leave of me.

Not one of them can look me in the eye.

But it isn't over yet. Her enemies are still not pacified. Spain heaps pressure on me, reminding me that the throne will never be secure while Elizabeth lives. Philip will not leave Spain and the marriage will not take place until justice has been served. I fob them off, promising that great headway is being made and that she is close to a confession. In truth, my ministers report that she continues to defend every accusation laid against her with the deftness and wiliness of a fox.

"You must remember, Your Majesty, that she is not without power. I wonder what it would take for her supporters to rise against you? She certainly does not lack the wealth to pay for it."

My head aches. I wish they'd shut up but they are right. After me, Elizabeth is the richest woman in the land, her coffers are overflowing, her estates are vast, and she is far more skilled at winning men's loyalty than I.

She does not lack the wherewithal to rise against me but even if I wanted it, I wonder at the wisdom of sentencing her to death.

Richmond Palace – April 1554

On the eleventh day of April, Wyatt faces his death on the scaffold. Trying not to think of the events taking place, I bury myself at Richmond. I know Wyatt of old; he is a few years my junior and formerly a merry member of my father and brother's court. His father was one of Boleyn's many lovers who somehow

294

managed to dodge the axe. Despite not wishing to hear of it, they bring me news of his death.

"He died bravely," Rochester tells me. "And before he did so, he swore the Princess Elizabeth and the Earl of Devon to be innocent of all involvement."

He lied, of course, but I do not let Rochester see that I realise this. If I destroy Courtenay, I have no option but to execute my sister.

I cannot do that.

Trying not to dwell on the healthy young body that has been quartered and his innards drawn, I pretend to meet the news of my sister's innocence with relief. But my council remains divided on the matter. It seems they are never in accord. Gardiner, who once swore love for my sister, now argues against her, while Paget, who was formally her direst enemy, now speaks in her defence.

I am torn between the two. I feel as if a rope is tied about my middle and each side pulls in an opposite direction. I have become a royal tug of war. I don't know what to do. The people love her. *I* love her ... albeit reluctantly.

The whole realm is divided on the issue of Elizabeth. With my mind in chaos, I look about me to gauge the feelings of those I should trust. The people love Elizabeth; they remember Jane Grey and fear my sister is to suffer the same fate. If I let her die, she will be hailed as a martyr, an innocent victim, and I will be viewed as a vengeful queen. If I let her live, the Catholics, particularly Spain, will think me weak.

Every household, every tavern is alive with speculation as to whether or not I bear enough bitterness to kill my sister.

Let them wonder.

But, I *must* act. She must either be condemned as a traitor or freed. Questioning her is getting us nowhere. She was clearly aware of what Wyatt was planning but there is no proof that she condoned it, or had any part in it. It is not as if she handed over coin to be rid of me. I am relieved yet disappointed that no proof can be found. As always, the love and the hate I bear her are in conflict, and I *cannot* decide the best course to take.

In the end, I release her from the Tower but set her under house arrest at Woodstock, where a sharp eye is kept on her. Her every movement, every letter, every word is reported to me, and if she lets slip one tiny inference of treason, it will be her last … I think.

With Elizabeth safely stowed at Woodstock, I can at last look forward to the arrival of my future consort. My former reluctance toward marriage is forgotten and I can barely contain myself as I wait for our first meeting. The new extravagant gowns are ready and I have ordered equally extravagant gifts for Philip. I select a huge diamond; a poignard studded with jewels; and gowns, the most richly embellished I've ever laid eyes upon. On the day of his arrival, I send a white horse trapped in wine velvet and gold to take him to his well-appointed lodging.

By ten in the evening, dressed in my finest, I am waiting at the Bishop's Palace. Flanked by my ladies and councillors, I listen to the arriving horses, clenching my fists when I hear the heavy footsteps as his retinue mounts the stairs. The doors are flung open and I draw in my breath, hearing his name announced and his unhurried tread across the floor.

I look up.

Does my heart move? No; not as I had expected it would. Instead of joy, I find I am a little disappointed.

I see grace, certainly, but sense no warmth behind it. I suppose I had hoped he would display eagerness, perhaps a flourish of excitement, a dash of romance. I kiss my fingers and reach out to take his hand, feeling myself tense as he moves forward, grasps my shoulders and kisses me on the mouth.

I do not close my eyes. His lips are wet and rather thick, his breath tainted with an odour I do not recognise. As we draw apart, I note that he is very young. I knew his age, of course, but somehow hoped it would not be so apparent. I feel like a crone in comparison.

We are of a similar height, and he is slim with fair hair – *our children will be blond*, I think, before hurriedly suppressing the indelicate direction my mind has taken. But, he is well made and we are of the same stock, and I am grateful to discover that at least he is not revolting. It will not be too difficult to accept him into my bed.

He is polite and, over the next few days, he escorts me around the gardens and joins me at supper in the hall where all eyes are upon us, speculating and gossiping.

I place spies in his apartments and instruct them to report every overheard remark, regardless of whether it will please me or not. So I quickly become aware of the unkind whispers that are bandied about. I learn that his attendants describe me as a saint who dresses badly; they fear my youth has passed and my skin no longer fits me as it should; I am pale and appear older than my years.

Despite giving the order that he should be spied upon, I am wounded. While I am happy to take this young, fresh prince into my bed, his countrymen pity him the task. I had thought they would be honoured. No inkling of Philip's own opinion reaches me and I hope with all my heart the cruel views of his household do not reflect his own. There is, of course, nothing I can do about any of this, but I dearly wish I hadn't demanded to be told.

As my women disrobe me, I stand before my looking glass and see myself as the Spanish see me. I survey my small breasts; my flabby stomach; my spindly limbs; my thin, lank hair; my pale, sagging cheeks. No man will ever lust for me and I am filled with bitterness to have been denied marriage for so long. In my youth, I was comely; Philip would have looked forward to my bed then. I indulge in the fleeting memory of another Philip, long ago in the palace garden – my first kiss, my last kiss … until now. I can still vaguely recall the unfurling lust in my belly, the joy the sound of his name instilled in me. It would have been better to have wed him, at least he had the wit to pretend a passion for me … but this is feeble talk. Philip of Spain is kin. It is what my mother wanted. He is a good man and will do his duty.

I have faced worse trials than this.

My wedding day passes in a blur. Afterward, people tell me of the extravagant decoration in the cathedral, the superb voices of the choir, the triumphant spectacle of Philip and his grandees. All I can recall is that my new shoes were pinching my toes and that the Earl of Derby, who bore the sword of state before me, had sat in something sticky and carried a stain on his cloak.

If they weren't still hanging in my closet, I doubt I would recall the clothes I wore as I swore an oath to be Philip's true and loving spouse. All I remember is emerging from the cathedral with my arm in Philip's, the bells crashing overhead, the joyous cries of my people who waited so patiently in the steadily falling rain.

There is feasting afterwards, of course, and dancing. I sit enthroned while a stream of nobles and dignitaries from home and abroad offer their blessings and gifts. I give stilted thanks and replies, for all I can think of is the enormity of what must come later.

I have been a virgin for so long that I imagine my fear is far greater than a young woman's would be. A girl has the armour of confidence and youth to fortify her. All she need do is surrender her body, close her eyes and think of the children she will bear. At my age, I have other worries.

As I am made ready for bed, my women tease and make crude jokes, nudging and giggling as is tradition, but I cannot stand it.

"Silence," I bellow and they fall quiet, duck their heads and quietly turn their attention to my toilette.

The bed is huge. When I am helped into it, I pull the covers up to my chin while Philip, boyish in his night clothes, climbs in beside me. Gardiner blesses the bed, and my cheeks grow warm as the English courtiers give vent to further crude jokes, while Philip's Spanish attendants look on, surprised at the bawdry.

Acutely aware of my nakedness beneath my thin linen shift, I flinch from the man who is equally as naked beside me. Susan curtseys low and wishes me good night. As she leaves the room, she flashes an emphatic smile. I try to take heart from her unspoken advice. *Philip is handsome*, she says silently, *get of it what you can,* but at this moment, I would rather be anywhere else on earth than in this bed with a man who neither knows nor likes me.

Of course, I knew what marriage meant. I am thirty-eight years old and have heard all the stories, the grubby tittle-tattle. Susan and Jane have made quite sure I fully understand what is to happen. I know the - roughly what will happen, it is the execution that comes as such a shock.

When the night candle is doused, we sit silently in the dark, listening to the distant sounds of celebration drifting up from the hall. I jump like a startled hind when he places his hand on my thigh, and my breath increases with my rising fear. His hand travels upward but before he reaches his target, my courage fails and I fidget away.

I am not ready for a stranger to touch my quaint. *No one has ever touched my quaint.* So as not to offend him, I slide down the bed and toward him so his palm shifts to my hip. I smile tightly in what I hope is an encouraging manner, although I know he cannot see me clearly.

He sighs and his hand roams upward, fumbling for my breast; his fingers are cold against the warmth of my skin. I hold my breath, waiting for pleasure. I close my eyes and will the desire to come. As he starts to tug at the hem of my shift, my mind screams against it, but my knees part instinctively at his unspoken command. Surely he can hear the pounding of my heart; it is hammering like a drum. *Why doesn't he speak? Why doesn't he say something?*

I am going to die of shame.

He rolls and I tilt my head, waiting for his lips as he clambers on top of me, but the kiss doesn't come. Instead, he fumbles between my legs, probing places that even I have never explored. My body is rigid. Shock knifes through me. I crane my face away and a shameful tear drips onto the mattress. His touch burns as he pushes his fingers into me. And then he pauses.

Was that it? I think. *Has he finished?* But no, after a moment, he raises himself and thrusts hard against me, shocking me to the core.

My heart is bruised.

In the morning, when my women pry into the events of the night before, I find I cannot tell them the truth. I cannot confess to having made such a horrible mistake. Nobody shall ever know of it. Instead, I find myself smiling and blushing like a maid, making coy references to a delight I did not experience.

In Philip's absence, as I go about my day, it is easier to forget the crippling embarrassment of our coupling, and I pretend to love him. As my women attend me, I prattle on about how wonderful he is, how gentle, how magnificent. Once I am dressed in my finest and my hair has been brushed and tucked beneath my cap, I send for the court jeweller and order a collar to be made commemorating our joining. As I wrap it in fine tissue, I speak loudly of the sweet love between us, my devotion to my husband, and my joy that our marriage is a success.

But the truth of it is, Philip is a cold fish and I am filled with resentment that he does not even pretend, as I do, that our union pleases him.

Hampton Court – November 1555

While Philip takes the apartments that my father's consorts lived in at Hampton Court, I take up residence in the royal chambers that my father and Edward used. It is an unusual but appropriate arrangement given that I am queen and Philip is to have no power in England. His role is to support me. He will sit on my council but he will never rule. His opinions will be treated warily, and I reserve the right to veto them. If I die before him, he will have no leverage, no further claim to power here. I am the only one in this marriage to have supremacy over England. I imagine he secretly resents this as he seems to resent so much about our union, but he makes no verbal complaint.

We pass our first months together like distant acquaintances and all is well until bed time, when we are expected to couple and produce a prince of the realm.

The act has become a little easier now I know what to expect but I still find it uncomfortable and rather disagreeable. I have long given up dwelling on the dream I once harboured of marriage. I do not require his affection; the crux of the arrangement is to get with child as quickly as I can. Once I can be sure I am carrying England's prince, my duty will be done and Philip will not be required in my bed again.

Of course, I continue to act as though I hold him in the deepest regard. I couldn't bear the gossip, you see. We make a strange pairing. Privately, I liken us to Janus – welded together in marriage but while he looks to Spain, I look to England.

The one thing in which we are in accord is England's return to Rome, and Philip will be useful in this. He is the best man to take charge of the delicate negotiations and, when I make the suggestion, he cannot hide his pleasure at being given such an honour.

After months of negotiation, it is an immensely satisfying day when my cousin, Cardinal Reginald Pole, arrives in London. It is a breach of my father's making that should have been healed long ago.

Philip sees the return of the cardinal as a personal triumph. For twenty years, Pole has been exiled, he has seen his family destroyed for his sins, yet even when all guns were against him, he never wavered in his support of me, or the true church. His reward will equal the depth of my gratitude. I know he has always hankered to become the Archbishop of Canterbury and I shall ensure it becomes so.

I have not seen Reginald since I was a small child; in fact, I am not even sure if I remember the occasion, or if I simply remember my mother speaking of it. When he takes the knee before me, I go forward and bid him rise.

"My dear cousin," I say, "you are most welcome to England." A tear slides down his cheek and I my eyes are also moist.

There is so much to discuss, matters both personal and politic and, during the next few weeks, I am so much in his company that I do not heed the first rumblings of sickness. I am so often ailing with women's complaints that I dismiss it as the onset of my megrim.

On the last day of November, I stand tall and proud as Reginald absolves England of our years of sin and heresy and welcomes us back to Rome. The schism is at an end and the first thing I do is write to Philip's father, Charles, to inform him of our kingdom's return to the obedience of the Holy Church. My heart is so light that I am certain Mother is looking down and applauding me. Before I became queen, I compiled a list of changes I intended to make when I ascended the throne. Today, that list is a little shorter.

At the banquet that follows, I eat very little. I feel nauseous, my belly rolling with disgust at each dish the ushers place before me. I shake my head, waving it away, and chew only on a piece of bread.

"You didn't eat a thing, Your Majesty," Susan remarks as she combs my hair that evening. "You must keep up your strength."

"I think I am ailing," I reply, watching her face in the looking glass. "I feel sickly and have no appetite at all."

She touches my shoulder and I look up at her. She flushes pink and puts her lips close to my ear.

"Your Majesty, remind me, when did you last see your courses?"

My head reels, bells ringing loudly in my ears as the inference of her words penetrates my tardy mind. Realisation dawns. I grip her hand.

"Oh Susan, you don't think? Could I be with child … already?"

Her laughter echoes about the chamber.

"I rather think you might be, Your Majesty! We shall have to wait and see."

Hampton Court Palace – February -July 1555

I am filled with joy and can barely contain myself until the day comes to announce my wonderful news to the world. Etiquette demands the matter is kept secret until the child quickens in my womb, and daily I cradle my growing stomach in my hands and will the child to move. *Just one little kick.* But even before the child quickens, I feel replete, bursting with life, and know I have done my duty.

I am queen of England, a child of Rome, and now I will have my heir, my son. If he could see me now, I know my father would be pleased and proud of me.

"We must plan the prince's household," I say. "He will need a wet-nurse and rockers, a launderess, and we must have the royal cradle brought down from the attics … or have a new one fashioned." I lie back in my chair, stroke my belly and smile widely at my women.

Recently, the atmosphere in my chambers has changed, or it seems so to me. My whole world is brighter. Winter sunshine streams through the windows, the fires dance in the grate and my women are gay because I insist on calling for musicians and dancing every afternoon. I cannot wait for spring to arrive; this year it will not just herald warmer days and lent lilies but the birth of my child, a prince of England.

"Do you think I should name him after my father? *Henry the ninth*, he would become in time. Or would Philip be more suitable? England has never had a King Philip. I think it would please my husband, and his father too."

"Perhaps a combination of the two, Your Majesty. Henry Philip, or Philip Henry – both have a very nice ring to them."

"Philip Henry…" I try out the sound, repeating it over and over in different combinations to see which I prefer.

Months pass, and my lying-in chamber is arranged. Suitable tapestries are hung, plenty of cushions and soft fabrics are put in place. When it is time to enter, I bid farewell to Philip, whom I will not see until the time comes to present him with his son. It is clear from his expression and his chilly kiss that he will not miss me. After issuing orders and reminders to my council, I take up refuge in the shuttered chamber. It is dark, and warm, and quite oppressive. Barely a day has passed before I yearn to peek outside at the brightness of the garden.

A midwife is brought in, and my youngest maids are chivvied from the chamber with only my closest, more mature household women permitted access to me.

"Make sure the announcements are prepared," I say. "Leave a gap in the script that we might fill in our prince's name and the date of his arrival once he is born. It is not long to wait now." As she turns to go, I call her back. "And send for my sister. I would like to have Elizabeth attend the birth."

Then I sit down … and wait, barely able to contain my patience. I wonder if Philip is as excited as I. Not for the first time, I regret the lack of love between us. I remember my father when Jane Seymour retired from court to prepare for Edward's birth. He was playful and chirpy, buoyant with hope and never for a moment imagined she would fail in her duty – it certainly never occurred to him that she might not survive the birth.

The memory of Jane brings a cloud. I suppress a shiver and thrust the thought firmly from my mind. I am made of stronger stuff than Jane. I might be nearing forty and my fertile years may be numbered but I am the queen and God loves me. He will not fail me.

The womb-like chamber is supposed to soothe me but the warm airless space is dark, and the atmosphere as thick and slow as honey. It is more like a tomb than a womb and sometimes I feel I cannot breathe.

Elizabeth is with me nearly every afternoon. She lounges on my cushions, eats the dainties my ladies have placed beside me, and conceals her boredom, as she conceals everything. She does her best to divert me with gossip about family members, or childhood

306

memories of her and Edward. One day we even go so far as to indulge in naughty criticisms of our father.

But we do not mention Jane Grey. She is not to be spoken of.

I send Elizabeth to fetch things for me, ask her to rub my temples when my head aches, and if part of me remembers the days I was forced to serve her, well, I am only human.

I lie back on pillows, my hands resting on my stomach, my eye fastened on the cradle in the corner and dream of my son.

My prince.

"I think he will be blond, Elizabeth," I remark. "I am sure of it, and well-built like Philip, not spindly-legged like me."

"He will be beautiful whatever shade of hair he has, Your Majesty."

Elizabeth has a way of making statements that say absolutely nothing. Neutral comments that flatter until one analyses them. I flick through a few pages of my book.

"He will be an intelligent boy, quick to learn all he requires to be a great prince. I will ensure he is able in the saddle, and bright in the schoolroom and nimble of foot on the dancefloor."

"Yes, I look forward to it, Your Majesty. I have never had a nephew before. He will call me Aunt Bess, I suppose. I hope he will be fond of me."

I frown, disliking the thought of intimacy between my sister and my son. I'd not want him tainted by her hidden heresy.

"Children come into the world unformed and it will be up to me, as his mother, to shape him into the perfect Tudor prince – Prince Philip Henry, heir to the throne."

She smiles widely with no visible hint of resentment. I wonder what she is hiding from me. Elizabeth is always the enigma – I love her but there is always this dreadful sense of distrust. I would love to see inside her mind, unravel the mysteries therein and read her true thoughts.

April arrives. Although I am not permitted to look outside, I sense the sky is bright blue, the trees slowly turning green, tiny white flowers emerging beneath bare winter hedges. It will not be long now. I place my hand on the mound of my belly, and wait for him to kick.

"The child has been quiet for days," I say. "Do you think that is a sign he is about to be born?"

"I am sure it is, Your Majesty, but I am woefully ignorant of such matters. You must ask the midwife."

The reply is the same to all the queries I make of my women. They seek to soothe me, lull me to sleep, to rest and relax and wait. I am tired of inactivity. Tired of waiting. So very, very tired.

By the end of the month, I am so restless I could scream. I pace the chamber floor, ignoring their pleas for me to rest. I no longer feel in the least queasy and my appetite is returning. I turn from the pinkness of Elizabeth's youth and peer into my looking glass. My face is pale from lack of fresh air, my eyes are shadowed and dull, my jowls droop like a jew's purse. I look every one of my thirty-nine years. I hate myself.

Everything is going wrong. Swivelling on my heel, I dash the mirror to the floor, sending shards of glass exploding about the room. Wrenched from her usual annoying calm, Elizabeth leaps to her feet and my attendants come running as I knew they would.

308

I am trembling, head to foot. My women are full of calming words, their cloying hands inducing me to sit, to lie on the bed, to take a draught of wine. Each word, each touch drives me into a greater rage. I dash the cup away.

"How long am I supposed to bear this?" I scream. "I have been incarcerated for months. I am suffocating in here!"

"Your Majesty, you must calm yourself; think of the child…"

I wrench back the thick curtain, fumble with the shutter and push the window wide. Closing my eyes, I breathe in deeply and drink in cool fragrant air, listening to the pealing church bells.

I open my eyes, stand up straighter.

"Why are they ringing the bells at this time? Has something happened? Send for Gardiner."

I turn suddenly, in time to glimpse a dissolving smirk on my sister's face as murmurs of shock ripple about the chamber. Gardiner is a man, forbidden to enter the lying-in chamber. I wave a hand at them. "For Heaven's sake, I am your queen! Do as you are told."

A little later, Gardiner creeps sheepishly through the door, reluctant to look at me, his bovine cheeks as pink as a maid caught with her paramour.

"I heard bells, Gardiner. Why were they sounding?"

He clears his throat, gulps the air for a few seconds.

"They were rung in error, Your Majesty, there have been rumours…"

"Rumours of what?"

He swallows, and when he smiles it does not reach his eyes.

"A rumour has been circulated that the prince has been born. The people became over … erm … excited, Your Majesty. I have sent orders for a retraction."

I turn away, cross the chamber to stand before the open window again. *Supposing the child never comes, supposing he has died in my womb?* He has been very still of late; the regular kicks and squirms ceased days ago. I dare not voice my fears. Without turning, I address the window.

"Very well, Gardiner, you may go."

"Shall I send your attendants in, Your Majesty?"

"No. I have no need of anybody."

The door closes softly and I am left alone with my shrivelling hopes.

1556

I don't know which is greater; the grief for my unborn child or the humiliation that I was mistaken. *How can I have been mistaken?* My belly was huge and my breasts were full and painful … the physicians assured me.

At first, I cannot summon the strength of character to venture beyond the gardens. They will all be laughing. I cannot bear to be seen by anybody but I know I must return to court at some time. Even though there are none brave enough to mock me openly, the fact of their private ridicule is torture. But I do not feel weak or sad, and my tears have long stopped falling.

I am angry … furious. I have done *nothing* to deserve this.

All my life, I have put my duty to God first. I have stood firm for the true church, I have tried to be a good, honest woman, and a conscientious queen. But, it seems that wasn't enough. I am constantly punished, and the knowledge that I am still found wanting fills me with a fury such as I have never known.

Unable to look on her, I dismiss Elizabeth from my presence and shut myself away from those who love me. From now on, I will concentrate solely on ruling the country and persuading my subjects to embrace the Roman church.

No matter what the cost.

The older I become, the faster the days and months seem to pass. No sooner is it summer than the leaves are falling, and I realise it is winter again. There is no time; no time for reflection, no time to gather my thoughts and consider my future path. Thick and fast, problems are hurled at my feet and I must jump and scramble to avoid stumbling over them. Court activities, visiting dignitaries, matters of state rain down on me like confetti at a celebration. But there is little joy in it.

During my confinement, I've been blind to those who continue to resist the reinstatement of the church. I have made it an offence to deny the established religion, punishable by death, but I have been lenient with transgressors. From now on, it will be up to me and my council to enforce their obedience, but it would be so much easier if they would cooperate freely.

The terrible anger in my heart does not fade. Daily, it grows stronger, and when Philip tells me he is leaving court to lead an army against France, it grows stronger still. It becomes an ungovernable force within me and I vent it at any who dare cross me. I cannot even bring myself to be kind to Susan and Jane. My women creep about my chambers as if there is a wounded lion in the corner, liable to pounce at any moment.

I do not fight the rage. I have to let it loose. I shout and rant and cast punishment on the subjects I swore to love, and all the while I can see myself doing it. Shame and anger vie for position in my broken heart.

The good, tender, loving Mary has been usurped by a bitter, angry Mary and the good queen hovers just above, watching with great disappointment while I allow the bad queen to destroy us both.

I do not want this. I want to be kind. I want to lead the sinners away from heresy but they will not listen. Nobody listens! They leave me no choice.

It is three years since the trial of Bishops Cranmer, Latimer, and Ridley. At the time, they were questioned most rigorously by Gardiner and the Bishop of London, Edmund Bonner, and their guilt was plain. The verdict of death by burning was issued right away but I have a soft heart and have put off their sentences … until now. All three are clearly heretics, yet only Cranmer recants.

I always knew him for a hypocrite.

He has been my enemy since I was a child. It was Cranmer who supported my father in his divorce, and was ever a friend to the goggle-eyed whore. Since then, I have never been able to look on his face without a shudder of revulsion. Now, I have his life in my very hands.

So, why do I hesitate?

A memory stirs of my mother's misery, the great shuddering sobs she shed when she finally realised she had lost her husband to a whore.

"My pearl!" I hear my father's voice again as he tosses me in the air, catches me deftly before planting a great wet kiss on my cheek. It is sunny, the verdant garden bright and full of joy.

Cranmer spoiled all that. He *stole* it from me. He destroyed my mother and had me named a bastard, all so he could lure my father into the hands of a witch; his fellow heretic.

Cranmer is not deserving of mercy.

I order that Cranmer be made to watch while his friends, Latimer and Ridley, burn. He must know beforehand the reality of what he is to suffer. In early October, he is taken to a church tower from which he will bear witness to the heretics' end. During the six months in which he will be imprisoned, he can think of it before he himself is led to the pyre. It is meet that he should suffer, and I will brook no argument.

But, on the day of his death, I wish I'd given him a swifter end, or had him silenced in the Tower. Had I done so, I'd have robbed him of the opportunity to fashion for himself a martyr's end.

Rochester pulls off his cap and holds out a rolled parchment. I look at him. He is miserable these days, as if he bears the weight of England on his shoulders. But it isn't he who must carry that burden. It is me.

I take the parchment and turn away to quickly read the transcript of Cranmer's final words. Then, I move into the light, and read more slowly the words that are scored darkly on the page:

'And now I come to the great thing that troubles my conscience more than any other thing that I said or did in my life, and that is the setting abroad of writings contrary to the truth which I thought in my heart, and written for fear of death and to save my life if it might be; and that is all such bills which I have written or signed with mine own hand since my degradation:

313

wherein I have written many things untrue. And foreasmuch as my hand offended in writing contrary to my heart, therefore my hand shall first be punished, for if I may come to the fire, it shall be first burned. And as for the Pope, I refuse him, as Christ's enemy and anti-Christ, with all his false doctrine. And as for the Sacrament...'

"God damn him to Hell!" I scream as I dash the paper to the floor. *He is dead but how I wish he were not so I might punish him further.*

He has the victory. With his last words, he turns himself into a victim, a wronged man of God, and in doing so, he condemns *me* as a monster. This is how I will be remembered. A vengeful queen, steeped in the blood of her foe.

For a long time I stand at the palace window and instead of the tranquillity of the privy garden, I see the horrors of the heretic fires that are burning at Smithfield. The ashes blow east across the city, glowing red in the heretic wind and, when the embers settle, they are scattered at my feet.

I am not doing this for *myself*. I am doing it for my country, and for God. The people who are dying are sinners in the greatest degree, they refuse to renounce their sin. I would gladly pardon and embrace them back into my church if they would only recant. I begin to tremble. I cannot make it stop. It was not supposed to be this way.

I bury my face in my hands.

"Your Majesty! Your Majesty!" Someone is tugging at my hands, pulling them from my face. I gape into darkness, grip their wrists, and blink in vain in my effort to see. There is nothing; nothing but blurred outlines, black shapes against a deeper, bleaker darkness. A cold sweat breaks upon my forehead. I am in Hell.

"Susan?"

My heart hammers, an anvil of iron. Someone sits close to me, takes me into their arms and rocks me as if I am a child. At first, I think it is my mother, but then I remember she is dead ... long dead.

Of course, I recall as the present trickles back and is made solid. I am at St James', in my sick bed, likely to never leave it. I am safe and warm, and a few loyal members of my court still remain. Just the last few who have lingered to see me through the last hours. The rest have gone, run to ingratiate themselves with Elizabeth.

The next queen.

The hell of the last few months clarifies and I recall the fires at Smithfield are still smouldering. I have not completed my task. I have failed in every degree. The Catholic church is not yet secure in my realm, the people do not love me as they should, and I have failed to bear a son to rule after me.

I cough feebly and painfully. My mouth tastes of ashes. There is little breath left in my body now. What will happen once I am gone? Will Elizabeth revenge the blood of the heretics I have shed by punishing the Catholics? Will she hack open the schism with Rome once more?

She will no longer need to pretend to embrace the true church. I know her obedience was always just a ruse to appease me; an instinctive desire to preserve her life and liberty.

Oh, Elizabeth! I only wanted to be loved, to make the people see the error of their ways. I could not let my subjects burn in hell. I had to try to save them.

Susan's bosom grows too warm, I am suffocating. I pull away and draw the edge of my sleeve across my nose, dab my wet cheeks.

"There," she says. "You see, all is well. I have sent for the physician again, just to be sure you are..."

"I am tired of physicians, tired of the fuss."

My voice cracks. She moves from the bed with a rustle of petticoats and someone else takes her place. I wish I could see clearly, if only I could blink this damned mist from my eyes — this blackness.

The darkness conceals so many dangers, so many secrets. I need to see clearly. I long to look upon a face and see for myself if it is trustworthy or dishonest. The truth that lurks like an assassin in the shadows glides closer.

"Who is it?" My voice is sharp. A smooth hand slips into mine.

"It is Anne, Your Majesty..."

My spirit calms, I breathe more easily at the touch of a friend.

"You must be tired, child, have you been here all night?"

"All day, Your Majesty. It is just coming on to evening now."

I slump into the pillow, let misery roll over me.

"My world is always dark."

"I know but ... perhaps..."

"Oh, don't say it. They will not be able to cure me. I am beyond the help of physicians. We all know that."

"Hope is a powerful thing, Your Majesty."

"Well, I hope you are right then." I laugh bitterly at my poor attempt at humour.

Silence falls in the chamber and I subside once more into my own thoughts. The last few years have been a hell on earth. Everything I tried to do for the good of my people, the good of the church, was thwarted. I did *all in my power* to make them see the dark path they were following. Gentle persuasion didn't turn them. They are immured in their sin but I could not stand idly by while they perjured themselves. I had to *force* them to turn before it was too late. It was a case of the heretics burning here on earth, or for eternity in the hereafter.

Why would they not listen?

I cough, swallowing bile. I must try to continue with my tale ... while I can.

"I think I went a little mad then. Perhaps I still am. I was at a loss, do you see? I did not know how to help them...

"For a while, after Philip left the country, I tried to boost the royal coffers, reinstate the churches and some of the monasteries. There were other state matters too that had fallen into chaos during my brother's time. I tried to right his wrongs as well as my father's."

"I am sure, you did, Your Majesty, no one could have cared more than you..."

"Don't patronise me. I am not a child."

The coffers were almost empty but it was hard to be economical; after all, I had my status to maintain. Nobody will have faith in a queen who dresses like a pauper. I had to bind the people to me, persuade them that I knew best. It cost a lot to live up to my father's image..."

The child makes a soothing sound that is almost as irritating as her platitudes but, deep down, some part of me realises I must cherish those still loyal to me, for they are very, very few.

"In 1555, they tried to unseat me again. Members of my own council this time. They were dissatisfied with Philip and squeamish at my punishments of the heretics, and teamed up with France against me.

"I'd been too lenient after Wyatt's rebellion. I should have hanged them all then. This time, they didn't find me so forgiving. No one can accuse me of not learning lessons."

"No, Your Majesty."

Her fingers tighten on mine, pressing my rings deeply into my skin. I probably deserve the pain.

"I was sure Elizabeth was involved but as usual there was no proof. More than twenty men were arrested and we placed a ring of guards around my sister's house. We took her servants and after a little teasing in the Tower they soon revealed that they'd all known of the rebellion ... and supported it. I'd have taken Elizabeth too, and put her to the sword like her mother before her, but Philip advised against it."

"King Philip believed her to be innocent?"

"Well, no, but she has always been popular with the people. He was wary of punishing her too harshly. With her out of the way, the road would have opened for my cousin, the Scottish queen, and even if she is Catholic, nobody wants that. So, I delayed arresting my sister. Instead, I sent her a diamond, and invited her to court."

"You were reconciled?"

I remove my hand from Anne's to scratch my scalp.

"I need a drink; I've a headache and my stomach feels like it's been kicked by a donkey."

"I will order up a powder, Your Majesty." Susan's voice issues from the hearth. I had mistakenly believed I was alone with Anne.

I take a sip of wine, pass the cup back, and hear the clunk as she places it on the table.

"Elizabeth and I weren't reconciled, as such. She refused to come to court, pleading sickness again, and I was too ill myself to care. By then, the headaches had become so bad that sometimes I couldn't raise my head from the pillow. The doctors couldn't decide what was wrong."

"You've been ill all that time?"

"Oh, off and on; not all the time."

"So, she didn't come."

"Not until Christmas – fifteen fifty-six; I think that was the year. It seems longer than just two years ago. She made a real show of herself too, all airs and graces, a silent reminder to the people that she was the heir and they'd best remember it, for she would not forget a slight against her."

"The reunion was successful?"

"Not really, no. She stayed barely five days and then set off back to Hatfield in a peculiar state of mind. Philip wanted me to arrange a match between her and the Duke of Savoy, but she baulked against it. It was something she clearly deemed beneath her.

"You'd have thought she'd be glad that we regarded her as my successor but ... well, I have never determined what really upset her, but something did. Perhaps it was the fear that with Philip due back in England, I'd get with child again. That would have irked her.

"Oh, I would have given anything to fall pregnant and birth an heir right at the last minute. One small child would have thwarted her every hope."

"You must have been happy to have your husband back in the country, Your Majesty."

I cock my head, alert for innuendo, but I sense none, not in this child. I squeeze her fingers and smile.

"I was … for a while, but so much of my time was taken up with war. I was reluctant for us to be drawn into it but in the end the rebellion by Stafford forced my hand.

"France was behind it, of course, damn them all. Their persistent interference and support of traitors against me left me in little doubt that they were involved. The council was against the war because of the costs involved and the limitations it would place on trade, but Philip persuaded them. There are limits to what a monarch can stand."

"Indeed, Your Majesty."

Susan clears her throat. "I've brought you a powder for your headache, Your Majesty. You really should try to sleep; it will serve you better than all this chatter."

Anne shifts uncomfortably in her seat. I pat her hand.

"Don't listen to her, Anne. I like our little conversations."

"Well, don't say I didn't warn you," Susan sniffs.

I'd take such insolence from nobody else, but Susan has been with me for far too long for formality to come between us. She is the keeper of my deepest darkest secrets, my night terrors, my innermost fears. I wonder what she will do when I am gone – what will any of them do?

"Of course, it was that war that lost us Calais. The people loved me even less after that."

I sigh and let my mind trickle back to the day I mark as the beginning of my end. Was it really only a few short months ago? Philip and my council were at loggerheads, rebellion was always around the corner. There was no *peace*. Sometimes, when I dwelt too long on the things I'd lost, the mistakes I'd made, I thought I would go mad, and end my days a raging lunatic.

"After that, I grew so ill I could think of little else but my own survival. The headaches, the recurrent bouts of nausea – it was awful. It still is. The doctors, in their wisdom, suggested I might be pregnant, but I was loath to believe it. I didn't want to bother telling Philip but the council insisted."

"Such a shame, Your Majesty." Anne strokes my fingers, the touch softening my reserve, making my eyes prick with tears.

"I took to my bed but I didn't order a lying-in chamber to be prepared. I was afraid ... despite my women's assurances that my swollen belly indicated a child ... I was afraid. I knew I was sick ... unto death. Perhaps it is God's punishment for my failure to bring them back to the true church. A pregnancy would have been a mark of God's favour. I would welcome some sign even now ... of his favour."

Silence rings in my ears. Nobody speaks until Susan hurries forward, snatching my hand from Anne's.

"Your Majesty, we did not mean to mislead you! I was so happy at the prospect of an heir for you at last that we were ... I was carried away."

"Even when Philip wrote to tell me of his joy at the prospect of a prince, I did not believe it. I did not feel pregnant, not like before – I felt leaden and full of pain. I am old before my time. I blame the suffering I've endured; they say grief ages you. From the beginning, I sensed something was not right but ... the doctors are fools."

"They will heal you yet, Your Majesty."

"No. No, they won't."

I turn my blind eyes toward them, and a shudder of dread washes over me. *What is waiting for me in the darkness?* I grope with my other hand for her.

"I think they knew. I think everyone knew really, and few were sorry, least of all Philip."

"Your Majesty, that is unjust!"

"Is it? Is it really? Why then has he not returned, not even when I have written to him privately of my encroaching death? He doesn't care. He has never had any love for me but he has plenty of affection for my throne. No doubt he writes to Elizabeth instead; what could be better than a ready-made king to fall into her lap? She could not do better if she tried; he is handsome, powerful, the perfect match. She would relish being queen of England *and* Spain – how the Howards would welcome that! You can be sure neither she nor Philip will mourn at my passing."

"I will mourn, Your Majesty. I don't know how I shall ever bear it."

"Nor I!"

Susan and Anne cling to me, our tears mingling, and some strange instinct urges me to comfort them. I am dying, yet I need to protect them from beyond the grave.

"Fetch my casket." I pull away and point across the shadowy room. Reluctantly, Susan rises and brings my jewel coffer to the bedside. I feel inside and draw out a handful of trinkets, press them into Susan's hand.

"When the time comes, you must accompany Jane Dormer and Feria to Spain. Do not linger for my interment. Leave this place as quickly as you can. Things may quickly become difficult for Catholics."

If it does, I am to blame.

I fumble again and know by the touch when my fingers alight upon the rosary I carried as a girl. It is a priceless piece, crafted in gold, and adorned with pearls and rubies. I grope for Anne, let the thing trickle into her palm. I hear her gasp.

"Your Majesty, it is too..."

"Be silent. It is my wish that you prosper after I am gone. Susan will protect you but this will give you independence. Go with her and make a life overseas. If you should decide to take a husband, then choose him carefully. If I have learned anything in life, it is that there is nothing so damaging as a bad spouse."

"Your Majesty." With a few sniffs and whimpers, she pushes the rosary into her pocket.

The chamber is full of tears. Susan is prostrate on my bed, her face buried in the pillow beside me. In the next room, I hear further sounds of weeping and realise that the remaining members of my household are weeping for me.

A bell begins to toll. A priest mutters at the foot of the bed.

I must be dying. I turn my head, searching for a friendly face, but I am blind and cannot see.

"I had always meant to be so kind..."

My mouth feels tight, my tongue stiff. I cannot form the words; they gurgle in the back of my throat. I am a paralysed, voiceless wreck of a woman.

I meant to be so kind.

Someone is holding tight to my hand. I recognise the small palm, the smooth fingers and the voice whispering my name. My last human contact is with a girl named Anne.

I try to laugh at the irony but my lips won't obey.

<u>Author's note</u>

As always, I must stress that *The Heretic Wind* is a work of fiction. I carried out lengthy research to help me get inside Mary's head and, of all the women I've written about, I think Mary is the most tragic. After all the harsh things that have been said and written about her, I hadn't expected that.

I haven't attempted to whitewash or excuse either her character or her actions. I have simply tried to understand, and imagine the events of her life from her own point of view.

If you leave aside the religious bigotry and the cruel punishments she inflicted on heretics in her latter days, and consider her experiences during her formative years, it is little wonder she became the woman she did.

As I delved more deeply into Mary's personal life, the one aspect that stood out from the rest was her isolation. During and after her parents' divorce, Mary had few friends, and no equals. Later on, she had faithful servants in Susan Clarencius and Jane Dormer, but they were not her equals – they served her, they loved her but they could never really have understood.

The only person with whom she might have enjoyed an equal relationship was Elizabeth, the daughter of her enemy, Anne Boleyn, but for all her pretentions, Elizabeth was a Protestant. Although she was often suspected of treason, Elizabeth escaped full punishment because Mary went to great lengths to avoid it. This could have been due to fearing the backlash of the populace, but it could also be simply because Elizabeth was her little sister.

For a time, they had been close, sharing the same roof, the same father, and similar fractured childhoods. Their relationship was always complex, fraught with suspicion and probably more than a hint of jealousy. But, I think, empathy and shared blood proved stronger than Mary's resentment.

During her youth, Mary experienced rejection by her father, separation from her mother, Catherine of Aragon, banishment from court and the loss of her title, her status. This was followed by the death of her mother, and the execution of two stepmothers, and two who died after childbirth. During her father's reign, Mary was mistreated, bullied and derided as a bastard. During her brother's, she faced religious persecution. Happiness and security were always just out of her reach.

Even when the crown of England finally became hers by right, she was forced to fight for it and her early reign was smeared with violence, and the execution of her cousin, Jane Grey.

At this point, safely on the throne, she might have imagined her trials were over. But an unsuccessful marriage to Philip of Spain followed and, hot on the heels of that, came the humiliation and disappointment of two phantom pregnancies.

Catholic to the point of fanaticism, Mary was determined to turn her subjects to what she regarded as the true church. In Tudor England, the punishment for heresy was burning, something that Mary took to the extreme, but the actions of the past must not be measured by twenty-first century sentiment.

In studying the character of Mary Tudor, I discovered a woman who endured relentless misery. She was driven by unshakeable religious faith, and the desire to be true to her God and her church. I think, in the end, ravaged by sickness, blind and old beyond her years, Mary's self loathing and disappointment was perhaps exacerbated by a touch of dementia.

After her death, Protestant England inflated Mary's actions and subsequent popular history has turned her into a monster. In *The Heretic Wind* I have taken her pain, her hopelessness, her disappointments and her anger and tried to present a rounded character; a cultured, pampered infant princess, a strong-willed warrior queen and, in her last days, an angry, thwarted and isolated old woman.

Judith is the author of twelve historical fiction novels:

The Heretic Wind: the life of Mary Tudor, queen of England.
The Beaufort Chronicle (three book series) tracing the life of Lady Margaret Beaufort.
The Sisters of Arden: on the Pilgrimage of Grace
A Song of Sixpence: the story of Elizabeth of York
The Winchester Goose: at the court of Henry VIII
The Kiss of the Concubine: a story of Anne Boleyn
Intractable Heart: the story of Katheryn Parr
The Forest Dwellers
The Song of Heledd
Peaceweaver

author.to/juditharnoppbooks
www.judithmarnopp.com

Judith Arnopp's books are available on Kindle, Paperback and some are on Audible